ETCH

ETCH

STONE SOULS
BOOK I

J. A. L. Solski

JALS
Books

Venturing from the forested path to brave
the mountainous one.

It was terrifying.

And it was worth it.

Contents

Prologue

The town bell rang out. In the rafters, where the loud dongs echo, a shadow lurks in the darkness. A lone elf races, heedless of any dangers, towards the bell tower. Her dark hair flying behind her. Her legs pumping to the beat of the bell tolling. One question keeps ringing in her head, *Where is my father?*

When she reaches the doors, she swings them open wide, making quick frantic observations. There were signs of war. The hall was piled full of corpses. Bodies someone deliberately dragged in here to hide from sight. It was a trap.

So many elves, so many lives lost. The dark-haired elf's eyes begin to water at the sight. One body in particular brings her to her knees. "Father." she cries out loud, sobbing hard into her hands. He's gone, killed in action, and she can do nothing but let the blood soak her knees, and tears roll down her cheeks. As she mutters incoherently, a new thought takes shape in her mind, *Who did this?*

The elf stands, new determination surging through her, she searched for a way to the bell that had tolled only moments ago. She would make whoever did this pay. Not only for her father, for every elf in this city, for every elf in Zoriya. This murderer would answer to her.

She crept along a passageway to her left, and up the spiral stairs that led her to the top of the bell tower, towards the shadow. Moving with her back against the bricks, she pulled her longbow off, and held an arrow in hand. Stealthily she nocked the base against the string, leveled her fingers towards its point, brought it to half draw, and rested the line against her arm guard. She reached the door to the landing. Before she could consider her next course of action, the handle turned and the door opened.

A shadow stood in the entrance, over their shoulder sat a bright red and gold bird the size of a small elf. The bird was the most entrancing thing she had ever seen. It shot towards her, and she let out a scream. The bow vibrated in her hand. A sensation she had never previously felt consumed her. The elven magic within her flowing differently. Before she knew it, her body moved to protect itself, as if she was a puppet on strings maneuvered by magic. It pumped her blood harder fueling the adrenaline that aided this new magic. Her body flashed into stance, walked the string rapidly into position, and fired.

The arrow flew straight through the being, as if it were a mirage. The bird flapped overhead back towards the shadow, it turned and glared at the elf. Tiny fires danced in its eyes. The shadowy figure loomed like a reaper, gauzy black fabric covering their tall frame, darkness cloaking their face. They picked something up from a slab table near the gargantuan brass bell hanging above them.

Whatever they had picked up began glowing pink through

their thin wispy hand. Without warning golden flames burst from the item. It was growing, and growing. The light blinding. The tower shook and crumbled. The shadow laughed, watery gasping sound.

The elf loosed another arrow, at the bird this time. It fell, turning to a pile of ash that still held a small glow. Running towards the cloaked being the elf threw her bow overhead, slinging it across her chest, and then leapt for the shadow. She grabbed the burning orb, tried to peel it from the shadows grasp, they wrestled with it in a foolish looking fit of yanking and tugging. The elf jerked hard, and the boney fingers broke free, she had whatever it was now. She felt her body fill with ferocious energy. She was being swallowed up by a flame, burning all around her. No, she was the flame. Flicking and snapping out of control. She began sweating from the raging heat.

All at once, the pile of ash that had been the red bird became a flame as well. One that seemed to unfold in layers as it grew. Then, as the red-orange parts of the fire reached white, wings shot out and fanned the flames into the rest of its body, as it shook the last of the feathers smoothly into place the flickers of heat sizzled out. It was reborn.

Black dots were drifting across the dunes on the horizon. She tried not to let them distract her from the fiery bird and their eerie master. The dots became more shadows, moving fast towards their location, and within mere minutes they floated up to the tower. Hundreds of new shadows leapt up from all around them, with flowing wispy bodies, some were rushing through the door, while others came swimming up from outside onto the open bell tower landing.

In that moment, when all the shadows were floating around her, she let out a wail like the call of a siren. She sang fire out of her body, like a dragon breathing flame. She felt the waves of power in every note. Every beat of her heart a drum, leading her voice, until it felt like all of the air had been expelled from her lungs. The singing stopped abruptly then and the elf went slack. Sinking to her knees, still soaked in the blood of her kin, her magic depleted, her arms draped at her sides, knuckles resting upon the stone floor.

She looked up to see what had happened but everything was a blur. The elf could barely make out the cloak that appeared to whirl off the edge of the terrace, before the red bird swooped to grab them mid jump, then they flapped off to the West. The other fainter shadows followed them. Like a wave of dark across the sandy dunes. All of them just drifting away. As the elf strained to watch them leave, eyes turning white with blindness, the shadows on the horizon grew fainter, and so did everything else.

Chapter 1

As Ilva walked briskly down the damp leaf covered paths, her wavy auburn hair swayed against her sun spotted cheeks. With amber eyes, she saw reflected flecks in the autumnal colours that were beginning to change. The Nilfin forest was exceptionally beautiful this time of year. Ilva's favourite time of the year was fast approaching. She loved this part of the season, colour and nature. Although autumn also meant traditions and rituals, ones that mattered little to Ilva. Whenever she thought about spending time with her kin, she became acutely aware of her disapprobation. Her family was not what she felt a family was meant to be. She fixated on these thoughts as she also tried to find salvation in the nature encircling her.

Ilva believed that families were meant to be something harmonious and happy. She wanted to laugh freely. Laughter at improper times, such as near her father, was strictly discouraged. "Stone elves must be stoic." He would always say. Ilva saw the world through her emotions, which were often as unbridled as a wild beast, and she thought it was natural to feel this way when living with such confinement. Though most of the time she thought of others more than herself.

She thought of why her father was such a stiff unless he was pining over her mother, why her mother looked so sad all the time, and why the elves in the village rarely seemed content.

When it came to family, it was hard for Ilva to see her sentiments as anything but reasonable. She thought her father wasn't a fair ruler, that he didn't give the people anything they needed, and that her mother clearly wasn't happy with him, but she was too afraid of persecution to leave. Then they had her, and they probably only had her for this one reason, to carry on a legacy. She was nothing but a name and a face. One that had to live with infuriating expectations and obligations.

This is not how we should all be living. My father is a jerk, my mother is a coward, and this life is depressing. What do I do with it? What is my fate? She slumped down on a log beside the path, put her head back, and groaned miserably. Her face wrinkled in frustration, her mouth turned down with stress, she thought she might cry but she did not. After a few moments she hunched forward, resting her elbows on her knees, and placing one hand on her temple she thought hard about her situation.

Ilva was one hundred and six. Old enough to attend the village festivities for the last half dozen years, but not yet old enough for adult ceremonies. It was at one hundred and fifty that she would be brought to the stone sanctum to ensure her lineage, through the induction to her craft, should she possess any magic. She would then be allowed to find a husband from a list of esteemed elves, and then they would be expected to produce an heir for the stone nation. *I will be expected.* To Ilva bearing children was a responsibility that weighed far heavier on her than it would on any future husband. Something she never wanted, and still didn't want, possibly ever, was to have children. *Nothing in my life will ever be a choice.* Ilva almost began crying again. Then she stiffened her lips, got up, and started pacing.

In order to be inducted she had to possess some sort of magical ability. Preferably stone. Which was rare among her kind. She estimated only a quarter of the village had the skill to use stone magic. She was afraid, being a bi-racial elf, that her magic might not manifest as stone. Her mother was a sylvite elf, and as lovely as sylvite was, Ilva thought her mother weak. She also knew her father would not be pleased if she wasn't able to ensure stone lineage. He would likely be happier if she had no magic than to have her mother's sylvite magic.

The stone elves are currently the weakest and smallest of the nations, after the recent annihilation of sylvite as a nation, and the disappearance of the stolzite elves almost two centuries ago. The silver elves took over everything, stealing the sylvite artifact that provided the race their magic, draining sylvite elf powers. The weakened elves rebuilt, and there was peace again for over a century after the initial war, though the sylvites were resentful of their magicless lives. This last month a sylvite elf infiltrated Karna, stole the artifact back, and returned it to Mila. The silver elves were furious. They marched on Mila the next day. And wiped out every single soul.

The rumors Ilva heard around the village say that the

sylvites had tried to trap and attack the stone and silver elves in a building, no one from Mila survived this time. Ilva's father was ordered to fight alongside the silvers during both battles. If he refused, he would have risked the safety of his own race. And so, he led the stone elves to war against Mila, upon his return much sorrow was felt when the death toll was realized. *Our elves were the first line of defense on the battlefield, and our race had suffered the most casualties, aside from the enemy. The race my mother belonged to before the first act of war. And my father helped slaughter them all.*

Her father was a terrifying looking elf. With a large scar blinding his left eye in contrast to his ocean blue right eye, a mohawk of dark brown hair, a grin that sometimes gave Ilva nightmares. She respected her father. But did she love him? He always gave her a terrifying vibe when he was around. There was great distance between her and her parents.

One thing is for sure, she thought, *I will never let any children I'm forced to have feel this lonely and unloved.*

She strongly believed in love. That real honest kind of love which could nurture anyone. Heal any affliction. She even believed that any two elves could love each other if they tried hard enough. *Maybe I can find love among my list of suitors,* she soothed herself with small hopes. Wishing for a life where she would no longer need to act. As her heart beat against the inside of her chest, and she ached over the fear of her parents never loving her, or expressing anything other than negative emotions towards her, she became angry. *As if I would get first pick. They'll chose my husband for me. I get no choice. No choice. No choice!* She raged and paced harder. She wanted to rebel from this, she wanted a life filled with truth and openness. *I want out. I want to get away from this life. I don't care what happens to any of them! I want to be free.*

She turned on her heel, despite her itching reservations, and began the trek back towards Falil. *I'll run away,* she thought, *I'll run and hide somewhere deep in the Nilfin forest. They don't love me enough to miss me, and even if they did it would take them centuries to find me in these wilds.* It was almost a full day's run to get home from the edge of the wood. She had run all night, just for a glimpse of the sun rising through the canopy. Ilva didn't mind spending her whole day running back to Falil. As she passed Ivarseas village she scanned it. Looking to see if anyone was staring at her, their lord's daughter, running at full speed down the dirt path.

Her father, Lord Ediv, was from Ivarseas village. He was lorded after the first battle with Mila, then he was appointed to live in Falil for ease of communication. Ilva thought Falil was a gossip ridden place. Negativity and judgement echoed in every corner. So, whenever she could, she would slip out for these runs, despite the danger. This run brought her the focus she needed to sort out her thoughts. Although, at times, that was easier thought than done. More often than not her thoughts would trouble her, as they did today. For all she could think about were her own judgements.

Some days she wished for even more silence than that which the forest provided her. She wished to turn off the cruel voice within her head, which sounded like a mash up of all the elves who had ever criticized her. Crueler even were the original critiques that she created herself. *How did I ever come to be so hard on myself?* Ilva wondered this occasionally, yet those thoughts continued, over and over.

The village came into view, far off in the distance, she was almost home. *The last few hours passed by fast,* Ilva thought. When you become lost in your mind, time becomes a relentless thief. New thoughts and fears bombarded her now. As the cobblestone path to Falil emerged, seemingly from under the dirt path, and dread crept over Ilva at the concept of being in this foreboding gloomy place, Ilva could think of only one thing; *I just need to get through tonight. Then I'll run one last time. Far away from all of this.*

Chapter 2

Syli watched her daughter carefully, inspecting her movements for any falter. "Ilva!" she proclaimed loudly from the balcony overhead "Watch your steps. Angle your chin outward. Why are your toes pointing in?"

Ilva was performing a dance that many her age had performed in her mother's homeland. It was upon Ediv's insistence that Syli teach Ilva how to be beautiful and intoxicating, in the hopes that more suitors would show interest. Image was everything. The dance involved a series of fluid soft movements, catching rays of sunlight in ornamental sylvite items, which would power the magic within the sylvite flecks of pinky orange. Her mother had sylvite encrusted fans, the very ones Ilva was using to practice now. Ilva felt no connection to the fans, and felt even less connection to the dance, but practice she must. Relentlessly.

Her mother was a sylvite elf who took great pride in her heritage. Her kind were very few, and most were slaves in Marka, maybe a handful were respectfully married to silver elves. Ilva had never met another sylvite besides her mother. Syli was quite old fashioned. Ilva hated it. In fact, she hated it so much that no matter how much effort she put into the dance, it was passionless and forced. She would move too quickly, jerking her body, there was no grace to what she was doing. It wasn't dancing.

Ilva seethed and grunted.

Sensing her daughter's frustration, Syli decided to use a softer tone, "Here let me show you how to do it slower."

This angered Ilva more. For every time she was not performing perfectly, her mother had to jump in and make her feel like she just didn't understand. She understood. Understood that there was no way to teach her to be something she simply wasn't. And she wasn't a dancer. She would never dance. *Watching you do it perfectly every time is not going to help me,* Ilva thought with misery.

Deaf to Ilva's thoughts and feelings, Syli stepped onto the platform. A massive stump in the centre of the estate Ilva's father had built. The village had grown quite a lot since the first war, and now since the recent deaths, houses sat empty. They were beautiful homes, with big sloping roofs, and tall doors. She looked at them all, counting the vacant and occupied ones, ignoring her mothers dancing. All she felt from these streets and homes and civilians was pressure. Pressure to conform to a society in which she was born. Pressure to dance, to allow young elven males to court her, to manifest magics.

As she turned to watch her mother, still performing the traditional dance with ease, she felt a pit of contempt form in her gut. She didn't want to feel these things; they came nonetheless. With every soft tip toe and sway of Syli's lavender skirts and golden hair, she appeared more and more beautiful. Her smile bright as the rays that touched her fans. The flashes of her peach coloured eyes sensual and lost in time. She looked magical.

When she stopped the dance and rested in her final position, the fabric in her ensemble easing slowly back into a still shape, her face contorted to the pained one Ilva knew best. The one that meant the fire within her soul had passed. Ilva used to long to see that smile when she was young. Now it just broke her heart to watch her mother trying to keep a dying culture alive, only smiling when she was dissociating, and it burned in her that she would never be as beautiful as her mother, sorrowful Syli.

The seed of contempt was growing into resentment. After years of trying, she was tired. She felt her essence of self slipping away. How could she tell her mother what rolled about in the caves of her mind, and in the pit of her stomach? *I cannot,* she thought. A firm decision. An affirmation that affected the love she could have felt for her mother, or for herself.

"Wonderfully done dear!" Ilva turned to see her father, Ediv, who was walking down the carved wood steps from the terrace of their home. His mohawk was greasy and slicked over to one side, his expression stoic and firm enough to be addressing soldiers before battle, and every step he took was intimidating. The steps he descended curled around and down into the tree stump, carved right from what the tree had once been. He marched off the final stair to face them both, giving them a look of what Ilva considered falsely affectionate scrutiny, he addressed them each with a nod.

"Thank you, Ediv." her mother's reply came out slightly

slipping. Her breath was laboured. Ilva noticed the dance must have been straining for her. Lately her mother had been unwell often. Her lungs failing her at times. One year she had caught a cold and it had almost killed her. Ilva recalled the memory with silent sympathy. She cared for her mother deeply, even if she buried those feelings.

"You do that dance as well as when I first saw you perform," Ediv exclaimed with what looked like a moment of true pride.

This made Syli blush, only a fraction, before she tightened her sashes and responded with, "You need not commend me so my Lord." She curtsied.

Meanwhile, Ilva would have given all her heart for a compliment of the same caliber to be directed at her. She was shocked to find this only seared hot fire into that growing seed in her stomach. "I am going to the square for a bit," Ilva stated, and walked across the stump, away from her parents.

Before she could get to the base of the stump her mother grabbed her arm, "We are not finished! The sun has not yet touched the sea. Two more sets." Ediv stepped towards the women to interject. He often did when he could tell Syli was pushing too hard, and she always pushed too hard. It was a circle that their family grooved into a pattern. Syli would push, Ilva would resist, Ediv would try to appease both, and none came out satisfied. Ingrained in these behaviours were all three.

Ilva was, once again, triggered. "Oh, to hell with your training. If you enjoy it, then you do it. Stop trying to make me a dancer. I hate this stupid dance." Then she ripped her arm from her mother's grip and stormed away. With every step she felt her breath push from her, and then rush back in. She was full to the points of her ears with anger. She knew when she felt this particular emotion it was better to walk than talk. So, she walked, pounding her feet into the dirt until she reached the cobblestone ground of the square. As she approached the civilians, now looking at her like she might hurt any one of them, she straightened herself, plastered on a falsely content face, and walked around the small space with gentler steps.

The streets of Falil were bustling with the usual activity; the stalls and carts of various eats, and handcrafted items. As Ilva walked past one of the carts she smelled the sweet scent of strawberries and pastries. She glanced to see what treats the vendor had, and was delighted to see tarts with crème and berries filling them up. Her mouth watered. Practice often made her hungry, and she wanted nothing more than one of those delicious tarts to stuff in her keen face. She walked to the cart and the elf greeted her with an overzealous sales pitch. She gave him a small smile, and made her purchase.

Walking from the cart she barely took two steps before indulging in the tasty treat. It was so flaky, and soft that it broke gently under her teeth, almost spilling the contents. The berries were sweet and sour, the crème soft and buttery. Focusing on the taste, she found every hint of its flavour, as it burst into colourful tangs upon her tongue. She chewed and savoured its decadence. She was reminded of the simple comforts she would have to do without when she left this place. This small pleasure she awarded herself brought her such joy. She was grateful of the distraction.

She stuffed the last morsel of crust and remaining fruit

into her mouth and continued to wander lazily through the tiny town. Children ran about with hoots and hollers of excitement, the occasional elder elf grimaced as the elflings passed. She found it strange that some would choose to frown at smiles. She so enjoyed watching anyone experience joy. Especially here. How could anyone find it in them to be unhappy with happiness? She tried not to let that behaviour trouble her.

Some stalls began to pack up their goods as the last light of the day was turning shadows long. The darkness that began swallowing the streets made it slightly cooler, and Ilva enjoyed that miraculous change. The sun was an everyday spectacle, but it did not make it any less magical to her every time it rose and set. Her mind was always filled with the simplest of joys to be had.

She turned a corner to walk down a thin walkway between two homes, and bumped straight into a young male, he bellowed grumpily at her, and continued walking briskly away. Taking the encounter to heart she began telling herself to be more alert. Then she walked on more carefully. She made it to her last stop. Every day, as the last light left and the skies were covered in darkness, she sat at a fountain of water at the entrance of Falil.

This place was beautiful in the dark, with the serene sound of water, and the glittering ripples it produced as the moonlight hit it just right. If you looked close into the water's still areas, you could see the stars reflected just before the ripples broke the vision. Just watching the illusory water move brought her clarity and rejuvenation. Her emotions balancing with each moment she focused intently on her daydream.

She stood up after feeling the calm take her in, and felt ready to return home. As she walked back through the familiar places that she had known for decades, she contemplated what other wonders the world held. She had been to Marka once with her father, and had on rare occasions escaped into the Nilfin forest to adventure. This was considered a dangerous and rebellious act. Not many were brave enough to wander the ancient forests. *Soon to be my new home.* Ilva smiled again.

There were many terrifying tales about the forest. Rather than let it frighten her, Ilva was fascinated by all of these. She found herself constantly saying she was brave enough to survive in the forest, and strong enough to fight off any monsters lurking in the dark. She was not troubled by simple stories. There was never any proof these stories were true, maybe there were no beasts in the forest at all. She did not encounter any on her frequent and unauthorized escapades. She slept that night, dreaming of the leaps she was about to take. *This life is mine. No one can take it from me.*

She toiled the morning away until her patience wore as thin as her silks, and she let her troubles melt while getting lost in daydreams, she said silent goodbyes to each task as she completed them. When the chores were complete, and she knew no one would question her about her daily run, she took off. This time with a bag on her back.

Chapter 3

As Ilva stepped along the forbidden forested path once again, and absorbed all of the splendor, she felt even more righteous in her decision to break the rules. She was comfortable with her choice. Sometimes the ones that got her in trouble were the most satisfying of all until the trouble came. Aside from fear of the retribution she would face, she felt a sense of power when she was making decisions for herself. Felt a strength rise within her. She didn't know her independence could be so freeing. She was obedient for the first hundred years of her life. So very obedient. She questioned things, but did not often disobey. Curiosity loomed heavy in her.

Before today she had a role to play in her community. The world was always trying to fit her into a little box. She wanted to smash the box to bits. Ilva tried to maintain appearances all her life, and was successful in the face of most others. It was her parents that saw her at her worst. She expressed herself regularly without a care of their disapproval. At least, she tried to convince herself she didn't care. She had feelings, and she knew from experience now that if she did not shout them out and have them heard, that they would batter her even harder from inside.

She knew the damage of retaining things could be immense. It was not worth holding back all this pain. She shouted into the quiet of the forest. No one to listen anymore. That was ok. There was also no one looming over her with high expectations. So, when she let her voice echo into the forest, she felt a wave of relief hit her. There would be no retaliation. She could raise her voice louder if she wanted. She did not. But she could.

As Ilva thought about her parents, she longed to know whether her mother ever felt as she did. *Did she ever wish she had another life? Did she long for the option of choice?* Ilva knew her mother did not have any say in marrying her father. Her father had seen her mother dancing at a festival just before the war, and he fell in love. He bought her. There was a lot of slavery in Zoriya after the first war with Mila. Ilva's mother, who was once of noble upbringing, was a bought slave. That was their love story. The story of a war lord and his slave bride.

It broke Ilva's heart to consider herself in the same position as her mother. She would have never gone willingly if she was bought. She didn't want to think her father was a cruel leader, it appeared that her folks were content in most ways, more so than a lot of other elves who had seen and survived wars anyway. Most slaves would end up dead as a result of rebellion. It made her rethink her belief that she would simply flee slavery. There were so many uncertainties in Ilva's life, even with her new found freedom. She wandered through her new home. Her precious forest of isolation and peace. Her own secret sanctuary. *Free.*

Chapter 4

Eighty Years Later

Ilva was sitting on a fallen log carving a bit of wood into a twisting, unnatural shape. She loved to create abstract objects, made and created only by her. Artistically carving wood was now her main pastime. Her hair had been chopped short. Cut away in messy pieces with a small knife. It helped keep it clean. Her face was always smudged with a bit of dirt, and she didn't bother using the rainwater she collected to wash with. It made much more sense to save that for drinking. She was content with her life in the forest. She seldom missed her home, and found more beauty and appreciation of her surroundings now then she ever had before. The peace she felt made her soul feel light and airy.

She looked up from her masterpiece, to see a figure walking down her path. No one came to this part of the forest. This sanctuary in nature belonged only to her. She felt the sharp pangs of frustration. The urge to throw this intruder who was approaching, at a very slow casual saunter, out of her realm of isolation, was deep-seated and strong. This interaction, with another, that was surely soon to be upon her, gave her fear she had not known in more years than she cared to recall. Nevertheless, the figure was encroaching.

As this elf came closer, Ilva could make out the large shining bow strung across her chest. Her long straight hair floating behind her shoulders in colours resembling raven feathers, her clothing as dark as a moonless night sky, and her heavy boots making surprisingly light feathery steps. She was lean, taller than Ilva, her muscles under her outfit were noticeably strong. She wandered down the path, and appeared not to notice Ilva hidden by the foliage in front of the withering log she sat upon. A small flash of fur, no bigger than a mouse, darted across the path from one side quickly to the other. Right in front of the stranger. The stranger was not startled. She glanced slowly at the direction the furry thing went, then brought her head slowly back to her surroundings. She was calm.

This intrigued Ilva. When she lived among others, she did not know them to be so cool, and collected. Everyone she ever knew always seemed to be full of fear, sadness, stress or anger. Except her father, he seemed emotionless most times. He would put on airs for many elves, but never her. Watching this stranger, Ilva noticed how she seemed as at peace in her solitude as herself. Seeing the way the elf appreciated her surroundings made her connect with this stranger, on a level she never had with any other. Then, Ilva noticed as she pulled back from her entranced state, the stranger was closing the gap between them.

Though she was sure she hadn't been spotted; the stranger was no less than ten feet from Ilva. She felt a panic lace its way into her heart as the elf crunched the dirt underfoot. Step,

step, step. Feeling her fear take control, she ducked behind her log, deciding she wanted to remain unnoticed. However, at this motion, the elf turned, as slowly as before. "You need not hide, I have known of your presence since entering this part of the forest."

Ilva, frozen in shock, found her voice hard in her chest, her muscles clenched so hard and tight she could feel her bones beg for movement. She debated on running away. She had run all her life. Running meant safety. Running meant she could stay as she was. Free. Her feet were rooted though, and the stranger did not appear to pose any threat.

The stranger was still looking in her direction, and Ilva noticed the dullness in her milky eyes. They appeared foggy and colourless. *Is she blind?* Ilva thought she could make out traces of an iris that was once there, but now seemed to be hidden by stormy clouds. She felt a feeling, was it pity? No, sympathy maybe? She could not place it. Emotions were fickle things, and Ilva had always struggled to name hers. She did feel one thing she could place however; curiosity.

This was Ilva's nature. She had always been inquisitive. The stranger moved to speak again, shifting her body to face the way her seemingly sightless eyes did. *Gods and goddesses those legs, those shoulders, she could really hurt me if she wanted to. Please don't let this turn to conflict. Should I run? No, she might be able to outrun me.* Ilva struggled with her faintheartedness. "Do you speak?" the stranger asked.

Ilva was terrified to, but she spoke. Her first word to another in decades. "Yes." This word that left her lips, left a stain of remorse upon her tongue. Her silent oath to never need speak to another again, broken. In all her stubbornness, Ilva felt like crying over this betrayal of her willfulness. She could never show anyone her tears though, another sign of her willful nature. She receded slightly, one step, one more, her feet feeling less like they were attached to the forest floor. Those two steps put the stranger on alert.

The unwelcome guest spoke again, "Do not be afraid. I mean you no harm. I'm embarrassed to say that I am quite lost. I was on my way to the ruins of Mila, on the other side of the mountain, do you know the way to the mountain pass?"

Ilva pondered the reason anyone would seek the desecrated city of Mila. This stranger seemed determined in her quest however, and Ilva would be only too happy to direct the lost elf away from her forest. This would require more than one word, and Ilva trembled at the thought. Speaking. Could she do it? Will her voice betray her? She wanted nothing more than to avoid sounding weak in front of the strong female before her.

She took a deep gulp of the saliva that pooled upon her tongue, which threatened to sour into nausea. She said with only a fraction of a shiver in her tone, "That way," and pointed South-West. Forgetting the glazed white orbs within the stranger's sockets.

"Forgive me," the stranger started, "I cannot see well, you blend in very well with those bushes behind you, could you come forward so I can better make out your gestures?" That answered the question, she had some vision. Ilva took unsure steps towards the path, not lowering her arm which pointed the way to Mila. "Ah, so this way then?" said the stranger, mimicking the hand motion.

Ilva nodded, curious if this stranger could see that.

"Thank you," her visitor responded. Yet she did not move down the path towards her destination.

Ilva worried that the stranger intended to converse further. Her worries always came true it seemed.

"I'm Vali, I come from Karna." *Karna.* Another clue about this imposing elf. *Did she really come all this way alone?* Ilva felt that same feeling that could not be placed, the stirring of empathy or something similar.

"Ilva." *Stupid! Why did I tell her my name?* Ilva thought with self-contempt.

"Ilva," the stranger rolled the name out, "I like it."

Ilva felt the heated blood rising in her head until it was to the tips of her ears. Embarrassed by the compliment, Ilva did not know how to respond. Vali was putting Ilva in an awkward position, and she wanted the stranger to be on her way. Then, all at once, she was.

"Well, it was nice to meet you Ilva." Vali said, rolling the name out with her soft voice again. Then she was walking down the path. Out of the forest, now filling with signs of the approaching dusk. *Out of my forest,* Ilva thought as the forest went quieter than ever before. She was surprised with a sudden feeling of loneliness. It was foreign and unwelcome, as the visitor had first been.

Chapter 5

Ilva woke to the light pouring through the canopy of lush trees. She was sleeping in a small cave not quite big enough for a boreal bear, but big enough for her and her small pack. She'd had this pack since the day she left Falil. She remembered suddenly that her birthing day had passed, she was now one hundred and eighty-eight.

Recalling the damp day that she strode from home, backpack in hand, she felt the memories of her past envelop her. Despite Syli not showing much emotion, there were definitely things Ilva said in anger that hurt her mother. Some days she wished she could go back and respond to things differently. Once she had called her mother a coward, it had angered Syli enough that she slapped her daughter, hard across the face. The sting still biting at her all these years later. The moment they broke each other. She would never forget it.

Silence would always be more of a comfort than the condescension, gossip and fighting Ilva was accustomed to growing up. She wandered day in and day out here, in the natural wooded lands, where solitude and silence could be found. Where there were no others but the flora and fauna to share it with. She had never been comfortable with her duty to being social in Falil.

On occasion she would speak, to animals or trees, just to remember the sound of her voice. To recall how the tone echoed within her ears. To feel it leave her lips. She once considered the idea of talking to non-responsive entities and beings odd, but now she did not give it a second thought. She talked with the forest as if it could hear her, and respond. Her imagination turned the wind into words. It comforted her to think the forest was as alive as her. In a way it was. She felt the pulse of nature. It was no illusion to her. She convinced herself of every reality she created, and it held her together on her hardest of days.

As she rose up from her bed of leaves, and her leather pack pillow, she peered out into her forest. Her home. She remembered the stranger that passed through the evening prior. It surprised her that Vali came to her mind, it surprised her more that she remembered her name. The name was pleasing to roll around in her mind. She liked the way it sounded. She felt a sense of longing, which she brushed off as she would an irritable blood fly at dusk.

As she emerged from her tiny cave, she looked around, not just for the presence of animals or danger, but for the beauty that the forest held in those early morning hours. Dew glistened, and light sparkled in droplets like tiny jewels. Something about the forest in the morning brought her the strongest sense of appreciation for where she was. She may be alone, but who would ever care when surrounded by such beauty. She suddenly wished however, that she could share it.

She adjusted her pack so it was comfortable. She didn't have much, so her pack was light, and after years of wearing it daily it felt like just another article of clothing on her. Her bag consisted of a belt and hunting knife, a very small piece of flint, a waterskin she had made herself, and a small bag of nuts she had gathered the day before. She had learned the importance of having food on hand at all times, hunting wasn't always easy, and foraging can be hard when competing with the animals at certain times of the year. She glanced at the forest path that trailed far beyond her cave, staring in the direction Vali went. She had an urge to walk that way, and before she knew it, she was strolling down the dirt and leaves and dew, heading South-West.

She won't be too far ahead if she set up camp last night, Ilva told herself. There was that curiosity, saturating her urges, pulling her feet forward. *Should I follow her to the edge of the forest? I could probably catch up if I sprint.* Before she finished the thought she was poised, ready to lunge forward. She pushed off with her right leg and flew down the trail.

She loved to run. Especially in the morning when everything felt so magical, even her. She felt free when she ran hard, wild, and untameable. As if she were just another creature of this forest, she dodged branches and hurtled over logs like a delicate creature leaping and bounding. The only sound was the wind rushing past her, and her feet tapping the dirt.

After running a little over an hour, she was nearing the edge of the forest, where it met with the foothills. There was a narrow mountain pass that cut through to the abandoned city. This was the way that Vali would have come. She looked around, and saw no sign of the stranger. Not even a sign of her stopping. *Did she not sleep? Did she walk all night?* Ilva pondered question after question.

She stood now at the edge of her forest. The mountains seemed to invite her. Pulling her from her safe woodland home. She fought with the urge to stay or go. Her curiosity threatening to override all her sense. She took a small step out of the foliage, and looked around at the sight of the mountains looming beyond either side.

This was her first step outside of the forest in the eighty years she has resided there. The sun was warm, it threatened to tire her already. She knew the beauty of her forest, how had she never noticed how lovely these mountains were as well? They rose up higher than she could see, rocky and jagged cones larger than the castle in Marka. The top most peaks broke up clusters of clouds, and the clouds swirled around as if stirred, revealing a cyan sky above them. She took in all the majesty.

Her bubble of isolation seemed confining now. *I left to have my freedom,* Ilva rationalized, *so, why do I hesitate?* She could always return to her forest, these mysterious and intriguing mountains pulled at the part of Ilva that could never say no. The desire to take in more sights took her feet and moved them. Her heart racing with the thrill of new places. Adventurous blood pumped in her veins hard and hot, infatuation fueled by adrenaline, she barely noticed her fatigue creeping in. Shouldering her bag up higher for her trek, she began hiking towards the thin pass.

When she had climbed about halfway up Ilva turned to

look upon her forest, which seemed small from way up on the mountainside. Did she really hold herself up in that miniscule looking paradise for so long? With as high as she was, she could make out the vast expanse of the land before her. From here she could see the ocean, a bluer than the sky line that ran from one side of the mountains to the other, and way off in the distance to her left, she could even see the faint tiny speck that would be Marka.

Marka was a huge city filled with elves, for it to appear just a speck on the land mesmerised Ilva. She pulled her vision across the world before her eyes, and thought she might cry when she realised how small she was in such a large place. *Have I really wasted all these years of my life, living in a speck on a map?* she actualized. She sighed so hard her shoulder sagged and her chest and stomach released enough air to make her lightheaded. *Maybe that is just the altitude?* She made to return to the pass, not wanting to take her eyes off the incredible sight of ant-hill sized cities, and gasped at the horrifying sight before her.

It was not the land or cities that caught her breath and pushed out the sound she made. It was a dragon. A massive beastly thing. Its scales brown and black, blending with the rocks of the mountain it now slithered across. It was sinister looking as it slowly slunk over the rocks, dragging its belly and gripping the mountainside with each step. Claws digging into the rock, tail giving the odd flick of enticement, eyes gleaming gold. They seemed to say *and just what are you doing here intruder.* Ilva felt a strong sense of panic. She knew a little about dragons, yet had never seen one. She was so entranced with her adventure, and the wide world before her, that she had forgotten caution. She was the cat, too curious for her own good, and there sat her death upon the rocks.

She gulped so hard she thought she'd choke, and sweat began to bead upon her upper lip. In that instant she was more afraid than she'd ever been in her life. The enormous obsidian horns upon his head spiraled like the horns of a large ram. His tail was almost longer than his body, muscles bunched and rolled under his scales at every movement, his shoulders sat at twice the height of this hips even when crouched. She was surprised the dragon had not attacked her right away, it was as though he was waiting for her to run; tail still twitching like an excited predator ready to pounce. It wanted sport. It wanted to show its prey how little of a chance of escaping there would be, only after giving it the chance to try. It was a game, and Ilva did not want to die playing it. This time, running was not her salvation.

She faced the dragon down. Wishing deeply that she had secured her knife to her belt, before her journey, rather than keeping it in the pack. *This is what you get for being unprepared!* She began doing battle in her mind, which was not productive now. It never was. Yet she bickered away with herself over the mistake. The dragon slid into the pass and began approaching her slowly, his front claws moving delicately through the narrow rocks on either side of its massive shoulders. His tongue flicking lizard like in and out, tasting the air. He was now close enough to lunge and grab her. She swallowed again, almost choking her throat was so tight, and then Vali came leaping across the sharp peaks.

Chapter 6

Vali shot her body fast and adept across the back of the dragon, running up half of his spine dodging spike after spike, until she was at the base of his massive horns. By the time the dragon had noticed her landing on his back, she had already wrapped her legs around one of his immense horns and hooked her feet together to maintain her spot of dominion over the terrifying creature. As she held on with just her legs, the dragon roared loud enough to send rocks tumbling down either side of the mountains, the thunderous sound threatened to split Ilva's ears.

Several rocks and boulders pummeled the dragon as they tumbled into the narrow pass. One large boulder plowed heavily into his back-left leg, and another struck his tail, he let out a throaty groan. The avalanche pounded the earth around Ilva, where she stood motionless in the path of the present dangers, one rock the size of her head came down and struck her in the shoulder hard. At first it didn't register how painful the crack was, then when she went to lift her arm she winced and held in a shriek of pain, almost biting her tongue at the resist. It felt as if someone had suddenly set her joint on fire and her blood rushed under her skin forming bruises she could not see beneath her tunic. The dragon, afraid of another avalanche of rocks, let out a deep unending growl, as he swayed and shoved his head against the rocky cliffs, in an attempt to remove the pest upon his crown.

Bow in hand, and body curled under the swoop of his horn, Vali aimed at the base of the dragon's skull with a huge black and silver arrow. Ilva watched her display of expert battle reactions with awe. Vali loosed the thick heavy arrow straight down into the dragon's scales, its eyes went wide with rage. The shot did not kill him, but it was obvious he was in excruciating pain, the way he reared and bucked now was frantic and panicked, rather than annoyed. He was less concerned about the pest as he was with the fiery golden stream running down his long face.

Vali took the arrow in both hands and pushed with what looked like incredible force, down further into the skull of the monstrous mass. At this the dragon engulfed the air in flame, so hot the air became heavy and was rank with a burning sulphuric scent. Ilva thought she would pass out soon, she looked up at the skirmish before her, and Vali slid her hooked feet off the curved horn, planted them on either side of the arrow and yanked it out. When she did the stream became a torrent, like lava bursting through the top of a volcano. It flowed fast down the dragon's snout, smoking and sizzling as it struck the path in heavy drops.

The great dragon fell, breathing heavy and laboured. Ilva locked onto an eye, and for a fleeting moment she registered pain in it, among other things, before his lengthening breaths became one final heave. The breath, long and shallow, echoed across the wind. The silence that followed was eerie, and the sight of death sent shivers over Ilva, and then the world spun. Her head became light and her body cumbersome, she fell forward, into the gravel, unconscious.

Chapter 7

Ilva woke to the sound of a crackling fire, and the scent of smoke and burning wood. There was another smell of cooked meat, and she thought she could almost taste it, it was so sweet. When her eyes adjusted to the darkness around her, she noticed it was night, starless and black. The only light the glow of the fire about four feet away from her. It was warm where she lay, resting on a large fur pelt, and it felt as if there were a cushion of soft grass beneath her. The comfort of this made her not want to move, yet she was on alert. *Did Vali help me after I passed out?* Ilva wondered. As she thought this, and looked around the small camp for another body, she saw another heap of fur with Vali upon it. *Why would she have gone to the trouble?* Ilva was riddled with questions.

The direction Vali came from across the mountain made it seem like she was ahead of Ilva. *Why would she turn from her quest to slay a dragon that was preoccupied with someone else?* Was the dragon valuable to kill? There was no way she would have done it if there was nothing to gain. *Elves don't do things like that. Elves are self-serving,* Ilva mocked to herself.

She shuffled to sit, and a single "Gah!" escaped her lips. She murmured and heaved a few sharp breaths. At the sound Vali was to her feet. The swift reaction startled Ilva, and took her attention off the pain now pumping her veins hard.

Vali relaxed her body and face, folding her legs under her she sat upon her pile of fur. "Do you feel rested? We should move at first light." Ilva strained to find comfort in those words, but instead found fear, as she did with most things.

"Why do we need to move? Are we in danger here?" The questions fell from Ilva's mouth before she could realise how cowardly they made her sound. Embarrassment coloured her cheeks as, once again, she wished she had not spoke.

"No. And Yes." *Straight and to the point,* Ilva thought. *I like it. The less words the better.*

"You said we," Ilva returned, interested in the affirmation this statement made.

"Yes, we. You are following me correct?" Ilva flushed. She had no response to this. The ones tumbling through her mind made her feel foolish. Vali continued. "I do not mind the company, though mine may be poor." Ilva considered the response carefully. This elf was not displeased with her, in fact, it sounded as if she was judging herself more than her company. Openly. Without hesitation, she stated a flaw of hers. It made Ilva want to open up too. Yet she did not.

"Are we heading to Mila then?" was Ilva's reply.

Vali nodded once. Then she stood up, a bag in her hand, pulled out a strip of dried meat, and handed it to Ilva.

Ilva took it, whispered a quiet, "Thank you," and began to bite and chew.

Ilva and Vali rose simultaneously from their beds the next day, and Ilva copied Vali's actions as she rolled the fur tightly into a small log shape. Vali tied it to her pack with a leather strap, and tossed a long strip of leather to Ilva to do the same. She was grateful for the efforts Vali had made to ensure her safety, and even her comfort, when it was not her responsibility.

Ilva wanted to express her gratitude and found herself struggling for the right words. She realised that gratitude was not something she often expressed to others, even before her isolation, and felt ashamed at that cognizance. She considered that her old self may have been a bit entitled. She then considered whether anyone in her life before had done anything to earn gratitude from her, and she bitterly assured herself they had not. She conveniently forgot about shop keepers who parted with their creations for mere coin, and the elves who cooked the food she once ate. She decided that Vali was the only one who had earned this feeling of indebtedness. She searched within her for something to break the silence that she usually treasured. Vali did not seem uncomfortable with the silence, this made Ilva relax a bit, and she continued to think of ways to express herself in silence.

Vali was kicking dirt over the coals in the fire pit, and brushing the ground to look as if no one had been where they had. Ilva did not know if this was because of potential dangers, or if it was because, like her, Vali felt things in the wild should be left as they were found. Either way, she appreciated her diligence and commitment in tidying the area.

When Vali handed Ilva another strip of the meat she

accepted it with another "thank you." At that moment, she found the words she had been searching for. "I don't know why you saved me, but you have my gratitude." The statement came out naturally, and this caused Ilva to be surprised at herself. She did not expect, after so much isolation, that she could speak to another with such ease. She smiled a bit to herself. Proud of her ability to express her feelings to this elf.

Vali seemed to shrug the comment off at first, but then replied "You were foolish to be in that pass, but I would never have been able to abandon you to such a cruel fate. You are welcome." This was going well Ilva thought! She was excited about the concept of a conversation thriving. Talking never used to feel like this. It used to feel constrictive, and forced. The authenticity of this interaction warmed her heart. It wasn't a long conversation. *Could two lines even be called conversation?* She felt content. As content as if she had never left her solitude in the forest. Vali felt like the forest to her.

Chapter 8

Vali held up a hand, off in the distance, about a three hour walk now, was Mila. The broken city rose up off the land hauntingly. Nothing else was visible upon the flat wasteland of dry cracking earth. Ilva stared at their destination with a breath of relief. It had been almost two full days since the dragon. It would be night time in a couple of hours. They both concluded they should camp for the night.

They had to traverse the dry rocky mountainsides, and set up camp along the foothills the two nights before. Vali lost a whole day of travelling caring for Ilva after the dragon incident and the guilt nagged at Ilva.

Vali felt her own guilt, about bringing Ilva along to this awful place. Ilva may have felt unwanted but, ironically, Vali wanted Ilva with her very much. She never wanted to come back here alone, and now she wouldn't have to. It felt selfish, wanting Ilva to follow her, for the company and comfort. Vali began digging up rocks to make a fire pit.

Ilva thought about why Vali always started to set up camp so early. Was it her eyesight? Ilva knew she could see a little, maybe she was more uneasy of the dark because of the loss of more of her vision? Ilva thought about Vali's eyes. Then her own. How would she feel if she could no longer see? The view from the top of that mountain pass, or the sunlight streaming through the trees in her forest. She loved seeing the world. She loved colour, light, and shape. Her favourite things in life were what she saw. *What an extraordinary reality, to not be able to take in sights.* She instantly felt a stronger sense of interest growing.

Does she feel sadness over the loss of her sight? There were so many things Ilva wanted to ask. She turned and looked into Vali's eyes, allured by their appearance. Ilva stared for a long time, until Vali said, "Paint a portrait, it will last longer," not in a biting tone, more a joking one. It still caught Ilva off-guard, and she felt ashamed at her rude behaviour. "If you are curious about my eyes, you can ask me about them."

The words shook Ilva's curiosity around inside of her. She did want to ask, the question was what did she want to ask? *How did it happen? Does it hurt? Do you hate it?* She settled on one she thought was not too invasive, but would still satisfy her meddlesome mind. "How long?"

Vali took a deep breath. "It has been just over eighty years."

Ilva took this in. Then it hit her; that is the exact time that Mila fell. Was Vali part of the War? Was that the reason for her journey to the ruined city now?

After a few minutes Ilva was spouting out questions faster than Vali could answer them. She was worried she might be annoying her. If she was, her companion did not say, or show signs of irritation. So, she continued her stream of interest, and the conversation grew to be effortless between them.

She asked her if it hurt, Vali said no.

She asked if it stayed the same or got worse, Vali said it depended.

Some questions got a straight yes or no, while others, like this last one, just created more questions. Ilva was dying for more explanation at times. To prevent more questions from arising she attempted easier queries. Ilva felt full of puzzles. She had never met anyone without sight.

"How did it happen?" Ilva finally asked.

Vali sagged her shoulders a bit when she let out a breath, as though she knew this question was coming, as if it was the one question she hoped to avoid. She took one more breath, sat on a boulder, and motioned for Ilva to sit too.

Ilva pulled out the sack of nuts from her pack. She ate a handful, crunching them casually between her teeth, appearing calm and collected, maintaining the aura of comfortable confidant.

Vali half whispered, "Magic did this to me."

Chapter 9

"Magic?" Ilva queried.

"Yes. Magic. The thing that divides us, causes imbalances in our world, and ruined my life. The thing we would all be better off without. Meddlesome nefarious magic," Vali vented.

Ilva didn't really want to go down this road in their conversation. Things had been going well. Ilva let her history with communication haunt her as she assumed responsibility for Vali's sudden shift in mood. "I'm sorry, forgive my intrusive questions," Ilva offered abjectly.

"Quite alright," Vali returned. "I do not enjoy talking about what happened, but I want to. It is just a bit of a long story, and a rather traumatic tale, I would not want to make you uncomfortable."

Ilva wished to comfort Vali, "I understand, thank you for indulging my curiosity, you only need talk if you want to. No pressure."

Vali was grateful for the position Ilva awarded her, the choice to share information. No one was ordering her to provide detail. *No pressure.* She soothed to herself. "Did you know silver elves create ornate weaponry from our element?" Vali shared, as she handed her bow to Ilva.

It was exquisite! *This is made of silver magic?* It was smooth, long, and the points where silver met string curved a fraction. There were leaves and vines detailing the entire piece, the string glittered as if it too was silver, most noticeably though was how heavy it was. Ilva could barely hold it up.

Vali took it back when Ilva had finished gawking. Then she added, "It took me a while to build up enough muscle to shoot it properly."

"Were you afraid when you fought the Dragon?" Ilva thought this was a safer question. *Avoiding topics that have to do with the past might be easier.*

"Yes. Fear is a necessary part of fighting. It tells you when danger is present." Vali reasoned.

Ilva thought on this, and found it to be sensible, despite the debilitating effects fear had on her. "How do you fight when you are afraid? How do you prevent freezing up, or running?"

"Sometimes I run and sometimes I freeze. If you face enough of your fears you start to overcome those urges though. You can learn in time how to fight your fear and your opponent at the same time," Vali admitted.

Ilva was content with the conversation once again. "I hope I can learn to fight someday," Ilva conceded.

"It is definitely a valuable skill, self-defence. However, learning to fight the way I did, with the intention of killing in battle, is less appealing." Vali, it seemed, had returned to the past.

Ilva wondered if she should say anything, or give her a moment. She decided on silence, turning her body towards Vali to let her know she was still listening, and waited for the conversation to direct itself.

Vali began to profess, "My father was going to war, and I was afraid for him. I knew the elves of Mila hated us, I knew that our dungeons had some held prisoners of the war too, though I never knew why. I was young and naïve. The details of the conflict were kept between a select few high ranked officials of each faction. No one told me, or civilians, why there was such hostility between cities. I wanted to know what all this fighting was really about. So, the day he was to set out, I grabbed my bow and quiver, and followed him. It's been a long time since I've made this journey."

Ilva shuddered. She was unsure of whether she wanted to know any more. *This story must be hard to talk about.*

Vali shifted her legs up higher on the rock, pulling one ankle up underneath of her.

Has she ever spoken of this to anyone else? Ilva thought about her role in the conversation. If she was the first, she felt honoured at Vali's trust in her. She wanted to be the best listener she could. The listener she herself had longed for. That's what she could be for Vali.

Vali continued, "It was several days before they made it to the place we are now. Many soldiers together move slowly. I was staying several hours behind the band of my father's company, sleeping among boulders and foothills as the nights came on. The morning of battle, when I went to spy on the company, they were gone. All of them. As I approached Mila,

I noticed the quiet. There were no shouts or screams. It was completely silent. There were no elves in sight as I entered the city." Vali stopped. Her face contorted with pain.

Ilva wanted to reach out to her. *But, how?*

Vali squirmed a bit, making it apparent how tense she was. Her stance was rigid and she gripped the leather belt around her hips. Ilva didn't notice her squeezing and releasing the leather over and over. A secret trick Vali used to calm herself and avoid panic attacks. She wanted to end the conversation quickly now. *Why did I even start talking about all this?* She went on, "I never found out what I wanted to know and my father died in battle that day. I lost my sight when I fought with, something. I don't know what it was. A shadow. A darkness. There was an arcane artifact in Mila, we fought over it, that's how I was blinded. I had it in my hands, and I lost it. It must still be out here. I haven't had the courage to come back. Until now."

Once again, Ilva was frozen, fear of failure to communicate dominating her subconscious. Deciding upon the correct response was almost as terrifying as the dragon encounter. Almost.

Chapter 10

Ilva gulped. How could she ever comfort someone who had survived so much strife? *She is probably so tough she doesn't even need any comforts from me. It sure puts my situation into a new perspective,* she thought. With no idea what to say, and the feeling that she had to say something, she shyly stated "I'm so sorry,"

Vali heaved a deep sigh. "No one believed me when I went back. My grandmother told me there was no shadow, that going blind had played tricks on me, and that if I kept talking about shadows she would have no choice but to declare me mad and lock me away for my own protection. I have not spoken of it in nearly half a century, but I know it happened. I felt the bruises of the battle. I can still smell the smouldering charcoal scent of that bird. I remember using magic." She made a mocking snort sound before adding. "The event was traumatic and I have no idea why I'm opening up like this. You make me feel comfortable I suppose. I appreciate your curiosity."

The compliment took Ilva by surprise.

Vali added, "Swallowing my truth was the only way to

ensure I would be able to find acceptance at home. This, talking about it, is most comforting." The conversation still hung over them, Vali sought the comfort of closure, "Thank you for listening to me. It means a lot to me." Her sightless eyes moved in Ilva's direction, as she said in a softer tone, "Let's get some sleep. We have a long day ahead."

Ilva blushed so brightly her cheeks felt hot, and stung a bit as if someone had pinched them. The softness and emotion in Vali's eyes had caught Ilva off guard. She bit at her lip and struggled to find something to say. Ilva was so uncomfortable she shifted in her seat and let out the most awkward, "I am out of practice with communicating, I can listen all you like though. Talk any time you feel the need my friend." *That sounded good, right?* Ilva thought.

Vali let out an exhausted grunt and appeared ready to pass out. The time had passed considerably as they had talked, the sky was shades of amber and amethyst. Sunset. As the last golden line left the horizon, navy began spilling down from above the clouds, slowly filling the sky with deep-sea hues. Though it did not feel like a waste of time to Ilva, to Vali that is exactly what it felt like. She cursed herself for wasting time talking about unchangeable history. She never even finished setting up camp. So, she jumped off the rock, began hastily unrolling their beds and grabbed her flint for the fire.

As soon as Vali had stood, Ilva was eager to give her a hand. This comforted Vali more than any words would have. She wasn't used to having physical help.

It was much colder on this dry open land at night. Though they spoke no more, Vali sat close to Ilva upon her fur, and wrapped hers around the two of them, claiming it was the easiest way to stay warm. They sat by the fire, shoulder to shoulder, feeling the flames and eating the dried meat Vali seemed to have unlimited stock of.

Ilva fell asleep like that, lolling her head until it dropped onto the silver elf's shoulder. She drooled a bit, and Vali smiled. *Maybe this is what it feels like to trust someone,* Vali sighed to herself. She liked the hopeful thought of a new friend in her life. The idea of trust. It also frightened her.

Chapter 11

When they awoke the next day, they were both still next to one another. Ilva was pretty much blanketing Vali with her left leg and arm. Their curves rested against each other comfortably. Upon waking, they both startled at the position they were in. They sat up, shifted a fraction apart, and tried to act as if there was nothing odd about how they slept. Other elves do it all the time. Why did she feel so shameful? It was not as if they did anything. The things that didn't happen flashed through her mind. Ilva, absorbed in her wildest imaginations, a nude version of Vali next to her, their curves meeting, almost didn't hear Vali say, "Let us pack up."

Ilva blushed so hard she thought Vali, even with her fogged vision, might see the flush in her face; bright as the crimson sun rising with them.

Vali stood up first, and began packing up camp, moving swiftly.

Ilva watched her and noticed it then; Vali was blushing too.

When they had packed up the last of their gear, and buried the pit of coals, they marched around to face Mila. Today, maybe they would find what Vali sought. Ilva was still following along with no idea what they were after. Vali seemed like a decent elf. Ilva thought they had a lot of things in common. Then the story came back to her. *Maybe not that much,* she thought, *she is braver than I could ever hope to be.*

"Ilva," Vali spoke.

The sound of her own name had never been so pleasing to hear. She loved the way her name sounded in Vali's soft sing-song voice, as if she had never before been called by it properly. She turned to face her. She was sure that Vali could still sense the movement, and appreciated the gesture. "I told you my story yesterday. I still do not know yours, however. Forgive my curiosity, but would you tell me something of yourself? Just to pass time on our walk."

Ilva was so taken aback she almost tripped over her own foot, but she managed to right herself before feeling too foolish. "I am not as interesting as you are. I do not wish to bore you with my rather uneventful life."

Vali smiled and giggled, "You find me interesting, do you?"

Once again Ilva's face was on fire.

"Oh, well...yes. Your story yesterday was fascinating, and so are you." Ilva shook all over, she sounded only a little awkward when she spoke. It took all her strength to maintain her composure.

Vali suddenly burst out laughing. Then Ilva joined. Unable to hold back, her face became sore from the strain on her cheeks and her stomach felt like she had never used her abs before. *Who knew laughter could be such a laborious thing?* Her lungs trembling under the short inhales she managed to take. The two of them laughed harder and harder. As one would stop the other would start again. After a couple good minutes, they had become raspy and had to stop. Deep breathing ensued, and the two of them chuckled down as smiles were still spread upon their faces, they walked on.

After another few minutes Vali spoke up again. "I did not mean to jest you. I had no idea the request would make you feel so pressured to respond. I am glad you find me fascinating. I also find you most interesting, and though I do long to know about you, mysterious Ilva, I would not press for it. No pressure, right?"

Ilva considered her words carefully. *She wants to know about me, and she finds me interesting too? I do want to talk about what happened to someone too. I can trust her, if she can trust me.* Ilva began "Well, I was never inducted. Never learned magic. My mother tried to force her traditions on me. I was a bit of a disappointment I am rather a childish girl I suppose. I am not well behaved, and as a result not well liked. So, I sort of, ran away from my life, like a coward.

"Not much else to tell really. That's my whole story. A spoiled rich little elf with controlling parents. I stayed in the forest for a long time. All alone. You were the first elf I had spoken to, in eighty years." The reality sunk in, and as Ilva opened up this part of herself she felt the hurt all over again. She had forgotten a lot of her pain and loneliness, focusing only on where she went and not where she had been. *Is that really how cowardly I am?* Ilva thought. She looked to see if she could gauge how Vali must see her now.

Vali's face was painted with an expression of soft sympathy.

Ilva felt surprised at this and found comfort in it. She spoke again, "I feel at ease speaking with you too. Even if I have not conversed in years. You don't judge the things I say, or berate them, or lecture me. You are not demanding, or pushy, or mean. You have my thanks for wandering into my forest, and leading me out. I did not even know I felt alone, until you walked away."

"Well," Vali soothed, "neither of us is alone now. I consider you the only true friend I have ever had. I do not care that we met only a few suns ago. You are my friend, and I hope we shall always be friends. I wish to laugh like that more," she ended with a light chuckle.

They reached the ruined place by mid-morning, and it was a frightful sight. Buildings were tumbling down, and dusty sand covered every inch of the city. Vali stiffened as they approached the large pillars that rose on either side. The first step into the city was daunting. Vali did not need to say anything for Ilva to know her reservations. She turned to her new friend, and grasped her hand. It was an unusual sensation. Touching the hand of another. She had not done this since she was small. She could feel, through the griping of her fingers, the relief it brought Vali, as her hand softened its grip. They took the first step into the city. Together.

Chapter 12

Walking through this abandoned place was frightening. Ilva was glad to give Vali support. She wished someone had given her a hand to hold many times while she was alone. Holding Vali's made her feel she had something to give. That she was needed. It was a good feeling.

As they passed home after home, the desertion was clear. No one else was here. There was no livestock, no farmable land, and no water. It was a formidable wasteland, and this town was part of the landscape now. The dust had battered the wooden doors down to soft shapes resembling driftwood. Ilva thought it was fascinating that sand could have the same effect on things as water.

The largest settlement appeared to be the bell tower, now sunk sideways into the ground. It was as if the bottom had crumbled, not the top. The bell hung at a permanent sideways angle, and looked like the base of it was resting on the roof of what might have once been another building. With the sand dunes rising up the sides of all the buildings it was hard to tell what any of them were before. What might have been double doors once was now simply a large gap between the sides of a massive doorframe. They walked over the dusty hills of windswept earth covering the steps and trudged inside an open ceilingless room. As Ilva's feet shuffled heavily and slowly over the ground she kicked something, then she let out a short high-pitched yell. A skull came into view under the sand. Vali squeezed her hand, quieting Ilva's fear. "It's ok. Come on."

They worked their way around the room to where the stairs had once been. Vali seemed unsure of where to go, and Ilva could tell she was too proud to ask for help navigating. Ilva looked around for where they might get to the upper floors. She saw an opening to the next story up and it was leaning. They should be able to walk up the slope to the inside of the tower from there. So, she pulled Vali's hand saying, "Come this way, we can make it up there from this direction".

Vali let Ilva lead her. Ilva hesitantly let go of Vali's hand to climb up into the cylinder. Then she reached back, but Vali was already beside her in the tube. They climbed upward, gripping bricks in the old stairwell and pulling themselves towards the bell.

What are you looking for here? Ilva wished she knew so she could help find whatever it was. As she was focusing on thoughts her foot slipped, several bricks fell out of place, and her leg now hung in the hole it created. She pulled it back through, paying more attention to the bricks and rocks under her still stable foot. *The higher we climb the more dangerous it would be if these bricks gave way. What if we get trapped under all of the debris? What if the whole tower comes down upon us?* Her thoughts tormented her with negative possibilities. Vali was so sure footed as she climbed, the sand covered buildings were the only thing that seemed to be difficult for her so far on their journey. She may not have been able to see things as clearly, but she made that problem seem irrelevant, the way she scaled the inside of the tower. One powerful leg pushing her up, after the other. Steady she went.

This gave Ilva a sense of competition she was not accustomed to. If Vali could scale this tower without fear, then so could she. She propelled herself higher and higher. Each foot pressing gently and feeling for the support under her as she went. Soon she was shoulder to shoulder with Vali, and they were at the bell before either of them realised the ascent was complete. They stood on the precipice of where the bell was tilting over, and the place that used to be a balcony now looked like one of the floodway slopes in the larger cities. The floor sat at an angle cutting into the top of the adjacent building. On the roof of the building being crushed by the bell tower landing sat a slab table.

As Ilva looked to her newest friend, who was squinting hard, attempting to see, she was impulsed to assist her. Ilva thought it might be rude, but she asked anyhow, "What are you looking for? Can I help find it?" She chose her words carefully, she didn't want to make Vali feel incompetent, but she also wanted to help in any way she was able. She was also still riddled with curiosity about Vali's quest.

The unscathed Vali answered, "I am looking for an arcane artifact. It will be made of pure sylvite, pinkish in colour, it resembles an unrefined hunk of crystal about the size of a fist. I don't expect I will have much luck. But I have to try." In her mind she added, *that artifact is the only thing that will make my truth undisputable. I will show my grandmother that I am not crazy. I wish I could hunt that shadow down to throw at her feet as well. Then she could deny my truth no longer.*

Ilva took in the description. *At least I know what to look for now,* she thought. She began scanning the area. Ilva wondered about the artifact. It amazed her, she had never heard of an arcane artifact, yet her own mother is a pure sylvite elf. As she puzzled more pieces of the mystery together, she walked back and forth along the top of the sloped edge that met with the roof below. Her eyes scanned all over for anything fitting Vali's depictions. She thought the crushed roof at the other side of the landing, near the fallen table, might be worth inspecting closer. She stepped onto the tilted floor, slipped on the dusty stone, and began falling towards the slab table.

As she slid down the landing, a few uneven cracks and juts scraped at her back and arms and her bad shoulder. She winced and cried out once or twice on the descent. Forcing herself to remain upright during the slide, despite the bumps and bangs under her, she slid foot first towards the roof. When her feet struck the clay tiles below, she winced at the pain that shot through her shins. It stung for a moment, then slowly her legs uncoiled and the pain receded some. Her shoulder still ached. The pain hadn't gone away since the encounter with the dragon. When she stood, she had to use her other arm for support, any pressure put on the pained shoulder strained the joint.

Vali yelled across the gap, "Ilva, are you okay? What happened?"

"I'm alright!" Ilva shouted back, "I slipped. I'm on the other side of the bell tower now. There is a big table down here and I thought I would check it out."

Before she began walking across the roof, Vali began running down the slope. Ilva turned to watch, both in fascination and in fear. Vali was tapping her feet off of each place she landed as if she were just a kid playing at jumping stepping stones in a pond, leaping from one spot to another. Ilva was terrified she might fall, or miss step. But she did not. Ilva realised she didn't give Vali near enough credit for how she worked alongside her disability. She was not looking at anything, her eyes fixed within her face, and her bounding remained resolute. It was as if she could judge the distance by some other means. Then she landed right in front of Ilva, feet planted firmly on the roof.

"How did you do that?" The expression of surprise leapt from Ilva lips before she could catch it. She burned with shame. She shouldn't ask Vali to explain herself in this.

But she had, and Vali replied, "I can still make out some shapes and shadows, and feel the closeness of things, I thought I had mentioned that. Elves and moving things are easiest to see, their tone, smell, breathing, heart rate, sometimes I swear I can feel the blood pulsing in someone's veins if they stand close enough. Also, the sound of your voice told me where you were. My others senses have made up for my eyes."

Ilva was amazed by Vali, enamoured with the information on how she perceived the world. Ilva realised she hadn't said anything and breathed out, "You are incredible."

Vali reddened and smiled a bit at the compliment. Her

senses felt fuzzy and distant at the sweet sentiment, and then she quickly and quietly regained her composure. She turned to the table, and began walking across the shattered terrace.

Chapter 13

Ilva walked across the roof in the other direction, towards the edge of the terrace, and almost stepped in a hole on the roof. *What made this,* she pondered. Peering into the hole, she looked all around the abandoned dirty building. There was rubble just under the hole, and everything in the building was coated with sand. She could bear her eagerness no more, she kicked the sharp bits of clay off around the hole, and jumped down to scout out the empty dust covered space. She caught herself on an exposed beam in the roof, and shooting herself farther into the room, as to avoid the rock pile under her entrance. Once landed, she felt that same shooting pain as when she landed on the roof. Her shins burned a moment, then the shock ebbed.

She began pacing the perimeter of the room, inspecting it thoroughly. It was a large open space. Long tables ran in two room length rows, with benches on either side. There were still bowls and plates and silverware, napkins and glasses and bottles. Some undisturbed, others knocked over by any wind that had blown in over time. Every inch looked claimed by nature, yet Ilva could envision easily how everything had looked before the years had changed it. She wandered to the corner closest to the damaged roof again, almost finished walking around the entirety of the extravagantly large room. She noted a large buffet cabinet against the back wall, four tall wardrobes in-between the large windows to her left and right, one of which was cracking. As she walked back to the hole, she looked up to study a way out, and was aghast.

A single grand chandelier, which seemed to retain so much dust it was indistinguishable, hung from an ornately decorated ceiling. There were large lush green trees painted onto the curving buttresses, they grew up into the ceiling and the tops faded away into darkness, a night sky speckling the sloped ceilings with stars beyond the boughs. It was like looking up into her own forest at night. It was stunning craftsmanship. Ilva was awestruck.

As Ilva lost herself in the stargazing, she tripped over the pile of rocks she was so careful to avoid on the way in. She nearly shrieked, but didn't want to alarm Vali, and chomped the pain down into a swallow that made her eyes water. She stood after a second and noticed her leg was cut open, one of the rocks had been sharp enough to cut well into her shin.

She winced at the pain, and noticed the small amount of blood that slowly seeped from the deepest part of the cut, then began to flow quicker. She didn't have anything on her to stop the bleeding. Frantically she looked to her right and saw dusty old napkins on the table, which she grabbed hastily and shook out before pressing it on her wound. The pressure was enough to stop the flow, so she wrapped it tightly around her leg and hoped the dust wouldn't cause any infection before she could wash it and dress it properly. She continued scouting the room, now very focused on finding a way out. There was a big double wide door at the far end of the tables. It was blocked by dunes on the outside, but she figured if she pushed hard enough the blockage would give way.

She pushed hard on the door to the left, and the entire thing fell out of the doorframe, her body leaned into the collapsing wood. It smashed under Ilva's weight, and the splintered pieces lay in the dusty earth that now spilled in. When she stood up, Vali was above her, head hanging over the roof, "What was that?" she chimed in a playful tone.

Ilva awkwardly explained, "I broke the door trying to open it."

Vali swung down, and although she landed smoothly, she stumbled awkwardly through the spreading sand into the doorway. "The doors are very thin. I'm surprised they were still in place," she said, as she touched the double door that was still in place. It shifted slightly.

Ilva stood next to her and looked back into the room. Vali opened the other door, broke it off the hinges as well, and dropped it into the room. Ilva turned and saw something reflect the light now pouring into the room. Her natural curiosity took over as she approached the glint. She rolled the rocks closest to where she spotted the glare and let them tumble onto the floor beside her.

Under the rock, nestled for all this time, had been the item of Vali's pursuit. Ilva called Vali over, they were both reluctant and full of overwhelm. Vali expected this to be a fruitless journey. To have found what she sought was an outcome that she had not exactly prepared for. She was so used to expecting the worst. For things to turn out like this, well, it was a lot to process. *This feels too easy.* Vali stepped gingerly to the spot where Ilva knelt on the rubble.

Vali quickly stated, "Don't touch it. This is the magic that stole my sight. Is there anything in your bag we can put it in? Or do you see anything in this room we can use?"

Ilva was already thinking ahead of Vali's next question, "There are cloth napkins on the tables, will wrapping it up work?"

"Let's try it," Vali replied.

So Ilva stalked over to a table and swiped up two, just to be safe, layered them together after a good shake out, and laid them cautiously over the sylvite. She tied the napkins corner to corner, tucking in every edge to hide the item inside, before handing the bundled artifact to Vali.

Vali accepted the precious cargo, bound within the cloth, she placed it in her pack and gently eased the straps onto her shoulders. Then, she pulled Ilva into an embrace that left them both glowing.

Ilva was elated to have been of such tremendous help to Vali. She felt, for the first time in her life, that she had done something right. She let the euphoria rampage through her. The two of them left Mila. Walking away from the ruins the same way they had entered, hand in hand.

Chapter 14

Vali stood over the fire, poking the coals and feeling the heat from each one as she turned it. Once she had made the bed of coals she needed, she rummaged in her bag digging things out, two pieces of the dried meat, some leather strips, a few bits of cloth, and a rope. All of which she put back in her pack, after retrieving a small wooden box the width of three fingers, a wineskin and a knife.

Ilva felt a bit useless whenever Vali cooked. She wished she had some cooking knowledge of her own. She was really more of a gatherer than a hunter. She wasn't even sure that she wanted meat tonight, but was afraid to turn Vali down after all the effort she put into hunting and prepping the fire, so she waited patiently and offered occasionally to help with things like cutting herbs or gathering up any small sticks she could find. There wasn't much vegetation along the mountains that met the desert. She managed to scavenge a few armfuls of dry twigs which burned quickly.

A small animal, resembling a rabbit with tusks, hung from a branch close by. Earlier she had cleaned the insides and buried them, then sliced and tugged the fur off. Finally, she brought the meat over, stuck it through one of the gathered sticks, and roasted it close to the coals as the fire dimmed. The food was cooked rather quickly, likely because it was a thin creature. Vali shredded apart portions with her knife, and passed Ilva a large piece.

Ilva hadn't had cooked meat in a while. As she sank her teeth in, chewing slowly, there was familiar flavour. Then she noticed the box Vali was heavily pouring on to some of the leftover pieces of meat. *Salt!* Ilva was thrilled for the sensation. Her tongue was tingling, her taste buds danced. However, after dinner her jaw hurt. Going so long without meat her jaw wasn't accustomed to the effort of chewing.

Vali was curing the leftovers, creating a kind of jerky. She finished the salting and then stuck the meat into the smokiest part of the fire. Letting all the smoke drift across the meat would help preserve it for the road, the smoking and heavy salting gave the dried meat another flavour entirely.

Ilva watched Vali work. Following every movement until everything was wrapped and stored. Vali got up, cloaking herself in her bedroll and furs, and came to sit next to her. In Vali's hand was the last item not put back into the bag; the wineskin. Ilva felt a chill of anticipation, hoping the wineskin held actual wine. She had only tasted wine a few times in her life. She recalled loving the fruity flavour, the memory set her mouth to salivating, before she began recalling darker memories of nights when her mother drank too much of it. When she noticed her drift in attention she snapped back to where she was. Safe. With Vali.

Vali uncapped the skin and glugged a mouthful of its contents. She gasped afterwards, coughed a moment, and then offered the skin to Ilva. With controlled hands, not wanting to come off as nervous, she reached for it. She took a sip, and almost gagged, it was strong, stronger than any wine she had ever tasted. It wasn't fruity. It was definitely still wine, yet it burned on the way down, and filled her nose with a strong alcoholic scent.

She thought back to the forest again, and how this was a life of luxury in comparison. Even if it was not as elegant as her origins, this moment itself felt rich. The strength of the wine did not deter Ilva from drinking more than half of the skin, at Vali's insistence.

Vali had sensed the satisfied vibes coming from Ilva. She was often understanding of the things that Ilva found pleasure in, and felt relief that they were simple pleasures. Things, she realised since meeting Ilva, that she herself took for granted. A warm bed, hearty food, a simple hug. Ilva was showing her all she had to be grateful for. She took her last sip with great appreciation. Listing gratitude's such as having the sylvite artifact in her possession, food and wine, and having a friend to share this moment with. She voiced the later. Ilva was light-headed from the wine, she smiled dopily at Vali. Then, out of nowhere, she hugged her hard. Giddiness escaping her, and laughter bubbled out of them both again.

They lay there tired, and only slightly winded after the hearty laugh. Vali released even more of her tension when Ilva said, "Thank you for everything. You have been exactly what I needed on this journey. Since I met you there has been a spark of light in my life. I am filled with the curiosity I had as a girl, and I find pleasure in many things we do together.

I enjoy your food too. I enjoy being your friend Vali." Vali hugged her back then. Holding tightly around her shoulders, she felt her whole body relax deeper, sagging into the comfort of the embrace. Ilva fell asleep first, it was more sudden then the night before, not being very tolerant of the wine it had fatigued her.

Vali pushed Ilva's reddish brown hair out of her face, and felt her features daintily with her fingertips. She touched the back of her ear as she placed the hair, and felt the shape of the small points of cartilage. She brushed her forehead and felt the smooth skin. Her brows were strong, her hair soft and dense. Vali noted the weight of Ilva's head upon her shoulder. She was enjoying the rhythm of her breath, heavy and deep as she slept on. Vali laid back with her on the furs, and shifted so she was still next to her, *It is comforting sleeping beside someone out here. So warm and reassuring.* Ilva rolled over and clutched Vali's abdomen. Vali took in a sharp breath at the motion, perhaps a bit nervous to be seeking comfort herself in the embrace. With the shared fur thrown over them, breathing deeply and steadily, they had the best sleep that either of them had in a very long time.

Chapter 15

In the morning Vali awoke first, Ilva still asleep upon her chest. Vali could sense the drool saturating her shirtfront, it did not bother her. She was happy to be comfortable enough for someone to sleep so soundly with her. She always worried she made others uneasy. She treasured the way Ilva treated her. Given their situations, they had both placed a lot of trust in one another, and Vali was very happy for that. It was nice to have someone to rely on like this, and to be this close to. Most of the elves she had been courted by were transactional relationships, in which the belief was held that there was no sense in having the relationship if there was nothing to gain from it. She did not have that kind of unspoken agreement with Ilva. There was no ceremony to this. No propriety. This made her immensely happy.

She started to think a bit too hard about her relations with Ilva then. *What will I do when I go home? Is she coming with me?* Vali shifted her foot slightly, then Ilva woke. She glanced around and noticed her position, she instantly said, "I'm so sorry Vali, I fell asleep on you again. I don't mean to invade your space," She moved to sit up.

Vali held Ilva's arm as she moved away, and said, "I don't mind, I was very comfortable both times." Vali was blushing so hard as she spoke, her face was blotched with patches of red all over.

Ilva looked at her with compassionate eyes. She realised how much she wanted to hug Vali. Ilva wanted to smother her with affection and giddy embraces. Most of all she wanted to see how many other surprising things she could make her companion feel. Maybe she could make her laugh again, she longed to see Vali laugh since she first heard the delighted tone. She felt thrilled at the news that she was not crowding her friend. *Where is Vali going now? Should I follow her? Does she want me here?* She let these questions eat away at her, it devoured all she was just appreciating. It ate at the feeling of security, and chewed at the trust that she was building.

Vali sensed the change in emotion. She decided to try conversing about their next steps, to gauge how Ilva planned to go forward. "I'm going home. Your reasons for being here, are all around the fact that I need you. I need you in ways I have never needed another before. I need you for your friendship, your perspective, and I need you because you keep me warm in more ways than you think. Reasons why I need you aside, I'm glad you came along, and I hope you will come with me to Karna. I understand if you wish otherwise in anything though. We are friends, and anything you want matters greatly to me."

Ilva was full to the brim with self confidence now. She did not hold back this time, and grabbed Vali up in a suffocating hug. After they felt sufficiently comforted, they packed up, and prepared to blaze their next trail.

They walked for a long time on the first day, trekking back through the mountain pass, still filled with the body of the great beast Vali had slain almost a full week ago. The corpse was as if it was from the same day, no decay had happened. The body was not swelled like warm blooded mammals might have been. The sight entranced Ilva. She stared transfixed, not looking where she went, and she fell over. Vali gripped her hand and helped her up. They didn't let go, continuing to hold hands for support as they moved up the side of the pass around the scaly heap.

There was an old male elf standing next to the head of the beast, he seemed to be mourning the creatures passing. He stood when he saw them traversing alongside the dragon. He had made an assumption that they were scouting the area as bandits and bellowed to them, "If you are looking for scales to steal, or other treasures to loot from this dragon's corpse, I suggest you walk on! He is mine. Whoever slayed him must have been a great fool."

Vali took this rough greeting at great insult, and rebelliously chimed, "I slew this dragon. If he had anything of worth to me, I would have taken from his hide suns ago." Ilva assumed Vali had meant to avoid conflict, and hoped the elf would let them walk past without any trouble. A new kind of threatening face appeared on the elf now. What was said had made him even angrier. The elf's eyes held such rage and hate. Vali seemed to notice the silence as dangerous too, for she was suddenly on alert, her hand tightening on Ilva's.

Chapter 16

"So, it was you?" The bearded elf spat sourly and with great contempt. As though they had wronged him worse than any other in his lifetime. His white beard shook with rage, his dark forehead beading with sweat behind a curtain of hair, and his orange eyes narrowed. "You are a greater fool for returning here, upon the day I discovered him. Europeas; my great fiery friend. You will pay for what you have done, dragon slayer!"

All at once there was a thunderous sound. A roar escaped the land, far louder than any bellow the defeated dragon had let out. It rolled across the rocky slopes with a screech most deafening, and the beast rose up above the pass from the opposite side. She was a large ancient looking dragon. Burned and battered long ago, her body covered in scars, scales black as a starless night, and her sleek body made her appear more serpentine than dragonlike. Her yellow eyes shone bright. She swished through the air cutting it with her sharp looking wings.

Ilva shifted her gaze to the male elf who was writing something down. He wrote and wrote and his pen only stopped when he looked towards her, meeting her glance with a malicious sneer. It set her whole body into a whirl-wind of motion, a combination of fear and action. She spun to Vali and said, "I think he is about to cast a spell, and there is an enormous dragon above us!"

Vali reacted, "Are you a strong runner?"

Ilva swallowed hard and said, "Go! I can keep up!"

Vali nodded, Ilva took another glance at the elf, now with his formerly belted sword in hand. His notebook was tucked in his tunic. The dragon swooped in low just as the bearded elf brought the sword tip down in a commanding gesture.

Vali suddenly catapulted forward with speed that Ilva could barely maintain. Ilva pushed herself harder than ever, her legs lunging her body from one rock, to another. She leapt with a precision that made her gasp at herself. She tried not to focus on how well she was doing, lest the confidence derail her. To her left, then her right, the serpentine dragon was blackening the rocks on either side of where she jumped. She tried to act wild and erratic in her movements to elude the great flying fire breather. It appeared to be working, however, the flames were still too close for comfort. She felt her leather cuffs melting on her skin.

Ilva could see Vali ahead jumping faster and faster. Ilva had to catch up, or risk losing her when she got to safety. She pushed her leaps farther, extending her legs further, jumping to and fro. Just when she was almost in step with her friend, the dragon came down upon them and raked a claw through the air. Although the claw did not hinder their steps, the wind that came off it did. The gust knocked both elves off their feet, and they fell into the rocks.

There was a small gap, they both became wedged within

the crevice. The two jutting boulders held them in place. They squirmed about, trying to untangle themselves in their panic. For as they were entangled in a mass of rock and limb, the dragon was snaking its way down, preparing a deep fire infused breath. Just as her flames ejected forth, the two elves rolled out of their bind, pushed together towards the bottom of the cliffside, and jumped.

They almost landed on the grass, but missed a few feet and collided with the rubble at the base of the mountains edge. The flames burst forth over top of them, it was searing the tips of their ears, frying hairs on their heads. Ilva felt the heat tinging her face with colour. They were almost to the forest. It was ahead of them. They ran harder, ignoring their scrapes and bruises, pushing their limbs to their very limits, breathing hard. They ran and ran, when they entered the forest they did not slow.

Ilva ran ahead now, in her zone, she pushed her legs and pounded the dirt, searching for a landmark. She looked all around until she found a large projection of dirt, with roots all knotted and gripping the ground far below, creating a small cave under the overhang. Ilva felt Vali following behind her as she approached it. Quickly, she reached back grabbing Vali by her leathers, and they slid in next to some of the tall messy roots. The dragon was apprehensive to enter the dense wood. It had lost sight of them as soon as they entered, and returned to the foothills. Ilva and Vali stayed still, focusing on controlling their breathing as they strained their ears listening for their pursuers.

After several minutes crammed tightly into the damp smelling earthy pocket, Ilva broke out of their cover. Guiding

Vali out as well, she surveyed the area. Ilva knew where they were, but she had only been to this part of the woods once, and it had been long ago, when she was first becoming acquainted with the forest. Normally she avoided this area, it always felt strange. Looking for moss on trees to direct herself, Ilva glanced in the direction of Lake Mara. Slightly left was the way home for Vali. Only, Ilva was already home, back in the forest, and it felt safe after evading the dragon. It also felt safe being with Vali.

It was peaceful, hearing all the familiar chirps and creaks and whispers of things hidden in their dens and nests and tunnels. She was elated to be back, even in the denser, creepier areas. The feeling of being home made her not want to go on, and she did not want Vali to go either. Feeling incredibly selfish, Ilva stewed over her thoughts. Vali stood patiently with her eyes closed moving her head around listening to the forest. When Ilva glanced her way, all those worries started to drift.

Vali smiled at each sound she concentrated on. Her body was less rigid at the light sounds beginning to rise around them. They meant the danger had passed. It was a reassurance that Vali loved about the forest. A comfort she had understood the moment she entered this place in her previous escapade, then again, a week past when she met Ilva in it. She understood well why Ilva sought refuge in such a place. She could not take that from her. Suddenly her face changed from its resting smile, to a lightly furrowing brow, and lines of worry began to form where her laugh lines were just exposed.

Ilva watched her face change, and approached her. "Are

you okay?" she asked. Vali shook the thought from her mind, and tried to compose herself.

"Just fine," Vali returned. "I was enjoying the serenity. It feels safe in here. Do you know where we are?"

Ilva sighed with relief at their unified feelings. So much understanding washed over Ilva in that moment. Vali understood her, and she felt the same way about the forest. "I feel at home here. I do know where we are, roughly. We will want to head north if you wish to return to Karna. If we head that way now though, we will not have much forest left to enjoy. Most of the forest lies South and East of us. Lake Mara is strait ahead."

Vali took in the information about her surroundings, "Thank you. Good to know. I have never been very good at finding my bearings. I am rather poor at geography, even though I appear sure footed in most places I find myself in, I'm usually running on instinct and not knowledge. You are very resourceful and have a great sense of direction."

Ilva thanked her for the compliment then asked with a small edge of fear to her voice which way they should go.

Vali thought, then said, "Well, you say my home is this way. Which way do you consider home?"

Ilva told her which way.

"Let us go that way then, I can afford to lengthen this quest, and I'm really enjoying it. Truthfully, I don't want it to end yet. Let us stroll leisurely to wherever you want, my friend. I'd go anywhere with you."

Chapter 17

Ilva and Vali walked without pause for what seemed like an entire day, only stopping when it was nearing the final hours of daylight. It was time to seek shelter and set up camp. Ilva knew this area but not well enough to know where the best spots to shelter were, though she did know a very thin stream was close by and an oddly shaped crevice she had seen. It was during the cold season when all things were blanketed in white, and the split in rock and tree had the most amazing icicles covering the entrance. She had no idea how the area would look without winter there, still she thought it the most reasonable place to go at the moment. She followed the sound of trickling water, knowing the way by instinct, letting the earth itself be her guide.

She came across the spot in a few moments. Beside the thin line of water was the cave like opening she had seen. There was a massive amount of moss on one of the trees growing into a slab of rock, its roots twirled up inside the sheltered area. The opening seemed larger than Ilva remembered. It had a tall open face, not ideal shelter in bad weather, but it would do tonight. The top of the crevice was covered by only the branches of the tree. The water streamed right alongside the tree and the roots were thankful for it. Though the tree was in no danger of weakening, it looked as if the boulder had tried its hardest to despair the condition in which it grew. Ilva thought she knew the feeling. That's why she remembered the place.

Ilva told Vali about where they were to camp.

Vali closed her eyes and listened to the stream while setting up a fire in the ideal location. Only a few feet away from their root crevice, which Ilva was describing in detail. The fire was ablaze in no time, and Vali dug in her bag again. This time she pulled out a length of metal wire, a bit of string, and her knife. She made a snare with these items, and set it up deeper into the woods, then came back. She left again when the sound of a large twang, and a high-pitched terrified shriek of a small animal sounded in the dark. She returned with another small tusked rabbit.

Ilva noted to herself that she still hadn't told Vali that she wasn't much of a meat eater. Although, she also could not deny some of the ways adding meat to her diet lately was a good thing. She felt like she had developed some muscle in the past week.

Vali set to work skinning and cutting up the hindquarters and backstraps. Ilva watched both curiously and with disgust as Vali sliced meat away from bone over and over, with fast precision and little effort.

About halfway through cooking, Vali rinsed her empty wineskin, then filled it with water from a rock drip near the stream. It took nearly thirty minutes to fill the skin with the little water that trickled down. She came back and flipped the meat. She pulled herself up, in her now accustomed place beside Ilva, and drank some of the water before passing the skin to Ilva. After she drank a few sips Ilva passed it back, and thought of how nice it would be if they stayed like this for longer. She did not want to hope for attachment like that though. She feared the pain that would follow was inevitable. No one would stay in this forest with her. She really didn't want to leave her world out here again, but the more she thought about it, *would it really be so bad?* If it was for this friend who saved her and kept her warm at night, she would do anything. Even change some of her lifestyle.

Ilva broke the silence. "I have never felt so close to some-one. I fear our separating."

Vali took her attention off of the warmth of the fire, and moved her face very close to Ilva's without meaning to, she decided to not retreat. "I don't want us to part ways either. I would like to spend more nights enjoying your warmth. I want to know how close we are meant to be. I've been think-ing that these feelings of friendship are amazingly strong."

Ilva was moved by this sentiment. She responded by em-bracing Vali, a gesture that was quickly becoming common for them. Not that Ilva got many before, but these were the most comforting hugs she had ever known. Ones that filled her with comfort and acceptance. Vali seemed to grip Ilva so hard when she held her, as though she felt the same. This time, Ilva squeezed harder too, locking them together, feeling their breath. Ilva noted that Vali was breathing heavily, and she tried to move apart so she could get more air, but Vali gripped her harder.

Vali whispered, "Just hold me a moment more."

Ilva thought she was crying at first, she pulled her face away enough to see Vali's, she was flushed and pink, her breath laboured, but quiet. She was not crying, but she looked as though she was unsure and struggling with strong emotions. Ilva comforted her friend in the cuddle a few moments more, her breathing eventually becoming more even. When they did separate Ilva told Vali, "Anytime you need a hug, just say so. I swear our hugs are their own magic."

"Indeed, I believe they are." Was Vali's reply.

Chapter 18

In the morning Vali woke before Ilva, again. She breathed in her scent, thinking of how she could get used to this. Ilva's face was so close she was breathing against Vali's cheek. Ilva made a small moan in her sleep, the sound setting off a torrent of amorous feelings. Her breath became laboured as it had during their embrace last night. Vali was embarrassed. She did not know what made her cling hopefully to Ilva. Or why she had promiscuous desire creeping over her. It might have been that she was afraid of their becoming close. What if Ilva had a boundary up that Vali herself did not? She knew she felt strongly, that the physical contact between them was healing something in her. The feelings of want that stirred in her when they hugged last night echoed in her now. What if Ilva did not feel the same?

With these thoughts on Vali's mind, Ilva's hot breath on her face, and their bodies so snug, all she wanted to do was close the gap between their lips. She thought of how she wanted to kiss Ilva. Desire deepening by the moment. She began recalling others she had kissed, a poor attempt to distract herself, she was trying to remember the sensation, it had been a long time since she kissed someone. The desire still deepening, she inched closer.

Vali had been quite lustful throughout her life, and experienced many elves of both sexes, though none of the previous encounters stirred emotion in her the way Ilva did. Every time they touched it was electric and calming all at once. She wanted to feel more of her. Wanted to touch her. To kiss her cheek, her shoulder, collarbone, waist, hip, thigh. The sensation of each curve tormented Vali's mind. The urge to caress the sleeping Ilva burned in her so badly. With her raging desire, and shallow needful breaths, she respectfully curbed her urges and tried not to wake Ilva.

Aside from the sensual feelings enveloping her, Vali's heart was full of appreciation, gratitude and she recognized another feeling. Love. Vali accepted the feeling as soon as it was realized. *I love her. I love this curious, sweet, adventurous elf. I love the way we talk, and laugh, and hold each other at night. I love her smells, her cute snores. I love how hard she pushes herself and how willing she is to try new things. I love her.*

Vali thought about how different things in her life were before their meeting, and of how it was Ilva who found the sylvite, and how many things could have gone wrong if Ilva wasn't there to help. *I owe her.* Vali committed to finding a way to repay Ilva, for all the joy she was bringing into her life.

The feeling of Ilva's arms against hers, and of their cheeks meeting, soft skin against soft skin, was the most comfortable thing Vali had ever known. Moving her face slightly, Vali enjoyed the sensation of their cheeks softly sweeping against each other, the gentle hairs on their faces sending shivers over her. Each time she shifted Vali felt a rush of excitement, she was starting to feel a bit guilty at her pleasure in this. Ilva moaned again, a bit louder, Vali's excitement rocketed through her for a moment paralleled by the fear of waking her still snuggling friend. Ilva's eyes fluttered and she nuzzled into Vali's nape, hugging her back. Breathing deeply, sending fierce shivers of release through Vali, undoing her completely.

"Good morning," Ilva said.

Vali was trembling all over. Ilva took in Vali's appearance, she was flushing just like last night, and seemed to be trembling as though cold. Ilva lay slightly over her and embraced her again. Vali shuddered deeply again, and Ilva sank deeper into the embrace. The deeper intentional snuggle felt good. Too good. Vali was still breathing hard when she asked, "Ilva, I want to kiss you, may I, please?"

Ilva was shocked at first, though she tried not to show it when looking at Vali's desperate face again. The desire in Ilva matched that of Vali's, and she realised she had wanted to kiss her since her first intimate thoughts in the foothills. Hearing Vali voice her own wants broke all hesitations within Ilva. So, she turned and lowered her head, brushing her lips gently against Vali's.

Ilva had never kissed anyone before. If she had known of Vali's experience, she may have been more timid of what she offered in her kiss. With their past experiences still secret, she kissed her with passion and love that kept them both grasping for more. Vali couldn't tell at all that Ilva was inexperienced. She was kissing Vali softly, and then wetly, and then firmly.

Vali lost herself in the kiss, releasing all manner of pleasure into it. Ilva was bringing life to every one of Vali's tenacious thoughts. She was kissing her so deliciously, it was devouring her sensibility, their tongues moved around making their minds and lips buzz. Vali had never been kissed like this. With such longing and wildness and seduction. She felt herself begin to squirm uncontrollably with desire when Ilva pulled away.

"I want to kiss you more," Ilva quietly voiced, before kissing Vali's cheek several times, and grazing her lips along her ear. She whispered into Vali's ear, "Can I kiss here?" Vali nodded, and Ilva planted her lips softly, moving them along her nape. She kissed lightly, and then with one firmer kiss she licked the skin underneath her still planted lips, and Vali cried out her pleasure loudly.

The moan that escaped Vali's lovely mouth made Ilva's confidence spike. She was so beautiful, and she was enjoying this. Ilva was so glad that her thoughts were not the only ones full of longing here. For several nights now she had dreamed of something like this between them, and what it might feel like. Now she was allowed to find out. She wanted to tug all of Vali's clothes off. To press her tongue along places that she only dreamed of being kissed too. Would Vali let her go that far? She slid a hand under Vali's tunic to test her limits.

Vali squeezed the furs up into her balling fist. Ilva trailed her hand over Vali's stomach, then her ribs, when she reached her chest Vali was panting heavily again. Ilva stroked her hand gently over Vali's breast, it moved her loosened tunic up, exposing the darker skin of her nipple just below the opening of the shirt. Targeting the peaked skin with her hand, and then lowered her head to kiss Vali's stomach. Following the trail her hand had made, she began kissing across Vali's breast, which was now fully exposed. Ilva stopped for only a moment, staring at the stunning figure under her who was now begging, "Please, keep going."

Hearing that she was desired made her long to hear Vali plea more. So Ilva came down quickly and kissed her exposed nipple hard, rolling her tongue across it, and sucking softly, tracing small wet circles until another steamy sound erupted from Vali's mouth. Ilva clamped her mouth over the moan and they moved together, as they shared a final kiss. Ilva gazed at Vali's face, her eyes shut and her breath leveling out. A weak smile tugged at her mouth as she panted.

Laid out beside her companion again, Ilva doing the holding this time, they kissed and nipped each other playfully, they remained like that as the sun moved across the sky.

Chapter 19

Later that day, Vali was preparing to hunt, and as she did so Ilva decided to tell Vali of her aversion to meat.

"I don't mind a bit, once or twice a week maybe, I actually prefer fish to anything else." Ilva explained.

Vali wasn't at all offended, "I wish you told me sooner. I'm sorry, I eat so much meat, I don't mind if you don't want any though. We can just eat what we like."

Ilva let out a sigh of relief, and offered to help Vali forage. They spent the afternoon picking berries, wild greens and some spruce to make tea.

When they returned to the camp, Vali refilled the skin with the trickle of water. She sat close to Ilva. Her need for intimacy as strong as it was this morning Vali turned and kissed Ilva, without warning.

Enveloped in the rapturous sound of their breathing again Ilva's mind was going blank, she wasn't the one in control this time, she had been filled with the urge to continue what they had started all day. Was this how she made Vali feel this morning? She gripped Vali hard when she kissed her deeper.

Vali pulled away to say, "I want to bring you such pleasure."

These words brought excitement to Ilva's body. A shiver rolled over her. "Go ahead then," she said coyly.

Feeling no guilt or shame, and without hesitation, Vali gracefully pulled their cotton and leather off in quick movements. She tugged at the string holding up Ilva's pants, the anticipation made Ilva kick them off.

Vali hovered her strong frame gently over Ilva, and kissed her lower, and lower. She nibbled gently, being a tad rougher than Ilva had been with her, she kissed harder and faster, pleased beyond comprehension in her ability to have Ilva accept her advances. Shock registered in every area Vali touched. She ached to know how to send waves of ecstasy through Ilva, as she travelled her tongue down her body. She parted Ilva's legs and dropped down between her thighs, Vali tasted her sweetness until Ilva's pitched tone could be heard echoing through the forest.

At this Vali relaxed her maneuvers until Ilva stopped shaking beneath her face, only then did she stop too. She kissed gently three times, then rose up to embrace the now equally satisfied Ilva. Smiling mischievously at each other, lazily letting the hours float by, they remained lying naked, in the middle of the Nilfin forest.

Chapter 20

Ilva and Vali's feelings of dependence grew stronger during their time in the forest. Ilva soon realised, that forest or not, she would be following Vali anywhere. Vali felt the same, and though she would miss a few elves back home, she would wander the world with Ilva forever. She was at home with Ilva, and Ilva was at home with Vali. It was that simple. They knew it the way one knew they were hungry, or the way one knew they had to run when being chased by a fire-breathing dragon. They both seemed to understand it as the beginning of something more.

It took them several days of enjoying each others company before they left their small creak camp. Travelling lazily through the forest from spot to spot. They stopped paying attention to the direction they were heading, enjoying their time together. After many weeks of travelling they spotted a small cottage. Ilva suspected they were somewhere near lake Mara, if her sense of direction was to be trusted, and Ilva's sense of direction could always be trusted.

Ilva was shocked to find another elf living in the forest. Embarrassment rippled over them both. They had been making love, loudly, less than a quarter of an hour's walk from the small cottage. They found themselves hoping the place was abandoned. It was a little dwelling, hidden by dense foliage, with a knee-high fence, a goat, three chickens, and a line of drying laundry in the yard. There were tiny shuttered windows and several circles of rock forming a little path to the front door. They approached with caution. Ilva spotted a small hunched over female elf sitting on the front step. She was eating a slice of bread and tossing a few crumbs to the chickens, who squabbled over each speck that dropped.

Ilva watched the elder female intently as they approached. She appeared harmless. Looking just as much at home here in the forest, Ilva wondered how long she'd been here. How long had she dwelled in this fantastic little cottage, in the forest that Ilva once considered her own private paradise. To happen upon this place, and reveal how 'not hers' this forest was, sort of dampened Ilva's pride, making her feel a bit less special.

Unsure as ever, Ilva did not know whether to approach the stranger, wave and continue walking, or say hello from a distance. She picked the third option. Stopping just at the edge of the path, seemingly the edge of the property, Ilva belted out an enthusiastic, "Hello! My name is Ilva, and this is Vali."

"Hello!" Vali added with equal welcome.

The old elf smiled lightly, as if it was a lot of energy to do so, "Well, ello! I'm Livy, ya travellers need any bread or water? 'Fraid that's all I've got."

Vali, knowing the limits of their supply, answered, "Yes, thank you! We would much appreciate your generosity."

Ilva was grateful for Vali's confident response, it came out smoother than her eager hello. She felt an urge to keep going, but knew Vali was being resourceful and brave. *Alright, let's do this then.* Ilva's thoughts urged her to follow her companion onto the cottage property. As they approached, Livy, who still sat tossing bread crumbs, looked up at them kindly.

Bravery to Ilva was being near other elves, being surrounded by faces that were all looking at you, judging you. She would rather it have been another dragon than a cottage. Thankfully Livy appeared to be the only one here. For some reason, Ilva did not want to go into Livy's home. No matter how nice she seemed, and how good that bread smelled inside, she was apprehensive. Ilva's stomach growled so loudly, it made her jump a little and clamp a hand over the rumble.

The old elf threw her head back then and laughed, a full hearty cheerful laugh. She sniffed like she was recovering from a cold, then said, "Come on in dears, I'll fix ya's up with what I can. These chicks already laid eggs for today, if only I knew before that you'd be showin' up...Ilva." The way Livy had said her name and just her name put Ilva on alert now. This elf might be dangerous. *Did she know I resided in the forest? How could this elf possibly know who I am?*

Chapter 21

Ilva studied Livy for several moments, she had a round little body for an elf and it showed in her face, her old pointed ears were wrinkled. Her eyes were so black and brown they were pits of darkness, save for the little twinkle she had in them. It was almost as if her eyes were her way of smiling. Her cheeks sagged and it seemed as though it took some effort to shape her mouth into any expression, her eyes did the talking.

The old elf guided them all into her home. Ilva let her gaze wander the interior of the cottage, and she really liked it in here. Moss was growing inside, and there were plants in every corner of the room. Windows lined an entire wall at the back of the cottage and sunlight poured in through them. It was lovely. The tiny sink Livy stood at pumped water slow, it was so small, but it was nice for a quaint home in the woods. Ilva was in love with the place, but still suspicious.

Livy waddled adorably into the room, with her small feet and wide hips, she brought them each a clay cup of water and three slices of bread. Two looked as though they had butter on them, the other with honey. Ilva bit into one of the buttered slices, it was soft and fluffy, and tasted toasty where the crusty edges rounded each slice. Each bite was heavenly, the butter a little salty, paired perfectly with the soft spongey bread. She tried the honey one second, and it had hardened the top of the slice with a crunchy glaze. Each bite into the crystalizing bread was like eating a chunk of honeycomb. Ilva liked it, and wished she had more. She was shovelling the other buttered slice into her mouth, when Livy brought her one more slice with honey. *You read my mind,* Ilva chuckled in her head.

After the fourth slice of bread they each felt satisfied. They drank several cups of water, and Vali used the sink to fill their skin, after asking for permission. When it was just them, Livy clasped Ilva's hands. "Dearie, I gotta tell ya some things. This visit brings me joy. Ya got a right to know why this is the first time I've smiled in ages. My little grandgirl. You've sure grown up."

Tears almost streamed down Livy's face. She tried to stiffen her lips, and Ilva swore some of those tears went right back into their ducts. She still glistened and a few tears had fallen. She smiled again. "You've no idea how long I thought...and who would've believed you'd stumble in here on me? Ya can just call me granny sweet pea. If it pleases ya."

Ilva swam in all her thoughts, grabbing up all the words and tossing them into the jumble in her mind. She comprehended, but focused on "grandgirl." *I am her grandgirl! I thought dad said she "wasn't around anymore,"* realising the vagueness of the statement as it echoed in her memory. *Ahh.* Ilva thought about her father, avoidant and blunt, she wished he would just be more forthcoming. Like his mother was being right now. *If that is who she truly is.*

Livy was an open book and couldn't hold anything back. She was still going. "I wanted ta be there y'know, but your folks, well they despise me. Just called me a meddler." She shrugged and continued, "I was against my son marrying a slave, things got all heated and personal. I just didn't like what my son was doing, buying the girl and all. I knew you when you were less than a decade old. Still so little. T'was around then Syli asked me to leave and never return to their home. She looked desperate. Something told me I should listen to her, so I left.

"I don't know about the pressures of leading, I won't pretend to understand politicking and other such refined practices. I'm of little use in a place like that. Can't even articulate things the right way, I just embarrassed my son most of his life. I figured ya's were better off without me. I didn't want to live in Ivarseas and chance awkward encounters with any who didn't want me. So, here I am. Crazy old elf lady in the woods."

Things were so confusing and sudden and difficult to process. Vali seemed to notice this as she walked back with the full skin of water. She tried to break the focus of the conversation by asking Livy about her livestock. As Livy was explaining the cycle of the egg forming in the chicken to Vali, and why it takes a full twenty-four-hour day for one chicken to make an egg, Ilva had a moment to compose herself, absorbing her new information.

She ticked off the facts;

Grandma.

Alone in the woods.

Angry at parents too.

Then her feelings;

I do not want to end up like that.

Dear gods and goddesses am I uncomfortable.

I'm glad they're not waiting for me to reply.

Then her questions;

Is she really the mother of the Lord of Stone elves?

Why is she so unrefined?

Why did no one tell me about her?

Her feelings started to outweigh the facts. Her questions became her focus to keep from ruminating on her feelings. Ilva really wanted to believe she had other family too. Especially family who loved the forest as she did. It was just a bonus that Livy disagreed with her parent's lifestyle as well. Livy's story didn't seem unlikely, and even if it was Ilva had always been the gullible sort, so she believed her.

Ilva cut off some confusing conversation about chickens and eggs and the order of their origin. "You know Livy, granny, I also disagree with their union. I left home because I was sick of watching my mother fake a relationship with my father, and I was tired of my father being more of a lord than a parent. Nothing I did was good enough for either of them. My mother was so quiet and controlled, unless she was speaking to me, then she'd change. She did to me what, I expect, my father did to her. I just don't want to continue the cycle. So, I left home. I will not be sold, or made into something I am not, I am no one's slave."

Vali's face darkened. Those words hit her. *I am no one's slave.* As she realised how free Ilva was, she felt a small seed of envy. *How can Ilva feel no remorse about leaving home? I still have not returned to Karna, and it eats at me daily. I do not want to part from Ilva, but I also do not want to keep my grandmother waiting. Why do I only care of what others want? What is wrong with me?*

Ilva did not notice Vali's reaction. She was completely focused on Livy's face, hoping for a positive response.

"That a girl!" Livy beamed ever brighter. "You're one smart lil' sprout. Left today did ya?"

Soaking up the praise Ilva chuckled, "No, I have lived in this forest for eighty years." Her tone became more sincere, "I am truly shocked to learn you have been here all this time. I mean it is a huge forest, it takes weeks just to get across it, and I didn't ever travel near the lake, so I guess it's not that surprising. I am nonetheless amazed at the irony and I wish we could have talked sooner. How different things might have been if I did not need to be alone all that time. Neither of us would have been alone. I am happy to meet you now anyways. It is an honour granny." Ilva smiled through forming tears, and reached out to hug Livy.

At the surprisingly tight embrace, granny went "oof" then giggled and cried with her grandgirl. Livy had needed a hug for far longer than Ilva had. When Ilva hugged her, Livy thought she might break all apart inside. Her tears suddenly became more violent, treading in all directions down her wrinkled face. Clear snot beaded at the tip of her round little nose. She then felt that she was at the extent of pouring out her pent-up emotion, and was ultimately embarrassed that she had exposed so much of her vulnerable self.

The old elf wiped her hand on her nose, recoiled a bit, and went to rinse her face and hand off. She came back rosy and bleary eyed, but with the same comforting smile she had on when she invited them in. She asked then, "So ya really lived in the same woods for almost a century and we both didn't know? Funny eh? We're just two stubborn peas in a pod!"

Ilva nodded.

Livy seemed to know now that Ilva was digesting her new facts. She took a deep breath and reflected on all they had covered, and looked Ilva's tired soul up and down. "Tired of talkin' eh? Stay the night, gals. I can give ya's eggs in the mornin'."

Ilva waited to see what Vali said.

When it was clear Vali was not going to speak, Ilva responded, "I am okay with spending the night if Vali is. We were on a quest and now we are, umm, sort of undetermined on our route I suppose?" She was awkward then, and looked to Vali for support or a response.

Vali seemed to sense that Ilva wasn't sure how to describe their schedule or plans proceeding. After agreeing on staying, she went ahead and explained their quest, and what they found. She could tell Ilva trusted Livy, still she spoke with caution.

Chapter 22

Retelling their adventure took time, Livy was patient, responding with hums and haws. It wasn't until they mentioned the artifact that Livy's dark eyes went wide. They were both shocked when Livy shot out, "Don't get that sylvite wet!"

Vali was suddenly very interested in conversing with Ilva's granny, "Why? What will happen? Do you know about the magic in it? Please! Tell me anything you can, I need to know more about it!"

Livy slumped a bit, "I'll tell ya on three conditions lovey. First ya both come with me ta market in the mornin' and help me carry things home. Second ya promise that whatever information I give ya's will not be used ta start another war. Third ya take good care of my grandgirl here when we part ways."

"Deal," Vali quickly launched out before Livy spoke the last four words of her conditions. It was settled.

They rolled out their furs on the floor that night, after a long day assisting granny around the cottage. She needed help patching a spot on the roof with sap, and milking the goat, and there were other various tasks that had kept them all working. It seemed granny liked to stay busy. They laid down, arms and backs rather sore from the labour, and waited for granny to come tell them the knowledge they had yearned to learn all day. Granny settled in a little wooden chair near the fireplace and passed them cups of heated up milk with honey in it. It was creamy and sweet, the honey that didn't melt enough stuck to the bottom of the warm mugs. Granny began her lecture on sylvite lore.

"When it's fully submerged in water the magical properties will die. That's only the case with sylvite though. Stone and silver are made of much tougher stuff, water takes a lot longer to break us down. Sylvite has always been a rare thing here. Your mother was very proud of hers."

"I know," Ilva muttered into the pause.

Livy kept on explaining, "If ya's really found that hunk of sylvite, ya have what's called an arcane source material, most just call em artifacts. That thing has different powers than the ones in your ma's fans. Those ones are just little specks of magic. What ya got is large, forceful magic, the fans pull from that larger source. Only sylvite folk can use it. There were rules about not mixin' with each others company, so that no one could merge powers and create stronger races. Two elves broke the rule, and then more followed. Only one race stayed pure up until the war. The sylvite elves."

"Mila wanted to stay segregated? Why?" Ilva was full of intrigue.

Livy seemed to enjoy questions, answering right away, "They were a small group see, and they worried we wanted ta weed em out by breedin' em out. So, most of em hated the idea of mixing the last of their race. Think it's why your ma felt so strong bout her traditions, being forced ta create the first-born mix of her race and all. She probly just didn't want em to die out, bein' the last. I'm glad you were born girl. I wish it wasn't done the way it was. I'm still happy you're here. Ilva you're the only half-sylvite elf in our world. You're somthin' special grandgirl."

Ilva suddenly felt very exceptional indeed, but burdened as well.

"There's an ol' story about them minerals bein' stronger together. But every time an elf that didn't have the power touched one of the artifacts that weren't their own magic, they'd get hurt. Or have all their magic drained. Just be careful where ya bring it, and what you do with it, whatever the quest you're on. Don't know how ya even got your hands on it. Could've killed ya both! Ah, well. Ain't my quest, is it? I won't meddle. Story time's over, time for sleep, big day tomorra'." With that Livy clapped her hands, rose up, and toddled off to her little bed. Out in seconds, snoring louder than any elf or beast ever could.

Ilva looked at Vali, who also appeared absorbed in all the info they had just learned. They sat in silence by the fire, until it was cinders.

Chapter 23

Ilva woke early to the smell of fresh baking bread. She rolled up out of her spot, realizing she was alone, and that it was her first night in weeks not sleeping with Vali. She looked over at the still sleeping temptress, and thought about when they would be on their own again. In an attempt to keep that part of their relationship private, she got up and followed her nose to the side of the cottage that held the kitchen, tiny sink, and little fire stove, the bread getting nice and toasty on top now. Ilva walked out of the cottage to find granny petting the goat and talking to him. "I see I am not the only one with that habit then?"

Granny looked up and said, "What habit?"

"Talking to animals," Ilva chuckled.

"Loneliness does weird things ta ya. Let's get headin' ta town now that you're up. Your lady friend up too?"

Ilva was a bit curious at how granny saw the two of them now. "I will go check." Ilva turned back to the cottage.

Vali was sitting up, and seemed to find delight in the smell of the fresh bread. She prepared her and Ilva's stuff, and as they were strapping on their packs, granny came in, and bustled the bread out of the fire. She sat it on the counter, threw a bit of sand on the hot coals, and gathered a basket full of cloth, and a small pulling cart. The bread stayed behind cooling on the counter, she gave them each a plate with an egg and a slice of the steaming bread. They ate quickly, then they were on their way to the market.

The walk to the market was fairly short, granny explained how it only came around here once every month, and they pitched up tents and then left. They went to a different location each week. There were fruit and vegetable stalls, meat stalls, ones with special squares and tarts and cakes. Ilva returned to the memory of a fresh strawberry crème tart. Vali was taking in all the wonderful scents. They threatened to overwhelm her sensitive nose. When she smelt a desirable aroma, she found herself walking towards it. Ilva followed her while granny bartered for a good price on some oats from one seller. Ilva stopped at the cart Vali was drooling over with all the pastries and baked treats. She asked what smelled so good, and the proud baker proclaimed, "You must smell my new pear sugar pies! Want a sample before you buy?"

Ilva and Vali both tried their bite-sized samples at the same time. There was a glaze on the pie, and the crust was flaky and thin. When Vali sampled it, her face swelled with surprise and then delight. It was exquisite! Sugary and sweet, the pear was soft and the crust combined with it made it a perfect texture. Vali whipped out her gold as fast as should could and bought them each a full one, thanking the baker they went back to granny. She had also bought one of the small pies for granny who was very happy to accept the charity. It seemed as if Livy thought it was the most kindness anyone had ever paid her with the pouty way she thanked Vali.

They walked back to the cottage, the wagon creaking under the weight of spice jars, baskets of rice and oats and flours. There were big baskets of veggies and fruits, a pile of seeds and nuts, and other various pantry items. Ilva was hauling a sack of potatoes while Vali carried a small barrel of wine.

Livy cheerfully chatted away, "Lucky the wine seller was there today! Last month he wasn't and I went without! Give ya's a nip of it before ya's have ta go, and maybe fill one of my old skins with a few glugs for the road too."

"Thanks granny!" Vali chimed with great glee.

She must really like wine, Ilva smiled to herself. She loved seeing the way Vali was with granny. They were a fun pair together.

"I could drink you down, you watch it!" Livy threatened.

Vali snorted a laugh just as granny was about to lose her own composure. The two laughed a good moment and Vali mused, "Oh yeah granny? If we had enough wine, I would totally show you my mettle! I've got quite a resilient liver I tell ya!"

Did Vali just use granny's backwoods slang? Maybe granny is a bad influence on her. Ilva grinned, partially to her thoughts, and to the mockery and foolery happening before her. Vali was mimicking a chicken, after first challenging granny to a real drinking contest next time they visited, she even offered to buy the wine. Which granny peaked interest at, then shrugged.

Vali was trying so hard, "Alright then Livy, what's your bargain?"

"I get ta rope ya's into another market trip next time ya's visit. Next time, stay a bit longer too. You's are no burden ta me. Not a worry that you're sweethearts either. You's do you's," Livy offered.

Then she winked at Ilva, and smiled a sly but still sweet smile. It was a perfect hint at the playful elfling that she once used to be. Ilva wondered again if Livy had heard them in the woods, her face filled with colour. She also wondered if Livy herself ever considered women the way Ilva and Vali did. It was possible. Her smile was knowing. Perhaps she just knew what it meant to love in any form. She shook the awkward moment off, and appreciated the blessing for what it was.

When they got back to the cottage, the goat still stood in a patch of grass grazing away. The chickens in the coop were all resting on their assigned nests. It was such a comforting place to walk into now. Not as daunting as the first time they had approached it. It was nice here. She would enjoy returning one day soon. For now, she wanted to head on her next adventure with Vali, intrigued to know where they might end up next. They had already been on the journey of Ilva's life. She would never live a normal life again, not after dragon fire and magic, not after the love Vali had made to her, not after meeting her granny, and learning how big and wide this world was. She was destined to go wherever her heart would take her. For now, her heart was going with Vali.

They thanked granny, and hugged her with equal fierceness. "We will visit again." Ilva called comfortingly to granny, as they walked towards the path.

Vali shouted back, "We will stay longer too. I gotta drink you down to size, *little* Livy!"

Livy, looking a bit harassed, but smiled deviously and bellowed in her old craggy voice, "Oh I'll see ya then girlie, and you'll be drinking them words ya hear! You watch it!"

Once the banter and love had been shared, Livy walked back into her cottage home to toil about. Vali and Ilva turned to head a new direction than the way they had come. Towards Vali's home Ilva expected. She didn't care. *I wonder what Vali's home is like?*

Chapter 24

They had been travelling for a few days. Taking their time. Sitting cozy beside Vali with a hot sweet potato in her hand, Ilva soaked the moment in. It was another perfect moment she wanted to focus all her energy on. For the first time in her life she felt a strong sense of belonging where she was. She wondered how Vali felt about everything, and if her heart was as full. She appeared very much as content, and she had become much easier to speak with the more they did.

Ilva's mind was running over thoughts by the thousand. The water wheel in her mind was rushing faster and faster. She found herself becoming afraid as the thoughts turned frightening. What if she lost everything? What if she had to go live in a hole all alone again? What was going to happen to her, and them, and that magic, and the world, and her family? Oh no. Thoughts of her mother's harsh demanding nature, her father's stoic rigidity, and the weight of their heavy expectation began crushing in on her. The panic she felt at grannies earlier was nothing compared to what was happening to Ilva right now. *What is happening?* she thought, panicked.

Vali, felt the stirring in Ilva. Felt her body tighten beside her, slowly at first, then she became fully rigid. Her breathing had changed, and her heart rate was up. Vali studied the change in her partner's body, focusing intently on the reacting nerves and organs. She listened with all her might, and felt everything as meticulously as she could.

She wanted to know how to respond, and these cues would give her hints. Then she recognized the pattern of behaviour. She was no stranger to anxiety attacks. She had many when she first lost her vision. It was so hard to focus when she had them.

Lucky for Ilva, Vali knew what might help. "Ilva." Vali reached around and gently laid a hand upon her shoulder. "Hey." She tried, to see if Ilva was present and responsive.

"Ya," Ilva shakily responded.

"Do you want to talk about what is on your mind? I'm right here," Vali reassured.

Ilva felt the strong hand squeeze her shoulder lightly, and she felt that small part of her body release a fraction of the tension. Vali noticed the reaction. She asked Ilva, "Would you like me to rub your shoulders?"

Ilva nodded nervously. It would be nice, her shoulders did ache, and the attack she was in the middle of was making the straining far worse. Ilva was even starting to ache in her stomach, her short breath stopping in her chest. She was going to throw up. Or cry? Or both? She was so overwhelmed.

Vali crawled behind her, splitting her legs aside the left and right of Ilva's hips. She gently pushed her hands under the back of Ilva's shirt and ran her hands up to her shoulders, lifting a little of the shirt when she did. This motion stopped Ilva's short breathing, holding for a beat, and then releasing an enormous exhale. Ilva shuddered at the shock of the cold air on her back, it felt soothing somehow. Ilva had no idea this was Vali's hope, that these factors would give her something different to think about.

Vali worked her hands over Ilva's shoulders and pressed the blades gently with her palms, a relieved sigh escaped Ilva, and Vali focused on the areas of tension, rolling her thumbs and knuckles over each one. She was finding spots that needed the pressure, and left each area feeling far looser with every application of her strength. Ilva's body melted into a hunch without noticing. Vali pulled Ilva back onto her chest, she stroked her hands down the front of the shoulders, and the top part of the chest. Ilva had never imagined such pressure could build up there. The sensation of Vali's hands working out knots, and leaving in its wake fully relaxed muscles, was heavenly.

Ilva fell asleep on Vali's lap that night, after Vali had rubbed her arms and her neck as well. She even massaged her hands and fingers, which Ilva found the most relaxing of all. She was running her hand through Ilva's hair now as her body let out exhausted sleepy snores. Vali was so entranced by the effect her being there had on Ilva. She loved that someone needed her for the same thing she longed for help with; her anxiety, loneliness, desire. It seemed neither of them had connections like this. No one else knew them so deeply and subjectively.

Vali let her mind wander. *Ilva's granny is far nicer than mine.*

Vali really liked Livy. She wondered about what must have happened to Ilva in her life, during the years she was alone, and when she was still at her home in Falil. About what Ilva meant when she said she was no one's slave. She wanted to find a way to comfort Ilva in hopes that she might share more about herself, which just felt like a silly selfish wish to cure her curiosity. Vali could understand Ilva being reserved about her past. She understood because it was hard for her to be confident talking about what happened to herself. She wondered what she could do to support Ilva in finding her own confidence, just as Ilva was helping her to believe more strongly in her own.

Ilva woke the next day, Vali was holding her atop her torso with one arm, her other arm lay straight out beside her. She was still breathing deep, mouth open. Ilva felt perfectly well rested. This was the second time now that she awoke before Vali. She did not know how something as simple as a massage could heal so much pain. Emotional and physical. It made her feel as though that loving touch were the most amazing magic she had known. She wanted to show Vali her gratitude, so she rolled over, and crawled up Vali's torso. As she straddled her hips Vali awoke with a smile, without opening her eyes her grin grew, "This is a nice way to wake up."

Ilva leaned in to kiss Vali's smartly curled lips. She still tasted like the wine they had drank last night, and her face was warm. Vali swept her lips against Ilva's softly, and Ilva kissed deeper and deeper in response, thinking all the while she could not thank Vali enough. She kissed and grabbed at Vali with desperate and craving hands. Rolling in the furs, lustful intent imminent, they giggled and kissed each other until they were contented to get on with the day.

It was a few more lazy days before they reached the town. Ilva was tired. She wondered how Vali felt walking up the dirt path toward the city. Slowly, the trees were thinning, the path opened up, and the forest was fading away behind her. She felt less entranced by the city than she did the mountains when she first left her forest. Now, a feeling of impending doom surrounded her conscience.

She looked back a couple of times. Her heart aching to turn towards those trees. She saw the determination and control on Vali's face. She wanted to support her on her return home, and to meet her family too. It was not only fair, but it made sense, and there was no logical reason to run, Ilva told herself. Yet her legs urged her to do just that, to leave while she still had the chance. Instead she stayed by Vali's side arresting her behavioural instincts. Walking towards the centre of the small town, Ilva swallowed her pooling saliva. They approached the doors of the royal house.

Ilva sucked in a breath, and stood very still.

Vali knocked.

Chapter 25

A small dark-haired elven boy with vivid and wide green eyes answered the door.

Vali beamed, "Krit! How are you?"

The elfling smiled from ear to ear at seeing Vali. His face was bright and shiny, and he had short points on his ears and a tiny nose. He was so delicate looking.

"Vali!" He lunged out of the door, hugging her around her hips. This sight made Ilva take a second breath. She was surprised, and fascinated watching the interaction between these two friends.

The elf boy walked over to Ilva and put out his hand.

"Marvellous to meet you, my name is Krit and I am the first son of the housecarl and his wife. What may I call you?"

Ilva found her courage again and managed to speak casually, "I am Lady Ilva of Falil. Daughter to Lord Ediv and Lady Syli. It is a pleasure to meet you Krit." Ilva bowed deeply and softly. One leg bent, the other swept gently behind her, she crouched elegantly down. Pulling herself back up after counting to three. It was a perfectly executed greeting. She was shocked at how proud something so simple as an introduction had just made her feel.

Vali was trying not to show the surprise that registered in her at the stately way Ilva introduced herself just now. *You really are full of surprises.*

Krit was thrilled by the presentation and returned Ilva's curtsey with a delicate nod and short bow. "What a great honour to make your acquaintance Lady Ilva. Will you come in?"

As Krit gestured, and the ladies entered the main foyer, he asked a less rhetorical question, "Would you like a short tour? I know a lot about Karna."

Ilva began "Sur-"

Krit launched straight into docent mode, "Home to several generations of silver Lords and Ladies, this building here is actually a historic castle, though it is only about an eighth the size of the several centuries newer palace in Marka, it was home to royal silver elves over a millennia ago. It is full of grand rooms, and delicate carvings adorn every wall as you can see."

Ilva did see. It was stunning. She gazed closer at a carving along the wall of a great hunt for a massive stag with wings that appeared to tower over trees. It was all made entirely out of bits of silver. The silver details adorned every surface. The walls, the floors, the ceiling. She almost lost herself in the craftsmanship when Krit's voice brought her back to the rest of her surroundings.

"We will see many more examples of ancestral art on our way to the library, Lady Ilva. I do hope I am not moving too quickly for you, do let me know if you would like me to slow down, or if you catch me rambling."

Ilva let Krit know that his rambling wasn't bothering her in the slightest. That she was quite enjoying her tour.

Krit took this as his cue to continue. "Good! Most elves find my fast-paced prattle annoying. Meeting new elves make conversation flow much easier I find. So much to discuss and learn about one another."

They walked on and on and Krit told Ilva many facts and showed her many similar looking rooms and hallways. It was getting slightly exhausting. *We have to be close to half done*, Ilva thought.

Krit directed the conversation back to personal interest again. It seemed to be a habit. "I usually prefer to focus on studying. Elves are easy to understand once you realise how alike we all are. It is the natural forces and ideas of the world that keep us in motion. I enjoy talk about science and literature. Which, sadly, are topics not many elves enjoy. That's why I love books. Do you love books? Vali loves books." he blanched, "Oh, I'm sorry, Vali."

Krit covered his face. He seemed to be really upset at the oversight of his friend's disability. Vali's face was calm and sympathetic.

Krit managed to say, with as much composure as he could muster, "I am sure Vali can show you the other side of the keep Lady Ilva. I am going to vanish myself to the library now. I beg your pardon, ladies."

"Oh Krit, you know I understand. You meant well. I appreciate the apology though. We will still come along to the library with you. That is, if Ilva wants that? Do you like books Ilva?" As they walked on, they waited for her reply.

Ilva thought on this. "I um, I have not seen books in a very long time. I did use to read a few books. I liked them." Ilva did not want to have Vali or Krit think less of her, so she added, "I once wished there were more books in Falil. There were only the ones each elf had for themselves, and my parents did not enjoy reading, so we actually didn't have any books in my home. I think if I were to give it another chance, and with more to choose from, I might like it more."

Vali smiled, and reached for Ilva's hand. She was shocked to learn Ilva wasn't much of a reader, inquisitive as she was, and then sad to hear it was due to lack of books available. Vali was suddenly thrilled at the idea of Ilva seeing Karna's library. She remembered its splendor. She really missed reading.

Krit watched Vali lace her fingers gingerly between Ilva's. He smiled knowingly, almost too knowing for one so small, no matter how smart he was. He began marching towards the library. All the while he was going on about facts he had read about minerals in their region and the effects they had on an individual.

He was getting very deep into his lecture when a voice shot out ahead of them, "There you are!" A very small girl with bouncy black hair yelled shrilly, "I thought you said we were playing hide and seek!" her dark blue eyes blazing.

"Were you hiding?" Krit responded coolly.

"Yes," she shrieked before Krit came back with, "Good, because I was seeking. Now go hide again. You were doing really well."

She thought for a second, then bolted back the way she had come. Krit snickered lightly, as he turned down a hall in the opposite direction the girl had gone.

A few moments later they entered a room full of books. There were books everywhere. Some areas looked neat, others messy. The shelves were all organized it seemed. There was a small three-tiered cart of books at a counter full of messy piles, and a few tables also had piles upon them.

"Sorry about the mess in here. I've not cleaned yet today. I have been reading in here since dawn," Krit apologized.

As he was explaining magnetic ability and lodestones, Ilva scanned her eyes into every corner of the majesty before her. The books were so well cared for. There was hardly any dust, and they all had such breathtaking bindings. Her eyes landed on a book with purple binding, a golden gilded edge shimmered on the spine. She plucked it off the shelf in front of her and flipped it open. It was a book of dragons. She turned page after page, studying the incredible beasts that had been hand painted upon each page.

Ilva stopped when she saw the dragon they had slain, peering back at her from the parchment. It was an exact replica, down to his curling horns. She studied the face of the dragon a moment before moving to the next page, which held text about this foe they had faced. From what Ilva read, that particular beast was a very large Western Dragon. The black serpentine one, covered in all those scars, was different. The book listed everything from Wyverns and Drakes, to Dragonets and Cockatrices. Most of the book's contents held new information for Ilva; however, that black sleek snaking dragon was not in this book.

What are you? Ilva contemplated with concern.

When she finally zoned back into the room, she realised

Krit was staring at her. Vali was also facing her direction. "Sorry, did you ask me something?"

"Well, no not yet. I had just noticed that you had an interest in dragons. I had mentioned just now to Vali that you were reading about them. Are you learning something?" Ilva was a bit awkward with this child's forthcoming nature. He was so very inquisitive. Even more so than herself.

"I did not know a Cockatrice was a thing," Ilva admitted.

Krit became very excited. "They are very rare. No one I know has ever seen one, nor do they know anyone who has dared look, one glance at it's eyes would petrify you. It is a fascinating illustration, is it not?"

"It is." Ilva stared.

Krit went on, "I love the looks of that Western Dragon best. He appears quite regal, and big. I cannot imagine what it would be like to fight something so frightening. Did you know that the dragons are actually allied with the elves of Evevale? The stolzite are so secretive. No one knows how they perform their magic. Someone wrote a reference journal here about seeing a brush in one of their hands. Like a paintbrush. They painted while on the back of the dragon, it was a fascinating and very old story. I am not sure about its basis for fact finding. Though I will see if I can find it for you if you like? Also, if you are as interested as I am in our magic, I have loads of resources on that too."

Ilva was happy that Krit wanted to share his knowledge, and she didn't want to dampen his spirits. She was feeling overwhelmed by his personality. She tried to reply kindly to the child. "That dragon is a fierce and frightening looking creature indeed. I would love for you to show me what you have found. However, I feel I have absorbed much already, and I need time to consider the new things I now know. I will come back to the library when I am ready to know more if that suits you?"

Krit practically leapt from the table with joy, "It does! I will leave a stack of books I think you will find interesting upon this cart."

Krit then reeled off with glee and purpose. He ran to the full cart and began putting books away at lightning speed. It was as if he had shelved and un-shelved them so often that he knew all of their exact places in the library. Now and then he would have to look the cover over more than once. He would check the isles for empty slots until he found the one he sought. He shifted many of the books still upon the cart to the top shelf as Vali and Ilva began to walk out.

"Nice to see you, Krit." Vali shouted into the library as Krit bolted off again, another chin high stack of books in his ambitious arms.

Chapter 26

Ilva and Vali left the library and walked down to the hall where the little elf girl had disappeared. They stopped when the elfling ran up to them.

"Is he in the library? If I go in there, he'll just hide and say he thought it was his turn." The elfling crossed her arms and grumped.

Vali looked at the elf girl sweetly. "Tila, you do a great many things very, very well, and I would have to say that your patience with Krit has been some of the strongest I have ever witnessed. I swear you both grew taller while I was gone. Has your reading improved?"

"Mother says it has. I don't believe her." Tila slouched a bit and her face turned a bit sour.

"Do you like the books they've chosen any better?" The question from Vali seemed to knock the wind out of Tila as she went stiff. Her eyes full of anger and overwhelm, she looked at Vali, then she changed her posture from rigid to slouched again. She cast her eyes to the ground.

"I don't enjoy the books they give me to read for lessons. They are quite dull. I want to read what Krit is reading. To know what he is so excited about all the time."

Ilva was surprised young Krit didn't fancy talking this elflings face off. She wondered how old the two of them were.

Vali thought the same as Ilva about the relationship between the two young elves, Krit would have to be mad if he did not see this elf's friendship as a blessing, and so she asked, "Why not go ask him for a book then?" At this idea, Tila took off for the library, and Vali smiled mischievously to herself.

Ilva thought about the elflings as Tila turned the corner out of sight. They couldn't be older than forty, which is quite young. Old enough to be dexterous and intelligent. Young enough to still have questions galore and sparkly eyes filled with wonder. In Falil, kids his age had rather heavy chores, such as hauling rocks for building, cutting down trees and making wood for cooking and heat, caring for livestock, and much more. The kids here appeared to have it good. It almost made Ilva jealous. Vali's easy friendships with these children. All of the freedom and comfort here.

Ilva and Vali walked down the hallway, turned to the right, and walked towards the end of the next hallway. As they passed dozens of rooms to the left and right, Vali mentioned their ages, to quiet Ilva's curiosity.

"Tila is thirty. And Krit is fifty-two," Vali explained.

Ilva took time to consider the differences between Falil and Karna and tried not to make it an area of contention. "Krit is so smart. I think it's nice of him to offer to find me some books," Ilva conveyed.

"Some? Ilva, that cart will be full of books! That is Krit's idea of light reading. He will fill the cart because you said you enjoyed knowledge. He is a bit overzealous at times. He means well, and yes, he is extraordinarily smart. And talkative," Vali giggled.

They arrived at open double doors to what appeared to be a spacious dining hall. Ilva was suddenly nervous. Was Vali going straight to see her grandmother? *I mean why wouldn't she?* Ilva was getting sweaty. *Is it warm in here?* Maybe there was a fireplace in this room?

She sucked in a deep breath as Vali walked through the doors and strolled leisurely inside. Ilva followed behind, her eyes scanning the room. It was an extensive room with no fireplace, just a large banquet table, and at the head of the table sat a queenly wraithlike old elf. Her dark grey hair curled loosely, cascading down the back of her chair to her hips, it was thick and teased back under a silver circlet, her ears were adorned with teardrop diamonds.

"Vali!" she spat, "Who is this elf? Where is her announcer?"

"Apologies, grandmother, this is a friend. She needs no announcer." Vali spoke with easy comfort.

"Apologies to you then. Might I at least inquire as to whom I am apologising to?"

"I am Lady Ilva," Ilva shouted out almost a bit too loudly, and flatly, before she squeaked out the a in Ilva.

"Welcome Ilva dear, I am Lady Dola, the head elf of Karna, and direct adjutant to High Lady Alix in Marka."

"Pleased to meet you." Ilva bowed.

"Vali, how did your mission go?" Dola shot out quickly, ignoring Ilva's pleasantries.

"Ilva is a very large part of our success, and I am only too thrilled to tell you the tale. Though I believe Ilva would like to eat and rest first. Might I come speak with you after that? I will tell you at least that I found what I sought." Vali spoke with a chilling cold tone. No emotion to it. Like a soldier addressing their captain.

Dola seemed both eager and annoyed. Her interest was obviously in the artifact. She seemed haughty at the requirement to address her guest first. "Yes, yes of course dear. Prepare one of the top floor rooms for her, and I will have someone bring up trays for you both. Come see me as soon as you are able. Please do not make me wait long."

As they walked across the room Ilva could feel Dola watching them with a predatory gaze. With her back to her she felt like fleeing. She walked steadily on though. The stairs to the next floor were on either side of the throne room door they entered through.

Vali guided Ilva to the open stairway on their left. Ilva didn't want to speak, afraid of being heard in the tower stairway. At the final flight of steps, they entered a hallway resembling the one downstairs, they made their way to the end of it and entered the second to last room on that floor.

Ilva flopped onto the bed and snuggled into the soft cool pillow. The many, now crumpled sheets and blankets below her looked like the most wonderful thing she had ever laid eyes on. She was mesmerised by the feeling of a down filled mattress on boards so much that she thought if one thing was to keep her from her old cave living days, this bed might do it.

She rolled around while Vali unpacked her bag, and organised things back into it at the same time. She put several items away in the room. A small knife, all of their leftover food, their skins, and other various travel related items. Ilva took note of how she had kept only the sylvite hunk, and her big knife in the bag.

Vali shouldered her pack again, and walked over to Ilva. She reached down. Misjudging where her hand was directed, she grasped Ilva's chest rather than the shoulder she thought she was aiming for. Realizing the position Ilva was sitting in then, Vali smiled and crawled towards her, hand still not releasing her, as it was her best guide to where Ilva was exactly. She knelt over one of her legs and she came down seeking somewhere to kiss. She was grateful that no matter where she kissed Ilva, it brought her obvious joy. She wished to keep bringing her just that, for as long as she was able.

Chapter 27

Ilva asked, "How long will you be? What should I do while I wait?"

Vali replied, "I will be gone for likely an hour, maybe two. You can go to the library if you wish to come downstairs with me. Or, feel free to rest here if you would rather, food will likely be up here soon if you wanted to wait."

Ilva decided, "I will just stay here, I'm worn out, and pretty hungry. I hope your talk goes well."

"As do I, Ilva. May I ask, that is, can I tell her about your grandmother? I want to have your permission if that is okay. Also, may I tell her some of the details of our adventures together?"

Ilva was a little unsure now. At first, she expected that was what Vali would do. She was asking her permission so Ilva considered what she was asking thoroughly.

"Which details?" Ilva suddenly let out, a blush covering her exposed chest, neck and face.

"Well, not all of them of course. I may mention our re-lationship though. I will gauge the situation first. Truthfully, I am nervous to bring that up. I do want my grandmother to know about my journey though and the things that have come of it."

Ilva considered Vali's position and the supportive blessing her granny had given them. She agreed, and Vali went off to give her account.

Once she was down the hall and descending the stairs Ilva got up from the bed and paced about the room. After several moments of looking around, trailing her fingers over the ornate silver designs that covered everything, she felt comfortable by herself again. She was fascinated by the silver that wove into all the wood. There were shimmering silver designs embossed into the door and the windows. It was beautiful. Ilva was mesmerised as she looked at the magical view she had in this room. The smell of food pulled her from her trance. She could smell it coming from down the hall before she even heard them wheel the cart towards the door and knock.

Ilva called for the elf knocking to come in. She felt like royalty then. There was a delicious toasted sandwich and steamy glazed carrots. Beside the main plate was a massive amount of strawberries and blackberries, some tea, and little cakes and cookies with icing. Ilva's mouth watered as the trays were brought in. It was the most extravagant thing she had ever seen or smelled.

Two elves brought the food in. The female one was pouring her a glass of water from a pitcher while the male sat the tray of food on a serving table with the tray of teas and treats. They both asked if there was anything else they could do for her to which she shook her head, and they left. The male had similar hair to Krit, and the female had a similar face with the same green eyes.

After scarfing down the sandwich and eating most of the carrots, Ilva shoved a few blackberries into her mouth. She savoured the cool sweetness cutting into the hot roasted flavour of the food she was just eating. She ate the rest of the carrots, deciding she wanted to save the berries for last. She got up, feeling far more energized now, and poured some tea into an empty tea cup on the dessert tray, refilled her water goblet, and loaded her plate with half the cakes and cookies. She sat back on the bed and sipped her tea gingerly, bit into a cookie, and smiled deeply with satisfaction.

This very well might be the most comfort I have ever felt in my life. She could not recall ever having felt so luxurious. She was sure there was more luxury than this out there, however, this was by far the most wonderful food, and the softest bed, she had ever experienced. The sweets were so flavourful. The frosting was creamy and sugary and the cookie was soft enough to think it was still partially dough. Every bite was so delightfully mouth-watering. She tried not to scarf all the cookies down at once.

She popped strawberries and blackberries, one after another, into her mouth in place of sweets, still practicing the control of savouring. She almost demolished both bowls of the bright and dark coloured fruits when she decided to try the cake, the frosting was so light and fluffy, and the cake sunk under the fork. Once cut, it bounced back into its fluffy, tall shape. She took a considerable bite, and tried not to squeal and kick with delight. She sipped small mouthfuls of tea to avoid rinsing too much of the flavour away. Life was wonderful.

She finished her tea and fruit and sweets, with one last cookie. She held the frosting on her tongue, letting it all turn melty in her mouth. She swallowed the final gulp with a mix of satisfaction and remorse. Fighting the urge to eat Vali's share of the desserts, she drank another cup of tea, and was just starting to wonder what time it was, when there was a knock at the door.

Chapter 28

Vali was in the main hall with her grandmother, feeling the air all around her for signs. It was the only thing that was hard with her grandmother. She was difficult to read. She wanted her to know everything, but where to start. Vali decided to start with the moment she met Ilva.

She spun their tale candidly, to the best of her ability. When she got to the dragon, Dola had many questions about the beast. Then she had questions about the sylvite, and the elf male who attacked them, and questions about the solitary old elf in the woods.

"You say she is a grandparent of Ilva's? What is her name?"

Vali decided not to tell her Livy's name, and so pretended not to know. This seemed to anger her grandmother. She could pick up on that much.

She continued telling of their adventures up to where they now were. She finished by saying, "I think I have fallen in love with Ilva."

"Enough!" Dola stood now. Vali could not see it, but she could tell that Dola was shaking with rage. She had been from the very moment Vali mentioned the word love. "I will hear no more of this fantastical delusion. You are tired and have clearly not rested since your return. Go rest, and reconsider your feelings. We will talk again when you are in your right mind." Dola shifted away, her armour clinking behind her as she exited the room.

Vali felt struck. She wondered how Dola could be so insensitive. After all the support she had given her grandmother over the years. She trusted her. Her anger roiled under the skin. She wanted to lift the table before her and toss it upend. She thought to sweep an arm across it and take out everything atop it. Instead she decided to walk away. There were so many aggressive thoughts clouding her mind. Taking control of her emotions had never been so difficult before.

She was used to being berated, but something in her snapped at the idea of being reprimanded for feelings of love. She had never felt so insulted. Maybe it was because Ilva's granny was so understanding that she thought hers would of course be as well. She felt a pang of envy for Ilva then.

Vali stepped up the stairs now and was heading back to the guest room. She had her own room, but she did not want to occupy that one. She wanted to be by Ilva. More so now that she had been denied of having her sanity intact for loving her.

She did love her. She loved her softness, and her smell, and her voice. She loved her conversation, her laugh, and the way she was always mindful of and curious about Vali's inability to see, and not insufferably overprotective of or unnerved by it. They were a good match. Vali knew it. Damn Dola for not seeing the possibility in that. She didn't need anyone else's approval to love who she loved.

Ilva was sitting upon the bed sipping her tea when Vali

knocked and entered. She could hear the sip and clink as she walked in. "How is the food?" Vali asked cheerfully.

Not a hint of the feelings Vali bared within showed on her face. She was a complete mask of herself. She was not as truthful with Ilva as they both deserved and she hated it. She loved Ilva, so why could she not tell her how she felt? Good and bad. She was always afraid of frightening Ilva. She wanted to protect her from hardship in a world that had already given her too much. She did not want to give her any cause to worry. How could she want to do to Ilva, the very thing she was glad Ilva did not do to her? She was angered by the conflicting thoughts she had.

She would keep her own dramas and troublesome feelings to herself. They were not Ilva's burdens to bear. *They do not serve to improve anything, so they should be ignored. They are not useful, and dwelling on them is just pointless.* She shoved them deep inside her heart. She tried to forget them. She made herself move on from the moment where she imagined leaving the feelings.

Vali approached Ilva with a smile, and a high-spirited wit that made Ilva chuckle. She came at her sweet and gullible Ilva with an intense need for affections. Vali did not know until after the deed was finished, just how much she had needed it herself. The intimacy washed her of her suffering. It made her feel like she could endure anything, so long as Ilva was there.

Chapter 29

Ilva woke first the next day, and washed her face in the bowl that sat by one of the windows overlooking the small city. It wasn't much bigger than Falil, but the homes were taller and housed more elves. The shops were bunched close together, and elves were bustling past each other tightly in the narrow streets.

She looked out and saw the forest. From way up here, it looked far larger than Ilva had ever imagined. The trees went on for miles and miles. She couldn't even see the end of the lush green wilderness. The sea should be visible. However, it was hard to see from here if it was water, or if it was sky that she was looking at. She could not see any of the distant mountains where her cave was, nor could she see the mountain pass. From where she stood, all she could see were acres upon acres of trees. Lake Mara was directly in front of her. It was barely visible from here, and it just peeked out through the edge of the forest. It was yet another new, breathtaking view.

It never occurred to her how much like a prison her old forest dwelling could feel, once she had a taste of this wide world. With only one way in or out of the forest, save for trekking through the wastelands, it was even more of a prison than her home had been. She realised that now. There was not as much safety as she once thought. Whatever she used to believe living in the forest brought her, she had quite forgotten now. She felt far safer with Vali by her side.

Vali woke to the sound of Ilva speaking with the housecarl. His name was Thon, her grandmother's silver swordsman. Thon was one of only a few silver warriors that had survived the war. Vali didn't want to think about Dola as the tyrant others often claimed her to be. She pushed the thought down to that place, the place she pushed most of her thoughts and feelings. As Ilva and Thon talked, Vali started gathering up their belongings into their other bag. Just in case. Vali always liked to be prepared.

She listened to what Thon was telling Ilva. She only caught, "I will be right back with your breakfasts then my dear, and I shall fetch Jyke to run you a bath as well."

He added, "Oh no, it will be our pleasure to aid a noble elf such as yourself. I am honoured to assist. Lady Dola is insistent that you are well looked after." He hurried along down the hall to the upstairs kitchen.

Vali sat up as Ilva closed the door. "Oh, you are up. Breakfast will be here soon." Ilva seemed the happiest Vali had sensed her feeling since their meeting.

"You sure are chipper today," Vali said, not unkindly, but not smoothly either.

"I am! I got to sleep in a nice soft bed last night, for the first time in decades, my meals are being cooked and served to me, and I have you. What in the world is there for me to be remotely unhappy about?"

Vali had no want to rain on Ilva's smiling soul right now. So, she said that there was nothing to be unhappy about. Nothing at all. She kept her thoughts and concerns about Dola's doting to herself.

When breakfast came, Ilva was overjoyed! Having food like this prepared for her, after toughing it out on nuts and berries, it was like the gods and goddesses were showering her with affection. She did not know what in the world she did to deserve this, but she was grateful nonetheless. Between bites she thanked Jyke several times.

Jyke was filling Ilva a bath with several pots of hot boiling water she had carted in. She then filled the remaining volume in the tub with two cold water pitchers she had put on the dresser earlier. The steam from the hot water subsided, slightly. Jyke stirred the water with a long wooden handled brush to adjust the temperature. Once it was not scalding, but still hot enough to leave your skin a bit red, she claimed the bath was ready whenever Lady Ilva was fit to get in.

She bowed upon exiting and briskly pushed the cart back towards their floor's kitchenette at the end of the hall. The pots and jugs clattered upon it with sharp metal twangs and bangs. The banging only stopped when the trays had been deposited in the dumbwaiter and send back to the main kitchen downstairs.

Ilva asked Vali, "Do you want to bathe first, or should I?"

Vali's face was coy and flirtatious when she stated, "Both."

Ilva looked sheepish. "What if Thon or Jyke come back?" she lazily protested.

Vali stalked up to help Ilva off with her things. Ilva obliged her, letting her drag her shirt over her head. Soon they both sat basking in the lovely warmth of the water. Ilva still feeling nervous.

The tub was huge, and they could easily sit the both of them in their own areas of the tub. It was perfectly square, and half seated into the ground. Mosaic patterns met each other, with silver engravings tiled all around the tub. They were blue and green, and shimmered like scales. The bathroom was cozy and calming. There were lush green leafy vines trailing from poles that went from one end of the room to the other. There was a small vanity table, and beside it a mirror almost the height of the ceiling. It was luxurious and the plants with all their vining and hanging leaves made her feel like the forest had followed her here. Breathing in the steam from the bath, she soaked into the comfort she felt.

Vali was enjoying the warm bath water too, and she dunked her head under to indulge her entire body with it's soothing effect. She always loved how she could feel her heart beat in the water. She heard both of theirs now. Ilva's was much calmer. Vali paid attention to their beats until they matched. Her face above the water still, up to just over her ears she was submerged, she could make out the sound of Ilva's exhale deep and satisfied.

Vali used the water to guide her to her destination behind Ilva. She reached for her under the water, and connected with her smooth skin. Their bodies touching beneath the surface felt softer. The atmosphere breathed a new romance into their passionate play. They enjoyed the bath. Immensely.

~

When they got out of the bath, Ilva felt a bit dizzy. She spun and sat on the bathroom floor, her breathing a bit heavy, and her face very warm. Vali knew that it was mild dehydration from sweating in the hot bath, as well as all their excitement. Vali got her a glass of water and brought it quickly over to her. Ilva drunk the water down, and Vali went to fill it again from the other room. When she came back, she told her to drink this one slower. Ilva swallowed the water back, sip after sip. Her breathing was already stabilising, and her face didn't feel as hot.

"Are you still dizzy?" Vali asked.

Ilva shook her head no. When she went to stand again though, she said, "Ok, I guess I am still a bit dizzy. I can make it to the bed now though."

Vali guided her to the bed anyhow, almost tripping on her own pants, which still laid on the floor.

Once Ilva was set up in the bed, Vali dressed herself and threw her bag from yesterday over her shoulder. She drank some water herself and then told Ilva, "I'm going to go speak with my grandmother once again. I'm not sure what she wants, but she wanted me to rest before asking it of me. Will you wait or go to the library?"

Ilva requested to go down with Vali and see the library and Krit again. "I bet he's got massive piles on the cart and the tables by now!" Ilva gleamed.

"The fact that this is exciting news to you is only somewhat frightening," Vali laughed.

They joked on their way down the stairs about all the

possible places the books would be piled, and how if they need to find her later, she would be buried under a mountain of them. One last wisecrack had them hunched over at the entry to the hall where Dola sat waiting. Their laughter echoed slightly in the hall as they entered. Vali's grandmother looked unamused by their antics. Ilva was suddenly worried for Vali's chat with her.

Vali bowed a good morning to Lady Dola, Ilva followed suit, then Vali reported she would escort Ilva to the library and return to discuss yesterday's matter with her. Then they were on their way out the big doors and down the main hall towards the library corridor.

Chapter 30

"Krit, are you in here?" Krit's footfalls could be heard rushing in their direction at the sound of Vali's call.

He lunged himself out from the bookshelf he was behind, and came up to greet them both with the same over-bearing exuberance. "Good morning ladies. How was your sleep? Restful, I hope. Nothing gets the mind more prepared for learning than a good night's sleep. A good breakfast is wise too."

Vali interjected when she saw the chance, "Krit, I have to confer with Lady Dola, Ilva wanted to come see the books you put aside for her, I will leave her in your care. Go easy on her though. Not everyone can process things as fast as you can, okay?"

"Okay!" Krit enthusiastically shouted. Then Ilva was alone with Krit.

"So where do we start?" Ilva said, looking at the too full cart of books to her left. She winced a little, when she saw Krit skip towards it.

"I have assembled many titles of interest," he declared proudly.

The first book he grabbed off the cart was titled, *The History of Zoriya.*

~

Vali traipsed down the hall towards the room that occupied her cranky grandmother. As she entered, she heard the sound of a wine glass taping back onto the table. Then she smelled the unmistakable scent, "Bit early for that is it not?" she disdainfully attested.

"Never too early to drink. Only too late. Like when all the wine runs out," Dola laughed to herself.

Vali did not find the joke amusing, same as how her grandmother did not think her and Ilva's joke was comedic earlier.

Dola sighed.

Vali placed the sylvite on the table between them. The ragged cloth napkins fell to expose the artifact tucked within.

Dola picked up the large mineral in her leather gloved hand and inspected it with hungry eyes. "Straight to business again then? Alright. I want to know more about the old elf living in the woods. You never did give me her name."

Vali winced before answering, "I do not see the importance. I want to know why you had me go searching for this hunk of junk that ruined my eyes. I thought you didn't believe me, but you seem oddly expectant."

Dola seemed surprised by Vali's resenting tone, and replied in her own, "I never said I didn't believe you, dear. I just didn't care for your ravings. Acting as if your trauma is centric. This hunk of junk, as you called it, is a source of great magic, and the race that once had control of it is almost lost. There are only a handful left in the world. I happen to know one who married the leader of the stone elves, the last female sylvite warrior, and they are willing to throw themselves and their lands to me for the cost of this hunk of junk. When I annihilate all the traitors in my midst, and assemble all of the arcane artifacts, I will be the most powerful sorceress in our world!"

Vali realised a few major connections now before she got spitefully angry with her grandmother, "What has gotten into you? Are you mad?"

Dola boomed back, "I am going to liberate us! I'm going to show Alix how powerful we can be. Why should we all have separate power? We should be united, and someone should take ownership and unite us all. That elf will need all of the artifacts, and the complete devotion of elfkind to do this!"

Vali, hit by Dola's greedy words, was too stunned to retort. Was her grandmother really this evil? What did she mean about uniting the powers? Vali was, for the first time in her life, considering that her grandmother might be indubitably dangerous. The guardian she depended on for so long to house and clothe her, she always believed there had to be some good in her, now everything felt wrong. Terribly tragically wrong.

Vali's thoughts went wild. *She cannot be this corrupt, she cannot be this cruel oppressor, this murderer. This is not her!*

Dola now had her hands on the one item that could help

her wreak havoc. The sylvite artifact, handed to her moments before by a beguiled Vali.

Full of venomous animosity towards her grandmother, Vali seethed. She didn't fetch the artifact so that Dola could barter elves freedoms with it. She didn't want Ilva's family to suffer as a result. *Why?* Vali kept questioning her reality, she realised how she had already smoothed over most of her feelings of invalidation by being around Ilva, who validated her, and how her pride in seeking that acceptance from one who could not offer it was a waste of effort. All that was left in Vali's bag now was the hunting knife. She considered taking it out.

"Dola!" Vali slammed her fist down hard upon the table. "Grandmother," Vali seethed through her teeth. The wine glass fell over and the clink sounded like a crack. "How could you? Selling something that is not yours, to one of the only surviving females of their race? In order to coerce them into working for you? Your swordsmen have become your wait-ers, and I your dog. I do not know what trials have brought you to this level of villainy. All I know is that I will not stand for it. I will not be your pawn in a grand scheme that is sure to get you and everyone around you killed. Or worse."

Dola picked up and inspected the wine glass, her violet eyes locking on the crack, sneering at it. She set it back on the table upright, and grabbed the bottle instead. She swigged back three large swallows, then told Vali, "You will learn darker secrets about this cruel world soon enough, you pathetic whelp, don't you worry. Now, how long were you going to try keeping that brat you brought home safe, hmm? Care to verify her identity, as a lady?"

Vali tried to appear puzzled.

Dola continued, "I happen to know that the stone elf leader lost his daughter some time ago, and they have a price on her head. Did you really not know yourself, dear? Blind in more ways than one I see. Too bad I was not with you to guide you along. Really dear, what would you do without me?"

Vali seethed as she took in this new information, she registered that Ilva had given those facts of her lineage to Thon's son, who happened to be the chattiest little elf in the whole castle. *Does Ilva know there is a price on her head? Not likely if she announced herself as nobility.* She had no idea what trap she had walked Ilva into. As pieces clicked into place Vali felt strangely sick. She felt her whole body stiffen. Something was indeed wrong. Terribly tragically wrong.

Chapter 31

Vali swallowed hard. She shifted her position. Giving her grandmother her full attention now. She wanted to ensure that no matter what happened between her and her grandmother that she at least made an effort. She tried to comprehend how her grandmother might be feeling.

Dola squinted at her granddaughter.

Vali paced towards her at the head of the table.

Dola stood.

Vali angled her chin and fixed her expressionless face towards the sound of Dola's movements. She gauged her opponent in this battle of confrontation.

Dola let out an unexpected laugh.

Vali cringed a little before asking, "What is so funny?"

Dola quieted her laughter, "I have always wanted to know if you would stand up to me, should I make this move. Now, I know. You are not with me. Do you wish to be a casualty of this war?"

Dola's comment caught Vali off guard. "What war?" Vali queried.

Dola looked serious then, "Do not be unprepared for the worst. The world is about to test us all, my dear. I am about to show you what it means to hate. You thought you were upset with me a moment ago. That was a mere introduction to our nature my dear. Oh, the things you do not know." Dola's voice had a dryness to it. It cut Vali to pieces as her grandmother showed her true colours. "There is far worse work going on here, my faithless dog. Bite me if you wish, but then who will feed you? You will hate others more than I by the end, so I am not worried about this small moment in time. Many elves have secrets, some are more dangerous than others, and some barely secrets at all. I hope you have something dangerous hidden within you too granddaughter, it will be what keeps you alive."

Vali shuddered at what her grandmother had said. She wondered what worse thing her grandmother could do than take over the world? She asked her what worse thing there was. The response she got instilled more fear in her than any idea of villainous treason she was just thinking of.

Dola told her, and it was a nightmarish statement that would haunt Vali tirelessly in the coming days. "Why dear, taking away *your* world of course. I'm not sorry. It has to be done. She has a price on her head, her parents are giving up resources, trade the stone artifact and, shall we say other things, for the safe return of their precious child."

Vali shuddered her lover's name, "Ilva."

Vali practically tripped into every chair on her way out, her senses deaf from fear. She stumbled forward and forward, racing to the library. *Please be ok.*

Chapter 32

Ilva spent the first few moments in the library pouring over every detail that she could retain from the books Krit was placing in front of her. She was working on three books at once, as she was reading Krit would talk between pages about things she had just read, it was annoying her. She thought, *for someone who likes to read so much, you would think he would understand the want to read things without someone talking to you.* Ilva focused her attention back to her task. She studied and studied. There was a knock at the door, and she did not look up.

Krit dashed to the door and let whoever had knocked in.

"Hello father! I'm assisting our guest Ilva. I hope you will excuse our mess."

"Fine, fine. Go have your mother fetch you and your accomplice a snack. I must speak with her a moment." At this Ilva turned.

Krit raced from the room.

Thon spoke, "Listen, Ilva, I mean you no ill will, but you may want to come quietly when the guards come to collect you in a few seconds. I wanted to come first and request this of you, I do not want harm to come to you should you resist. Not only that, but if you fight us then Krit will have to see that. I don't want him to think badly of us. It's only orders. You understand right?" he moved closer, "Your parents want you to come home. We have an escort prepared for you."

This sounded like a polite threat to Ilva. Another choice she did not have. *You do not sound like someone who means me no ill will. A threat is a threat,* Ilva thought. "If you wish your son to not think badly of you, then why engage in actions where he will think such things. If my desire is to not return home, then I think it is a choice I am entitled to have. Why should I not act in a way that respects my own choices and freedoms in front of your son?"

The answer Ilva just gave, which came out calmer than she expected it to, and made her feel confident, was clearly upsetting for Thon to hear. "If my son were acting as you are now, then perhaps I would want the same thing. For someone to return him to me. So that we might talk, and perhaps work through whatever separated us. What is the harm in going home, Ilva? Why do you not wish to? Your parents are worried. They're willing to pay a lot for your safe return."

Ilva began to panic. She wanted to know where her escape routes were. *Where can I run?* How did she not plan for anything? She used to be so cautious, lately she had been less careful and more impulsive. She scolded herself for getting too comfortable somewhere.

She made to bolt past Thon, and he gripped her by one arm. "Come on, please don't make my job harder. We're simply taking you home. Why are you acting like such an elfling? They are your blood! They deserve your loyalty and respect! Stop resisting!"

Ilva did not care if she was making Thon's job harder. She did not care about blood either. Ilva's mind filled with dark thoughts. *Being blood does not make your connection to each other unbreakable, brothers and sisters murder each other in this life. I once watched a widow drown her baby in the sea near our village.* Blood has never been reason enough for her. If her family really wanted her back, then why did they never step foot in the woods to find her? Was she just a pawn to everyone? She wanted to escape. She did not want to be forced to do anything, *I am no one's slave.* Her inner voice boomed the sentence out over and over. *I am no one's slave. I am no one's slave!*

She kicked, punched, and violently tugged on Thon's hand, which was gripping her bicep tightly. Peeling his fingers back with surprising force she yanked her arm away and attempted to run again. He grabbed at her again. He missed.

She tried to escape out the way they had entered the building, she ran down the hall to her left, and towards the front door. She stopped when two large soldiers blocked her path, along with two more running up behind her with Thon. She knew that was the end of the line. There was no escape. She could not fight off all these soldiers, armed for a fight. *Vali, where are you?* Another dark thought came and told her that Vali could not protect her from her life. No one could. She fell to the floor and cried.

Thon scooped her up, she no longer protested fiercely, she just cried. She shamed herself after the tears had flown. She thought herself pitiful and weak. She judged herself harshly, as she rode on horseback behind Thon, her arms tied tight enough to bruise. They rode hard and fast towards her old home. Towards the one place she vowed never to return to. There was no choice, she felt the weight of that reality crashing down on her. *No escape. No choice.*

~

Vali burst into the library, where Krit sat crying on the floor. She approached him, carefully. "Krit. Krit! What happened?"

He was incomprehensible through his sobbing. Snot was piled thickly upon his top lip, and when he breathed too heavily it bubbled out of his nostril. His eyes were beat red and puffy. Vali made out the words he stuttered, "S-soldiers t-t-took her awaaaay".

She jumped up, and without a comforting word to the distraught Krit, she lunged back into action.

Running down the hallway to the door, Vali nearly crashed into one of the guards in the hall. "Whoa! What's the hurry?"

Vali turned and gripped the front of the soldier's silver armour. "Did you help whisk Ilva away, from under my nose?"

"That stone elf? Yeah, she's going home to her parents. She shouldn't have run away anyways," the soldier grunted.

"What did you say?" Vali bellowed into every corner of the place.

The elf was afraid now, and he tried hard not to react.

Vali picked him up with the hand that held him, and in one smooth motion she slammed him into the hard floor face first. Her adrenaline surprised her, she was up and stepping over the disabled soldier in a flash, and out the front door rushing after Ilva.

Chapter 33

Ilva was surprised that even as the sun began to set, they galloped on. Thon, Ilva, and six other men riding with them. Not stopping. Maybe they had orders to get there as soon as possible. Not much hope of Vali coming to find her then, even if she was. Ilva wondered if Vali was the reason she was on her way home. She was not there to stop her being taken, and she seemed like she was having some pretty serious conversations with Dola. She was unsure what to make of anything in her life. There were so many endless possibilities and they all overwhelmed her. She just bumped up and down on the back of the horse, and let it and Thon take her to her unwanted destination.

She found herself lost in the endless possibilities she thought up. Did Vali sell her out? Did Dola hurt Vali? Maybe Vali never even loved her, and it was all a trick. What will her mother do with her? Did they miss her at all? Were they hunting her down to punish her? Did they want to talk with her? Or talk at her? What awaited her in Falil was nothing she could prepare for.

~

Vali noticed the deeply impressed hoof beats upon the path, and realised there would be no catching up to them, her stamina was fading faster from the anxiety. She could not run as fast as a horse, and certainly not for as long, and the soldiers had taken all of the stallions in Karna. Vali assumed it was so that their fleet looked intimidating and wouldn't be met with opposition.

She sat on the side of the trail, tears threatening her eyes, and wondered what she should do? Was pursuing wise, maybe she should she think of a plan? She decided to walk while she thought, sitting still was bothering her. She did not like to slump over in defeat, so she pushed herself up, ignoring her shaking legs, she began walking at a brisk pace towards Falil, as the sun was dipping into the sky lower and lower. At nightfall, she finally decided to stop as the chill bit at her. In her haste she had not brought any of her camping gear. She huddled on the ground behind a rock near the path. Then, the next morning she began walking again. Her bones aching, her heart breaking, and her head racing.

~

Ilva was up all night with the soldiers, galloping through the darkness. The rising sun shone on the mountains, it lit up their far-off peaks, foggy with the moisture of the morning, and made them appear to be bathed in a soft golden mist. Sad and defeated, Ilva appreciated the tiny moment, searching for hope or any happy emotion. She turned her body back in the saddle to face the sea that they were fast approaching. Ilva was sore, her legs were numb, and there was this sharp pain in her hips and backside. She tried to shift in the seat, but it only made the pain worse. She slumped back to her original pained position, enduring the jolt of discomfort shooting up her with every hoof the horse beat into the dirt.

The horses had been ridden through the night and into the morn. Foam coated their hindquarters and mouths. Their breath was laboured, and the poor beasts needed more and more reassurances to move. After a few moments of these creatures' consistent protests, they stopped. The horses were given apples and water was poured into an open leather feeding bag, then distributed to each one in turn. Their legs still shook from the obvious pain they were in, one collapsed and refused to get back up for several minutes. Ilva noticed Thon's steed seemed the most exhausted. Having two riders upon his back. Before the horses had a proper rest, they were on their way again. Her heart broke for the animals as they walked on.

In less than an hour they reached the gates into Falil. Ilva saw the large house looming ahead. Her heart filled with a dread she had almost forgotten how to feel. The memory of evenings dashing off through this small village, and then puttering home after, all came rushing back to her now. She remembered the way that she had felt before, and she desperately wanted to know how to make the feeling go away. The feeling of helplessness which overwhelmed her. She was so exhausted. Her, Thon, and the silver clad soldiers, walked into the main square of the village, after first tying the horses at the gate.

Passersby, and faces Ilva had long not seen, stared at them all as they crossed through the quiet village. They made their way through the main square, and walked up the large wooden steps to the familiar terrace of Ilva's parent's home.

Ilva's mother came out onto the terrace to greet them all. "Come in, the journey must have been tiring. Would you like me to send someone to attend your horses?" she preened politely.

"If it's not too much trouble, that would be appreciated Lady Syli." Was Thon's well-mannered response.

She urged one of the soldiers at her side to carry out the task. Only one of the village soldiers stood by her side now, she had been expecting their arrival. *How? Why?* Ilva wondered.

Chapter 34

Vali dragged her legs, at a slow pace, and let her mind whir with all the potentials and possibilities. *Was Ilva safe? If she is not, I am to blame.* The main thought that continued to nag at her. It pummeled itself into her consciousness. As she walked down the well-travelled dirt path, she heard a sound ahead on the road. The sound was a series of clunks and bangs, and there was an occasional sound of rushing, fast pumping water too.

As she approached the sound, she suddenly heard a booming female's voice beside the road. "Good morning! How are you! Coming in for a bite this morning friend?" the deep voice asked her.

Vali curiously responded, "Do you have anything to spare? I am afraid I have no coin on me."

The other elf took time to answer. Vali knew she was being assessed. She was probably wondering about how blind Vali was too. Despite her poor vision, she could see a shadow of the larger female, and tell she faced her at least. Eventually this stockily-built elf responded giddily to Vali's inquiry. "I am a place of business, so I have nothing much to spare.

If I spared every traveller who passed my establishment the burden of payment, then I would have no business left." She paused then added, "I could at least fill you a skin of water for your journey. Just fixed the pump here. Looks like you're mightily unprepared for your travels. The name is Llyr."

Vali thanked the elf, and at her request, helped her carry her tools back to her roadside tavern.

Now sitting in a bar at the crossroads, Vali stirred awkwardly in her seat, not paying any attention to the voices that swam in every corner, the patrons paid Vali no mind. She was embarrassed that she had been so unprepared. How could she have been prepared though? Her mind tried to make her see reason, over and over, it was a disciplined mind most days. She thought back about the interaction between her and her grandmother. Had her grandmother been building those prerogatives for power all along? Was she the first one to see it? She had no idea what Dola's undertaking was, however she was afraid of her now, and the hurt was unbearable. She could barely register with it.

Vali was pulled away from her agonizing thoughts. Llyr came hastily up to Vali, and shoved a few things into her bag, which only held her knife now. Into to rest of the space she jammed a full water skin, a small blanket, and a few honey smelling candies in a tiny little tin. Vali was full of gratitude. She thanked Llyr many times over, before moving on down the road shouldering the tavern owner's generosity. She would be sure to thank her properly one day.

Chapter 35

Ilva could not believe how much had changed, and how much had not, since she had last been in this room. She moved her eyes over the newness that had passed through her home; the new elaborately carved oak bench at the side of the doors, the new linen that adorned the windows, and the plants Ilva had once watered in clay pots had vanished. The things that remained the same drew less obvious stares from her, she glanced quickly, to avoid feelings of familiarity.

She flashed a look at the cup her mother used every morning, still the same one in the same place, and a door at the end of the hall that was still sealed shut. The door led to her father's stone cutting workshop. No one was ever allowed in there, not even Ilva's mother. She suddenly wondered why her father was not there to greet them as well.

Her question was already being answered, as her mother addressed their group once again. "I am grateful for you soldiers of Karna, for returning my daughter home to us, I am sorry my husband could not be here to greet you as well, he is taking care of some other business today. He is expected to return soon. Until that time I am the body of authority in this village. I do hope I can accommodate any of Lady Dola's appeals for payment. My husband will be overjoyed at the return of our daughter Ilva."

Ilva stood in the room, awkwardly, as her mother prepared to haggle their town's needs away, just to keep Ilva in a place she had tried to escape from. *Why?* Ilva thought painfully. *Why does she want me here so badly? Is it love? Possession? What drives my mother's motives?* Time moved slowly.

Lady Syli appeared only a fraction impatient when one of the soldiers handed over a scroll, she hated to read. She unrolled it quickly, and was struck with a look of panic and fear. What in this wide world would cause her to lose control in a social situation? This frightened Ilva. She was often moody with Ilva, but not with the Lord of the house or their guests. Syli did not ever lose her composure in these settings. *What is in that letter?*

Ilva's curiosity clawed at her. She could barely contain the urge to run up and grab it. Her mother pulled her mouth into the tightest line, and spoke one harsh cutting word in reply, "No."

The soldiers looked at each other. Thon nodded to each of them then. He spoke for them all, "If that is your answer my lady, we will take it to Lady Dola for you. I will humbly say, however, that I think it will be greatly in your interest to give her what she wants. The consequences of that response, I am afraid, are great."

Ilva thought she saw her mother shiver, she readjusted herself to a more defiant position, and firmly said, "I do not accept these terms. We must renegotiate."

Thon spoke again, "These are the renegotiations, you

said you would give anything else last time, this is what she wants. If you do not fulfill these demands, we have orders to assassinate you and your daughter."

Ilva froze.

Chapter 36

Vali walked hard and fast. She decided after seeing the first sign of Falil in the distance, to run again. She had been running on and off since she left the tavern, only stopping when she could take no more exertion. She was still a good hour or two of hard running away, but it was finally visible now, and it gave her hope.

She burst into the hardest, fastest run she could, urging herself onward. *Ilva, Ilva, Ilva.* The name of the elf she loved, sounded like a caressing coax inside her head, it propelled her feet, and it was in the throes of every step she took. She put all of her longing to see Ilva safe into every lunge. Her calves burned, and they were getting so tight, her skin felt as though it might split open. Her hands were swelling from clenching them at times, and her feet began to ache. Still, she pushed on, never losing step. She could not slow down. Not until Ilva was safe. She ran herself as hard as the soldiers had run their horses.

~

Ilva stared at the scene before her. Two of the six soldiers had stayed outside. The four in the room behind Thon began to spread out, covering all the exit points. This was bad. Ilva was a poor fighter, in fact she had avoided a lot of physical conflicts, opting for verbal ones instead. She thought her mother much the same. Now the two of them were trapped in this room, with no hope of escape, save for whatever Vali's grandmother had wanted of their village. There was so much at play that she did not yet understand. Just what kind of game were they all playing?

Ilva noticed Thon step towards her mother. "I want to help you, please. I know it is a lot of her to ask, but you will get your lives in return. She is wise, and she knows what she is doing, I trust her."

Syli sneered, "I do not trust Dola. She is a wretched old home wrecking hag. Tell her I said she can get over herself, and stop acting like anyone in this world owes her anything."

Ilva let the shock register in her. Then Syli did something even more amazing than insult her guests. She darted forward into the rays of light that were bursting through the windows, splayed the fans she was hiding in her sleeves, and danced two low to the ground sweeping steps. Her fans burst into flames, and her eyes snapped into a battle-ready glare! She rounded on Thon and slashed at his leg with the sharp elemental tips of the fans, rolling her body in a dancelike wave close to the floor. Ilva was stunned, her mother did have secrets. Ilva was all the sudden ashamed at some of her previous assumptions about her mother. *Go!* Ilva's thoughts urged and cheered for the very elf she often discredited.

~

Vali burst into the village, noting the guard's horses all still tied outside. She sensed them by their sounds and strong smells, she paced quickly now through her unfamiliar surroundings, and tried to figure out which way Ilva could be. She jogged through the streets, and heard many whispers around her. She heard many elves talking about the silver guards with Ilva. She quickly followed the streams of gossip, gathering info here and there, and found herself hearing the laughter of two familiar voices. The silver guards posted outside the door were subsiding their chuckling when Vali turned the corner.

"Vali!" One guard exclaimed.

"Where is Ilva?" Vali bellowed, her tone threatening.

The guard stammered, "Inside, we can't go in, they're negotiating."

Vali cut him off, "Ilva is the only one who matters in that negotiation! You robbed her of her own free will when you brought her here! I will not forgive any of you for that! She is not a good to be traded! She is not payment nor is she a way of securing payment! Leave! Go back to Dola. Tell her that there is no other I could hate more than her, and the danger lurking within me, will rain terror down upon her!"

The silver clad elf gave a quick nod, and backed away from the elf claiming herself dangerous, seeing in her the same look Dola had given the soldiers themselves time and time again.

Vali approached the door.

~

Ilva watched her mother disarm Thon, and then before she realised the intent, her mother flung the sword at her! Ilva fumbled the catch, but still caught the blade. She began working the rope on her hands free, nicking the inside of her thumb with the awkward blade. Before she could get the ropes fully shimmied off, however, one of the guards by the nearest window came at her. She forgot about the bits of rope still hanging from her wrist, and grabbed the sword hilt, defending herself.

She threw the blade up and blocked the swing of the other elf's sword. It made a loud clang when they hit, and the reverberation was a new feeling for Ilva, the shock almost made her lose her grip entirely. It shook her all the way up to her shoulders. She tried not to show her opponent the effect the blow had on her. She knelt under the pressure and dodged to the side, as she swept under the soldier, he turned towards her, and she lunged at him. She missed. He grabbed the sword with a hand and pulled it from her grip. His other hand was now gripping her throat. He squeezed his silver glove, balling it into a fist with her vocal cords inside of it. He was going to crush her neck.

Chapter 37

Vali pushed the doors open hard. Not caring about a rude entrance at this point. She surveyed the sounds in the room, and before entering, she knew Ilva was in danger. She called for her now, "Ilva!" She had no idea that Ilva was in fact, very much in need of her help, and very much not able to yell for it. In a few moments she would be dead. Vali noted the body rushing toward her, she sliced through the room to where Syli was, and her knife took down the soldier who had charged at her. Another soldier had been cut down by Syli, and lay on the floor behind her.

Thon seeing her approach shouted, "Vali! What are you doing?"

Vali was hurt by this elf's betrayal, almost more than Dola's, and she would kill Thon for his hand in this. She would do it now if she knew Ilva was, at this moment, clawing for breath. She decided to attempt reasoning with him, for Krit's sake. "Please Thon, don't barter with lives. Don't be Dola's dog anymore."

Thon wrestled with this. Syli took her chance and ran to Ilva. She struck the back of the strangling soldier with her burning sylvite fans, he fell screaming in pain, and Ilva clutched her throat a moment before grabbing his sword and thrusting it down into his flailing body. It took more force than she thought it would. She had no idea that the adrenaline rush, currently surging through her, was her reason for being able to sink the blade in. She was still coughing as she bent over the solider. Her face purple, her eyes bloodshot and blurry, her lips dry. Saliva pooled fast as air rushed into her lungs. She looked up at Vali and Thon through red watery eyes. *Vali. She came.*

Vali and Thon circled each other as they talked, Vali did not want him close to her, and she could tell he wanted to close the gap. He was talking casually to her, and it made her angry. "Vali, I am sure that if Lord Ediv was here he would be far more reasonable about this. I have no choice, when a citizen reacts with any sort of violence they must be controlled." he breathed deeply, "You are not educated enough in the subject of war to have a say. We are trying to prevent future division, and repair the damage after the last war between our kingdoms. Any elf who stands against us being united is a rebel. And rebels are what start new wars. She must be dealt with. Stand aside."

Vali looked disgusted, "I have no knowledge of the needs of greed, you are correct, I have my own knowledge. I did not feel it fair that Ilva be dragged here against her will and sold. I did not feel it fair when the elves of Mila were sold after the war as the spoils of it. I do not see the logic in these actions, no matter what they gain! Not wealth nor magic is worth the lives of elves! Why value such things over life? And how can we unite when we punish anyone who does not conform? There are better ways of doing this."

Thon appeared defeated by that statement. He appeared to be backing away from the situation now. Vali felt a flicker of hope. Then suddenly he attacked.

Ilva watched with horror as Thon grabbed the sword of the fallen soldier before him, and ran at Vali. A large bladed sword against Vali's hunting knife. They connected hard, and Vali almost lost control under the hit. His heavy blade slid off the tip of hers. The sound of the silver blades whistling in the air, clanging loudly when they connected, filled the house. Back and forth this went until their blades locked at the hilt. Vali would press and Thons arms would appear to struggle with the large sword. He took a few deep breaths and lunged his blade towards her face again and again. They wrestled, hilt against hilt, until his weapon cut deeply into Vali's cheek, and she staggered back. Her dagger still held up firm in a protective stance. Thon had less energy now, and so his sword hung to his side. He was not ready when Vali came at him this time.

She cut him across his ribs, before pushing past him, barely avoiding his wildly swinging sword arm. She stabbed him in the lower back, on his other side, then whirled around him again. He became enraged at his ineffectiveness and the blooming pain. This battle was with Dola's blind grand-daughter. How could he be losing? As his confidence faltered, he looked around for anything, and his eyes fell on Ilva, and Syli. He ran to them then, as Vali tried to register his move. Grabbing Syli by the arm he threw her in front of himself as a shield, and then pointed his blade at Ilva.

"I will kill these two as I was ordered! My last loyal duty before you attempt to dispel me from this world you faithless wretch! Long live the true high Lady, Dola!" Blood was in his mouth, his words slurred.

The sound of Ilva's scream, and the smell of blood, as it came pouring out of someone. Vali thought she realised what was happening, and she erupted. She rushed Thon, and punched him hard in the stomach, then when he crumpled, she sliced open his neck with her dagger. Pushing him over, not yet registering the lives that had been taken, she called out her only concern, "Ilva! Ilva!"

Chapter 38

Ilva was over top of her mother crying. Her mother had been stabbed, though it took Syli a time to register that it had even happened. Vali didn't know it happened, but Syli had tried to stab Thon with her folded up fan, and he reacted by puncturing her through her back with his sword. It had cut her clean through. The blade had then been yanked fiercely back out, cutting deeply into her organs, leaving her to bleed out quickly.

Syli lay covered in blood, her sight drifting very fast. Her final words came, "shh, shh, my girl. I know you are brave, and smart. Run to the mountains, go to the stolzite elves." she coughed violently, "I did many wrong things. I must now tell you the worst wrong I have done you, even if you do not believe it. You must not trust the lord of this house! We were both prisoners here you and I, Ediv is..."

Ilva watched as her mother's breathing became heavy and laboured. Her eyes flickered and spun as if she was dizzy. She coughed as blood stained her mouth, and coated her wounded stomach more thickly. Her body began to get heavier, Ilva was filled with all the regret she had long avoided feeling. Pain and guilt took over. She screamed sobs of furious agony until her vocal cords could handle no more. For the first time, even after her mother's curious last words, inquisitive thoughts did not come to her mind. Not for a while anyways. When she finally did consider what it could mean she was riddled with agonizing questions.

Such a quick goodbye. Not enough time. Not a chance to reconcile. Nothing but shame filled her memories. She was unbearably angry. Not at her mother's death, as much as at the soldier who brought it. She had the desire to run to his body and decimate it further. To stab Thon's wretched corpse again and again. The dark thoughts passed. After many long, silent moments.

Ilva and Vali stood in the room and Vali placed a comforting hand upon Ilva's shoulder. Ilva sighed deep and hoarse. So much had happened since the day Vali came into the forest. She partially wanted to blame her, and Dola. Yet she knew deep down the real cause of all her pain, was herself. If she was really honest about it, she was the one who left, and the longing to have had more time with her mother was brought about by her own choices. If only she had known her mother had felt imprisoned too. They could have run together. All this time. Things could have been different.

Ilva was torn between her feelings of anger and frustration with herself, and those same feelings towards others. In a hot moment, without thinking, she chose to lash out about it. She rounded suddenly on Vali, who was supporting her only a moment before, knowing it wasn't her blame to receive, and snapped. "Why did you take me to Karna? I thought I would be safe with you! I thought you were safe! This is all your fault!"

Vali removed her supporting hand. She was lost for words. *Ilva must be in so much pain.* Vali tried to rationalise that Ilva was just acting out.

Ilva yelled louder, "I do not trust you! How do I know your true intentions? I will never trust you or anyone else ever again! Not if this is what stands to happen when I do."

Vali gulped, then let out a meek, "I am so sorry, Ilva. I did not want any of this to happen. I would give anything to undo what's been done." She added with more of her voice, "I can be trusted."

Vali was near tears when Ilva only came back with a short venomous, "Get out." Ilva went to the study, kicked the door in, and stomped into the once forbidden room. Answers. She wanted answers.

Chapter 39

She stomped heavily around the room, ransacking, like a burglar upending a home. She shuffled through papers, and opened containers. She found a few maps, she took one that appeared to be of the Vozrek Mountains, and another that looked like the depths of Lake Mara. She found a large cross body hunting bag, in a chest at the end of the working table. She filled it with the things she found in the room which now lacked privacy. Her bag was soon filled with the maps, two long and thin knives, a small telescopic glass, a rope, a blanket, a piece of flint, and a few smooth stones from the working table. She did not know what these smooth stones were for, she just wanted to take everything out of this stupid secret room.

Why was it a secret anyways? Nothing seems that special? Ilva thought. As she thought this, the smooth stones in her bag clunked together slightly, they thrummed with power when they touched. Ilva did not notice. She was ready to leave. Leaving home this time was not as easy. It should have been. Now, she felt she had no reason to stay. Yet she did not move from the room.

She looked all around it. Gazed at the one secret her tiny village held. This one place that her eyes had never touched, soaked in her surroundings until she felt satisfied, she had seen all that was here. She wandered out of the room and Vali was not there. Ilva wandered the rest of the house, taking in memories, some of which now hurt her. Ilva ached over the loss she just endured. She avoided looking at her mother's body, she wanted to pretend it wasn't even there. The vision remained in her mind however, and she would never remove the memory of her mother's death from her mind. Every room held some memory of her mother and her. Ilva walked to a room between the study and the kitchen, the room she once slept in, and turned the handle.

The door was locked. Still fueled with adrenaline and despair, she decided to just break the damned door down. She walked back a few paces, gave herself the hardest push off, and propelled herself into the door with all she had. It splintered at the handle, and flung wide open, banging off a shelf and wobbling on it's now bent hinges.

Ilva walked into an entirely new room from the one she had known. It was another study of sorts, only this one had a single round table, with a map, and a box upon it. The map looked like it showed all of Zoriya, as well as other continents across the sea she had never before heard of. She opened the lid of the small box, and inside were letters. Many letters. From Dola. Ilva fingered through to the oldest one and read it.

Lord Ediv,

It has come to our knowledge that you may be in posses-
sion of two artifacts. This is not according to the terms of
the agreement made between our four realms ambassadors.
You cannot have two class powers in the same zone. If you
do not produce the sylvite crystal, so it might be moved to
a safer location, we will be forced to see this as an act of
war, and will respond with fervent aggression. We will be
awaiting your immediate response.
Regards,
Lady Dola

Ilva moved on to another letter, then another. It seemed through correspondence they had come to an understanding that, despite the fact that Lord Ediv was harbouring one of the only surviving elves of Mila, he was not in possession of the sylvite. They had also agreed that their elves should all come together as one. Ruled by one. It seemed that Dola and Ediv had been planning an uprising together by the end of these letters. They had set up several meetings from what Ilva had read, and she assumed some of them took place in this very room. Her room, had become a war room.

It was eye opening to Ilva, how much terror this place really did have, and maybe her instincts were right when they told her to run. So, after reading the last letter, and seeing that she only had a few hours of daylight left, she made to leave home. One final time.

Chapter 40

As Ilva opened the front door, Vali was sitting on the top step of the stump that Ilva once danced upon. Ilva remembered the lessons. Dancing in the dusk filled hours. They suddenly didn't seem like such terrible lessons. She wished for one more. Vali stood, she had heard the door, and now heard Ilva's approach.

"I am so sorry," Vali began.

Ilva stopped her, "No Vali, I am sorry. I said things I didn't mean. I must go now, to the Vozrek Mountains. I must know what my mother means for me to find out there. You personally have done me no wrong. I'm the one who didn't protect myself. It was not your duty to do that. Please take care of yourself."

Ilva did not truly want to leave Vali. She just wanted to find her answers, she was relieved when Vali responded. "Then that is where I am going too, if you will have me along."

Ilva let a small smile grace her face. She was quite surprised at Vali's loyalty, and dedication. She was moved by it. She thanked Vali, "I would love to have you with me. We make a good team. If not for you, I may have just been another body in that room. I am fortunate you came, despite the things I said. I am grateful for every moment since you found the solitary, lonely me, hidden in the forest."

Vali sighed her relief at her friend's fast forward thinking. It must have taken some serious resolve to come to terms with her feelings so quickly. Vali was impressed at Ilva's resilience. She was maybe even a bit envious of it. Wishing that she could process hers so efficiently, she thought to herself, *Ilva is remarkably brave.*

She walked towards the entrance of the village, Vali aside her. The two elves received more stares than either of them had in their lifetime. Blood covered them both. The large pack on Ilva's back, her face set and determined. They were an intimidating sight, and they were striking fear into the elves of Falil. They made it to the gate, and untied one of the rested horses, whose rider would never return. Once on the horse, Ilva gripped Vali's hand and pulled her up. Vali seemed unnerved sitting on the large mammals back, Ilva felt her grip tighten upon her waist, and she squeezed her hand over Vali's reassuringly.

Ilva turned the stallion to the gawking and inquisitive villagers. She shouted to them, "Lady Syli is dead, and your Lord is abroad! Appoint a temporary official. I, Lady Ilva, will not be returning. These horses' riders are all dead. The animals will need caring for. The bodies will need burying. I am sorry for the losses; I also suffer from them on this tragic day. If the day for war comes, I hope you choose the battles you fight wisely, for we all make our own choices. Do not lose sight of the freedom we all own. We all deserve freedom. We are no one's slaves!" The horse was pulled into a tight turn, and Ilva urged him into a less forceful run than before. They cantered off towards the forest, cutting straight across the land, forgetting about the lay of the road. Ilva wanted to be deep into the forest before nighttime cloaked the land. They rode at a steady pace, and reached the edge of the Nilfin Forest just as the sun dipped into the sea.

It was a short ride on the horse. They trotted down into a slow walk after a few minutes. The horse, appreciating the lazy stroll after the journey they had made from Karna, let out soft grunt-like neighs of approval. Ilva smiled at the sensation under her. The horse's body seemed to thrum when it spoke. The power of the creature fascinated her. She loved these magnificent beasts.

As the horse walked lazily, the events of the last few days clouded Ilva's mind. She thought earlier today that she hated Vali, she even wished she had never met her when she was coming undone with grief. The shame of those kinds of thoughts flooded Ilva. Her face lengthened, and her eyes began to unfocus, her mind drifting into a deep dissociation. The horse neighed. The vibrations struck Ilva conscious. She secretly thanked the horse for keeping her from losing herself to the depression.

They were entering denser parts of the forest now. By tomorrow they would be near Ilva's old cave. She decided she should tell Vali again that she really was happy to have met her, and that her words earlier were from a place of pain. She wanted her to understand how much she valued their relationship. She struggled to find the words, and was about to try. But, before she could speak, something came into view ahead that set Ilva into an instant panic. The black serpent-like dragon lay across the foothills about a twenty-minute walk away. She thought this would be a perfect place to stop for the night. Now this seemed like the wrong place to be.

She wished she had an idea where to go, no matter which way she looked she felt trapped. The mountains were on the other side of the foothills, she couldn't turn back to the town, and Dola would soon wonder where her guards went and send more. They couldn't continue on the path because it ran right by the hills. The Lake was very dangerous as well. The sirens in the Lake tend to lure in elves who get too close, and Ilva had avoided that watery grave for so long. What should she do? Ilva wanted to ask Vali, yet she was terrified the dragon might hear her.

She decided to chance it. To confer with Vali and come up with a plan. She turned in the saddle, came close to Vali's ear and told her, "The dragon that chased us across the base of the mountains is here. It's close. I can't see a sure-fire exit."

Vali seemed to assess what Ilva said, and set her senses on alert. She smelled the air and listened hard. She then suggested the Lake. Ilva felt this would be a road to regrets, yet she gently nudged the reigns to the right, and they walked around dense foliage and quietly left the area near the hills. When they thought they were in the clear, the horse stumbled on a thorny vine and let out a series of high-pitched whinnies. The dragon's eyes shot open, Ilva could see her agitated yellow slits from where she stood, and they filled her with terror. In her terror Ilva screamed, "It's seen us!"

Vali shouted in reply, "Run!"

The horse knew the command before Ilva could crack a rein, and it bolted through the trees.

Faster and faster they ran, the horse's eyes wide with fright. Its heart thumped so hard Ilva could feel it against her calves. They hit the water's edge, and ran fast alongside the sandy shores of the lake. Ilva pushed the horse into the trees a bit further for more coverage, to avoid the sand which slowed them, and the haunting lake. It was too late. A dark stony looking siren sat on a rock in the lake close to the shoreline. She had jagged horrible looking movements, and an eerie dark grin plastered upon her face. The stone body moved slowly, and crackled at every motion, she played notes on a lute that almost blended in with her body. The notes sounded like they belonged to a song Ilva had yearned all her life to hear. Desperation to hear more corrupted her. The gloom hit her hard, and swept through her whole body. Soon she was halting the horse, leaping off its back, and walking towards the siren. Vali was following, just as mesmerised now. The dragon was closing in. The horse dashed off. Ilva was up to her ankles, and the siren dove under the water. Ilva and Vali plunged in after her.

They kicked and swam and followed the gentle plucking sounds, now echoing in the water. They were running out of air, but the music pulled them deeper. They started to feel dizzy, but they kept trying to swim. Their lungs desperate to breathe, gasped in water. They sputtered in the deep blue liquid lake. Then their worlds went black.

Chapter 41

Ilva woke to the sensation of water rushing up through her throat. It stung, and it tasted awful, and she was coughing painfully. Vali next to her was heaving, and looked about to throw up. She was rolled up into a kneeling position, facing down, with her head resting on her balled-up fists. Ilva, still choking hard, looked around them with bleary eyes. It was pitch black out, night had fallen now. Her eyes rested on the creature that must have been their saviour. It appeared to be a woman. As Ilva's eyes struggled to find their focus, she noted the woman was nude, and her long hair flowed over her figure, all the way down to her ankles. It was a mix of silver and gold. Her face was expressionless and her eyes swam with various cool colours.

She eyed the two soaking wet elves, still hiccupping on the water lodged in their lungs. She was transfixed on them, and it was an eerie stare Ilva thought. Ilva finally had enough air to let out an exhausted thank you. The silver haired female did not respond. Vali, without speaking stood shakily. She bowed deeply to the speechless nude woman. Ilva faced her on her knees and bent forward into a bow as well.

Then their saviour replied in a watery voice that sounded

like a babbling brook, "I, Naiade, nymph of waters, have saved you. You are destined to remedy this world. My kind are counting on you. The other nymphs are Meliae and Oreade, of the forests and mountains. There are so many other creatures besides yourselves, like the sirens who just attempted to drown you. Kelpies. Dragons. Griffins. Ix. We are all here, a part of this world. Do not misuse this land as your predecessors have."

The water nymph then walked silkily back to the water, her body inching back under as she strode deeper and deeper, and then vanished beneath the glassy surface. It looked as if she had never been there at all. No damp footprints, no ripples to show she had just submerged into that blue realm. Ilva did not realise there were so many creatures. The sirens that tried to drown them she expected. But kelpies? She had already seen two dragons. There were griffins out there too, and other nymphs. She suddenly felt the lake wasn't the only place they were in danger. Perils were all around them. She wondered to herself. *What are ix?* She had never heard of them before.

Vali and Ilva walked away from the shore and into the dark misty forest. Scanning all around for any sign of the black dragon, who appears to have left the scene, along with their horse. Ilva wondered how long they were submerged. They were closer to the cave Ilva once resided in. They could have ridden there faster. The horse, however, was gone. So, they began their long day of hiking as the sun was rising. Upon finding their way back to the forest trail, they spotted heavy boot prints in the mud leading up towards the Vozrek Mountains.

As they walked, Ilva reached out and grasped Vali's elbow, holding her closer as they walked. At first Vali was surprised by the motion, then it was comforting. Vali had been wrestling with tough thoughts of her own since their ordeal with Ilva's mother and Vali's grandmother. Vali reached up and cupped her hand over Ilva's. Walking like this she felt like one of the noble male elves, who strolled with young females around the gardens in hopes of a courtship. The thought made her chuckle, she enjoyed walking like this with Ilva. She was always a bit masculine in nature, and had never truly thought much about it until now. She knew her feelings for Ilva, and feelings about her own sexuality that were unexplored before this. It meant a lot to her, that she could be so much of herself around Ilva.

Ilva felt the same way. She caught a glimpse of Vali's smile, and could see she was content.

The next day, in the evening hours, Ilva's breath caught when she saw the tiny familiar cave ahead of them. The small mossy overhang under the hill. It was going to barely hold the two of them. The same cave she had slept in for decades. The sun was setting, and the dark had closed in on them quickly, they hadn't paid attention to the orange glow across the land moments before. It had been a long night, and a long day.

Ilva's muscles groaned until she sat down, and her body did not want her to get back up. She slouched a bit, legs crossed, hand resting on her cheek, her elbow propped upon her knee. She might fall asleep just like that she thought. Vali laid down her blanket from Llyr, and Ilva pulled out her blanket from home to drape over the both of them. Then they crawled into a tight cuddle, Vali kissed Ilva's cheek, and they were asleep in minutes. Vali rolled over with an arm above her head, snoring loudly, and Ilva turned over until she was squashed up against her again.

When the cave brightened with the sunrise of the next day, Vali awoke. Ilva still breathing deeply into her collarbone. It felt good. Vali felt each breath huff hot across her, she flushed heavily. Unconsciously she squeezed Ilva tighter to her with the arm that still rested beneath Ilva's head. Vali breathed her scent in deep, the smell of her hair, of her skin. She kissed her forehead. It took such strength not to continue kissing. *Ilva is safe.* Ilva groaned sweetly in response, and that was the extent of Vali's control. She kissed her temple, her cheek, her nose.

At this Ilva groaned slightly crankily, and fluttered her eyes open. Vali was close, and her arm was holding Ilva in place next to her, she looked up at Vali and said, "Good morning," in the softest voice. Vali pressed her lips into Ilva's.

Upon waking they noted that their clothes were filthy, after the battle in Falil and the sirens attack they were covered in blood and swampy muck. They walked a couple hours to a stream and washed their clothes in silence. Once everything was clean they hung the garments in a tree to dry while they bathed in the rivers frigid waters.

Ilva dressed herself, watching Vali intently as she did the same. Vali's body was darker in tone than Ilva's, and she noticed it most when Vali was bare. Next to her own pale complexion Vali was quite a contrast, there were a few scars on her, that Ilva hoped one day she would learn about, the rest of her skin was that even tanned tone. It was soft and smooth. Ilva felt an urge to run a hand over Vali's abs before she covered them.

As the rough tunic was being put back on, Ilva suited herself, and did not deny the urge to show affection. She ran her hand over Vali's stomach, who let out a small sigh. Ilva hugged her from behind, keeping her hand under the shirt, she kissed Vali's back through the fabric. She released her, they finished dressing and walked back to the tiny cave. Vali felt they should stay in the cave only one more night, then move towards the base of the mountains on the morrow. Ilva agreed. She would miss her little cave, though it no longer felt as homey as it once did. The entire world felt different now, tainted with loss and hardship.

As Vali went out to hunt, Ilva began collecting fire wood. She had a large armful of sticks and was heading back to the cave, when she heard a snap from somewhere behind her.

She turned, but it was too late.

Chapter 42

Ilva awoke that night in a much larger cave. One that was so large there was a river running through it, and many stalagmites and stalactites adorned the floors and ceilings of this place. Ilva had no idea where she was, who had brought her here, or why? Questions, and fear of the worst possible outcomes flooded Ilva's head. She was beginning to panic. Her heart rate rising, her eyes wide in the darkness. A light began bouncing on the wall from a path down where the stream ran out. Soon the glow became a torch, and holding the torch was; the elf with the dragon. The elder elf approached Ilva with a casual gait. As he glided up, he stared down his nose at her. A contemptuous glare.

The elf began to speak. "I bet your friend would do anything to get you back. I plan to fight her, one on one. I did not think she would take the duel seriously without a little bribing."

"Why?" Ilva asked with fear dripping out of the question.

Her captor roared, "Because that silver elf killed the last Western Dragon in the world! The last one! She has no concept of what she has done. Just like the rest of the silver elf scum. Those elves are nothing but greedy tyrants. I should know." He paused before shouting, "Europeas must be avenged!"

Ilva breathed as deep as she could, and tried not to think of what she stood to lose, she was focusing on this elf's feelings. She wanted to understand. She wanted to help. Empathy filled her. She felt personally responsible for the dragon. *It was my fault he died, not Vali's. Vali would have avoided the dragon. She didn't want to tangle with it. It was all my fault.* Her face burned with shame.

She decided to try and apologize. "I'm sorry for your loss. It was my fault Vali fought the dragon, I froze up in the pass, and Vali just tried to save me. You did not deserve to endure such a thing. If there is anything I or Vali could do to right this, I would want to try. Tell me there is another alternative than more of us suffering great losses."

The elf stared with his orange eyes, his hard expression unmoved. He was cold and calculating as he said, "If you say that is her name, I have only one question. Vali, is her grandmother Dola?"

Ilva stared at this friend of dragons dumbfounded. She stumbled over a short, "Y-yes."

This set the elf's jaw into a tight clamp, his lips thinning as he clenched his teeth together. Ilva took in more of his features now that they were in close range, chatting like this. He looked terrifying before when he was filled with rage. Now his face exposed deep lines and wrinkles, he looked tired, Ilva wondered at his age. He seemed to be calming down, and trying to rationalize things, then abruptly he began to cry. He had the most painful expression on his face that Ilva had ever seen. She wondered what about mentioning Vali's name had sent this elf into such a torrent of emotion. Ilva thought him more childlike now. Sobbing as hard as he was, after venting his frustrations over Europeas' death.

She understood his fury. She thought she understood his pain too. She wanted to know more about what roots these emotions surrounding Vali and Dola came from. How did this old elf know them? Why does he hate silver elves? "How do you know Lady Dola?" Ilva was wrong to call Dola a Lady in front of this particular elf.

The roaring continued, "That tyrant, is no Lady! She is only a housecarl to Lady Alix in Marka. She does her bidding, and Dola's subjects in Karna are the same to her. She is not nobility, and she is not even supposed to have a city. Marka was their territory. Karna was ours! Lady Dola indeed." He made a tisk sound before mumbling the rest of his feelings, "Everything was always transactional with her, then it got worse when other elves lives stopped mattering. She sent her own daughter and son in law out on the front line. I will never forgive her for what she took from me. If that girl's name is Vali, and she is really her granddaughter, I thought she was dead, all this time." The elf began sobbing again.

Ilva had to know who he was. She asked, "Who are you?"

The orange eyes stopped flowing like rivers, and looked on at Ilva as he let out a weak reply, "I am Odys. Vali's grandfather. Exiled during the war for treason when I tried to save her mother, Vela."

Ilva was stunned. *Her grandfather?*

He told Ilva more. "It was Vela that Dola killed. Our own daughter. She did not consider my voice important in any of the decisions she made during the war. She ridiculed me in front of others at council meetings, made me look a fool, broke all my confidence. I never thought she would end up so mad in the end. That she would kill our beautiful little daughter." His tone grew fiercer, "Who kills their own child? That horrible, inconsiderate, tyrannical, villainous…" he looked like he wanted to keep going, instead he took a deep breath.

He appeared to be reining in a deep-seated hatred, before going on. "Dola has contempt for any creature that is not an elf. I imagine she never told Vali about dragons being allied with elves. In fact, I would not put it past her to insist dragons are to be slain. I prayed for her to change, in the decades prior to our war with Mila, I waited for it a long time. But you cannot change elves. It took me way too many centuries to learn that lesson."

He sniffed, wiped his face, and dried his damp beard. "I should not have stood by and allowed her to hurt so many innocent elves. I should not have taken innocent lives in her name. I did try to rebel against her in the end. I collected a band of elves with similar ideals. We evacuated most of Mila, then I called upon the wraiths, we had made a deal with them you see. I let the Wraith Wan of the Wastelands into this world to prevent Dola from getting her hands on the sylvite artifact. She would have destroyed us all! Dola sent many elves to their deaths trying to retrieve it. I could not stop her from sending all of our family and friends there, and I had already done my own horrible deed. If she had only listened to me!" He began tearing up again.

"Vali was pronounced dead. Eighty years ago. She died when she went after her father, Rolk. My informant in Karna told me Vali had followed Rolk into battle, then the great magic storm happened in the wastelands, there's no way she could have survived it. My informant waited, at my request, for many months. Vali was gone. Shortly after, my informant was discovered and hung. I lost so much hope." he seemed to shift his focus, "Dola, she always played the victim. I had to watch her change behind closed doors. That I believe is what hurt the most. Watching her put on a false personality for the world, and only share this corrupt and dark side with me.

"When our daughter died, she cried in front of others, then was secretly giddy over all the empathy and generosity others showered upon her. No one knew it was her that murdered Vela. It was as if she was glad for the death of her own daughter, for it made others sympathise with her. She took it to her head. Spun and twisted it up as sympathy to her cause. I was a broken elf, I would gaze at nothing, my heart sank every time I saw that grin on her. She tortured innocent elves. She imprisoned and sold sylvite mages. I had no choice, I had to try and stop her, but I made a mistake. She never went to battle that day. All those lives sacrificed, when she was the one that was supposed to die."

Chapter 43

Ilva tried to absorb this elf's feelings and understand. She did in a way, though she did not think it was a reason for Dola to die. She had her own ideals, and sure, they were wrong from where Ilva stood, but she could not justify more death. She thought she had seen enough of it already with the death of her mother, and all those soldiers. There are so few elves left in the world.

No matter how horrible Dola was, or her own mother, or the manic elf in the village who drowned her baby. Did they really deserve to die? She was thinking about this, yet she was keenly aware of her own hurt feelings. It was hard to walk that middle line, but she didn't want to fall to any one side of it. She wanted to focus on what she felt was good, and right, she just had to decide what that was.

She had to find a nice way to word her next comments. "I understand why you want to kill elves like Dola. They are toxic individuals, and they create ripples in the peace of the world. Sometimes they spread hate, and of course we need to fight it. But if we simply kill too, we are them. If we hate in return, we are them. If we oppress, shame or ridicule in return, we deny ourselves peace. If you wish to be something other than your enemy, then be something else. I do not think the answer to all the death that has happened, is more death. It seems counterproductive." she gauged his thoughtful face before finishing, "I wish you did not have to endure so much pain, at the hands of one miserable elf. And I agree with you, she is horrible, she tried to sell me to my own parents and her housecarl slaughtered my mother. I cannot imagine how many other losses there have been. I have barely begun to process my own." she paused again, thinking of what to say next, "What would your daughter have done? Tell me more about her. I want to know what Vali's mother and father were like."

Ilva listened intently as Odys told her all about Vali's mother Vela. She was a stunning elf with raven hair just like Vali, and her eyes were two different colours. Odys loved that feature. One eye was orange, and one was a violet-blue. Ilva was entranced with the description. She was painting a picture in her head. Odys talked about her love of fighting, and how the sword he carried was hers. He seemed to drift back to the negative now and then, and it took great effort on Ilva's part to keep directing the conversation back to lighter tones, with happier memories, and positive thoughts. It felt good, it felt like she was somehow helping.

She was about to ask another question about the past, when she decided to start on the present stuff instead. "So, Vali, if she is your granddaughter, what do you plan to do now? I mean, am I still being held captive?"

At that Odys jumped up. He began cutting away Ilva's bindings. Looking a bit embarrassed about their situation. He spoke quiet and deep, "You are a great listener. I'm sorry we all got off to a bad start, grief caused me to lose much of my sense. Dola really has sewn a seed of corruption into this heart of mine. She taught me what it is to hate, as she once said she would."

When he had cut away all of the ropes it surprised Ilva that he reached out and gave her a hug. "I hope Vali will forgive me. I did not know I still had blood walking this earth. All is not lost, I guess. There is hope, and I almost destroyed it. If not for you I may have made yet another grave mistake. Thank you for telling me. We can all use a reminder, at times, that things are not always as they appear."

Ilva let what Odys said sink in, as she rubbed her wrists where the bindings had been. She could have used a reminder like that, more often than she had realised. She was just as notorious for her negative thoughts. Just as pessimistic and unforgiving at times. She thought back on how angry she was when she first left home. How those feelings had changed now. She felt differently about her mother, and she was confused about what to feel towards her father. Her mother had said not to trust him. Life had become, to Ilva, an outrageous puzzle that she was truly struggling to solve. Ilva had no idea what she was doing.

Odys was walking back towards the back of the cave when he stopped and turned, "Come on...er, Sorry, what is your name my dear? I fear, in my ignorance, I have not asked you."

She spoke softly, "My name is Ilva."

As Ilva and Odys walked down the narrowing tunnel of the cave, Ilva could smell something burning and feel steam on her face. Odys spoke quietly over his shoulder to her, "This is where the hot pools are. They are all throughout much of these mountains, and are very dangerous. The water can burn you, and the steam can even become unbearable after too long. Dragons seem to like it, we elves prefer the high levels within the mountain. Although the heat that rises through the entrance is lovely in the winter time."

When he mentioned Dragons liking the hot pools, Ilva was immediately darting eyes all over the caverns to see if she could catch a quick glimpse of any that may be lurking about. She did not see anything in the inky darkness, and steamy clouds. What she could see was still interesting, almost as much so as a dragon she thought. The entire place glittered and shone. Crystals and stones adorned the walls of the caves. The ceiling's stalactites were dripping water onto all the surfaces around them, little holes appeared to be bored into them. She was mesmerised by all these naturally formed wonders. It was a whole new kind of environment to her. The forest had a majesty all its own too, this was just unusual and new and its mystery drew her in, as the foothills of the Vozrek mountains once did.

Ilva noticed the tunnel they followed was now curving upwards and to the right. She followed Odys up and up. It was getting cooler, and the air wasn't as damp now. As they made their way Ilva noticed how close the stalactites that hung above her were getting. She was desperate to touch one. Odys stopped her, "Do not touch them. You risk bringing it down. It took a long time to grow, and they are more fragile than they look. Breaking one might result in many more falling." Ilva was nervous then, she wondered desperately what they felt like, but had no interest in being impaled by them.

They moved on. Ilva's gaze caught another thing to be

interested in. There was a grand room ahead of them, the tunnel opened into a huge open space with rock walls that climbed to a peaked point. In the center of the ceiling was an elaborate light made from many crystal gems and what looked like a tiny flame inside of them glowing. The gems made the light dance all around. Ilva entered the room, the tunnel entrance was small and narrow, and she had to wait for Odys to go through first. Once inside she looked around to notice all the elves in the room. Then how all of them were turning, staring in her direction.

Odys addressed the crowd, "Everyone! This is Ilva. She will be staying with us temporarily. Make her feel welcome please. She is a friend." He turned and smiled at Ilva then. Ilva felt awkward as all the eyes remained on her. She turned to the many faces and bowed forward. Murmurs rang off the round walls. Ilva pulled herself back up and Odys turned to talk just to her. "I'm going to go find Vali. You will be safe here in Evevale. I am grateful to you Ilva, you have brought with you something special."

Ilva shifted uneasily and replied, "You are welcome."

Odys clapped his hands together in a delighted way. A female elf ran over. "If you have any needs just ask Bryn here."

Bryn had a slender boney figure. Her muscles were strongly defined in her lanky thin frame. Her shoulders were by far the broadest part of her. Her nose was long and narrow, and her lips peaked tightly under her philtrum. Her outfit was a brown cotton tunic and darker pants. Both were torn badly, looking rough and ragged, yet comfortable. She was barefoot, and her golden hair went straight as a pin down her back. Ilva thought she was striking. Her best feature had to be her eyes, they were a soft pink colour, and her pupils rather large. The black almost drowned the pink completely out.

Odys read the intrigue on Ilva's mind and said, "Bryn is a good sort, I was lucky to find her."

Bryn spoke in the strongest sounding female voice Ilva had ever heard, "You are a good sort too, and I was the lucky one to be found."

Their mushy musing made Ilva grin inside. She thought of Vali, and how lucky she was that Vali had found her. She understood this sentiment, and felt all the more comfortable with Odys and Bryn's company now. The comfort was replaced with worry when Odys left to find Vali. She found herself wishing Odys luck, and knew he must be nervous to greet Vali after their last encounter. She also wondered if she was still being used as collateral, having been left behind.

Chapter 44

Vali dropped the horned rabbits she had in hand. Ilva was not at the camp, and the fire hadn't even been started. She walked into a ghostly clearing where all their abandoned belongings lay. She called out, "Ilva!" No reply came. She was filled with panic. *I shouldn't have left her alone.* She kicked at her soul, and the dirt.

She picked up all of the items left at the camp, and decided she would head towards the mountains. Vali was in a manic state, hoping desperately, with all of her heart, that Ilva was safe. In her frantic searching she felt the night air cold and damp, she was not resting tonight. The idea of Ilva being harmed flashed through Vali's mind, and it made her move faster. She would search for Ilva all through the darkness if she had to. Though, she had no idea where she was to go when she reached the mountain.

Stumbling over a rock at the base of the mountains, she gathered up all of her senses, moving from one rock to the next. She focused on her footing the way she always did, by feeling it and trusting her gut. Her instincts were one of her best tools without her eyes. If she felt someone was watching her, there usually was, and she felt someone now. There were eyes on her, she knew it, and she could feel the eerie shivers run over her. She slowed her steps upon noticing the sensation, and then stopped when it was apparent, she was not alone. She listened all around for the sound of movement, anything that would give the watcher away. She heard nothing. The mountains and hills around her were silent. She decided to move on up the mountain, hoping she was going the right way.

After a few hours of climbing, Vali sat upon a large flat boulder. She was exhausted. She thought she heard the sound of a rock, rolling its way down the mountainside. This sound set her defenses back on alert. The rock sounded like it was much further down than where she sat. She was unaware she had kicked the rock that now tumbled. She wondered if the eyes she still felt were following her. Her heart beating rapidly, her sweat glistened, her breath laboured. It was hard with all the noise in her body to pay attention to her surroundings. There was a sudden movement to her right. *What is that?* Vali's senses ran amuck, she did not recognise any sounds or smells. Was this a creature she had never encountered before?

She had never seen these ix or griffins that Naiade had mentioned. *Could this thing be one of those?* Vali wondered. Cautiously, she pulled her knife out of her boot, a spot she assumed would be useful while climbing the mountain, now realizing how useful it was in other ways. She was ready for whatever came. She crawled towards the place she felt the breeze, all of the hairs on her body felt the air around her.

She stalked around the jutting rocks, surefooted and quiet. As Vali turned towards where she thought the creature had moved, she felt an overwhelming and ominous feeling, and sensed the danger. She was wrong, she had smelt this smell before, she had just forgotten. The creature was close to her now, smelling of decay and rot. It stung her nose and she could taste that unpleasantness with each breath. It took all her will to not vomit all over the craggy rocks underfoot.

The creature stood before Vali, they had baited her. She was face to face with them, and they grabbed her around the neck with a forceful grip. The dark shadow lifted her off the ground, Vali began to choke and tear up. She thought this was the end, cursing herself for not being more alert, and for not fighting harder. She had used so much energy on the climb. Gagging on the stench, she waited for life to drain from her. Her eyes were...clearing. Her vision. It had returned.

Chapter 45

Vali looked around, stunned. She could see again. The mountains, the trees, the sky, the lake, and tiny little dots that indicated far away cities and towns. She could see everything. She turned and saw the hooded wraithlike being. They were garbed in a heavy black robe that covered up most of their body, their face looked as though it were nothing but bone. Their heavy breathing came wheezing out grotesquely over a few rotting teeth. Their hands were mostly bone, except for the tips which appeared to be smoking black points, extending the length of each digit to look like massive evaporating claws. Eyes were not visible on their face. Vali swallowed, and thought about how she should thank them, as well as if she should. She remembered them. This was the creature at Mila that had attacked her.

This was the shadow figure with the strange red bird, they had witnessed the magic that took her sight, and now they had returned it to her. *How? Why?* She wanted to know. She knew the first thing she had to do though, "Thank you."

The red bird joined them, landing on a rock near the shadow. They did not speak to her. The figure only stood there, swaying. She was grateful for her sight. She wanted to express it. "I have missed sight. You returning my eyes is something that cannot be repaid in mere spoken words of thanks. I am truly in your debt." The creature smiled then, and Vali had an odd feeling that she may have been wrong to express her feelings of gratitude.

"In our debt are you? Indeed. If you truly want your eyes back, you will do as we command. You owe us, for stealing the artifact in the first place. We were so close to reclaiming it, and you little elf, stood in our way! It was ours long before it was yours." The dark voice seemed malicious and cunning.

Vali knew now, that she was still in trouble. She wondered who the creature referred to as *we*. What she thought was a kind gift was quickly falling into a coercive game of bribery and blackmail. "You will return what is ours. The arcane artifacts. If you bring us the stolzite, sylvite, and silver, we will help to grant you the gift of your eyesight back. We will need all of the proper elements to do it permanently. This is just a fraction of power child." Snapping with their hard to make out fingers; Vali's world went black again. Only this time, she could not even make out shadows. This time, it was total pitch black.

She wept on the mountainside. The Wraith Wan laughed. It seemed a teasing laugh, one a sibling may let out when they've meant to make the other sibling cry. "We will wait in the Vexian kingdom for you and Ilva." *Ilva,* Vali wondered, *what does she have to do with this?*

The Wraith Wan continued in mellow but still menacing tones, "The magic in this place will harm more than your precious eyes if you intend to keep the artifacts. Eventually magic will claim your very lives. Do not be so piteous! You are more powerful than you know. Whether you believe it or not, we are trying to save your world, before destroying it is the only option left. Make your own mind up about what you do, but heed this warning. We will not let you all suffer as our kind did. We cannot save any of you. In the end, you must save yourselves."

Vali was shuddering. The shadow was beside her. "A parting gift. Until we meet again. Be wise, Vali, and be cunning." Then the shadow pressed two wispy fingers on her cheek. Sight filled her hopeful eyes again. Just in time to see the sun rising over the mountain. Burnt orange and saffron filled the sky. She was grateful again. Even if it would not last. She was grateful.

She soaked in the land touched by the newly risen sun, watching it bathe only parts of the mountain in light, juts with hidden shadows painted the rock in various colours. Indigo, scarlet, amber, ochre. She kept watching them change, remembering how many there were, as the vivid green of the trees began to brighten up the valley below. The shadow bowed forward, the large bird plucked him up, and Vali watched them fly away. She watched with her eyes wide, the world painted brightly before her. She stared unblinking until the darkness came again. Her eyes softly closed. This time she was not afraid of it. She knew it would come. Though she was glad to see the world once again bathed in light, she was not going to be afraid of the dark.

Chapter 46

Vali walked gingerly down the mountainside, driven by her new purpose, she was going to return to Karna, and steal the sylvite artifact back from her grandmother. Vali would have to depend on Ilva's ability to handle herself. She would save her, if she had any idea where she was. She realised though, that walking over and around on the mountains was getting her nowhere fast. She was frustrated, hungry, and sore. She had almost forgotten what independence had felt like. She had been by Ilva's side so often. The night Ilva had been abducted and brought to Falil, Vali thought about her non-stop. She was doing so now. She would occasionally assume she was the cause of Syli's death. Not knowing or believing that she had indeed saved Ilva then. *Ilva doesn't need my help. And, even if she did, I would need help to find her. I feel so useless. What can I do?* Vali tried not to become absorbed in grief and self-pity.

She would do whatever it took to get her eyesight, and Ilva, back. She wanted to be able to see Ilva the next time they met. Vali was certain she knew what Ilva looked like, touch revealed a lot. She desperately wanted to see her though. To truly see the face of this love that life had bestowed upon her. The apricot sunrise, the sparkling lake water, trees, dragons, the artifacts, the world. She wanted to see it all. If there was a chance she might again, she was taking it. She marched unsteadily down the mountain towards Karna. Towards her chance to be what she once was.

As she went down the mountain, she noticed how much she relied on at least seeing the shadows. It felt like night all the time now. She still had much to learn. Now having complete and utter black shields lidding her eyes, she was far more reliant on her other senses, even more than before. She misjudged a couple of small leaps, but was getting the hang of it, when suddenly she heard the roar of the black dragon. Before she could assess its position, she was scooped off the mountain and carried through the sky. She kicked and yelled furiously at the beast. The dragon ignored her and brought her down to the foothills.

When the great lizard dropped Vali, she rolled away, and nearly bumped into Odys. "Whoa! Vali, please. It's okay. Ilva is safe."

"Where is she?" Vali spat at him.

"She's in the mountain. I was wrong to chase after you. But what is done is done. Ilva told me you would not have slain Europeas if you had another choice, and I believe her. I believe that we are allies now." He waited only a few moments before speaking again. "Please Vali. Let us talk. I know anger is an easy thing to let overwhelm you. I do it all the time. I did it with you. Please trust me now though, for we are blood granddaughter."

Vali took the news as a great insult. She thought this elf

was messing with her head. *How gullible does he think I am?* Vali raged inside. "I do not know what game you are playing *gramps*, but if you harm Ilva, I will kill you!"

The dragon sensed Vali's contempt and reared towards her. Odys put up a hand and the black dragon, Uroborus, seemed to rethink her idea to fry Vali to a crisp. She slithered into a curly ball of scales, much like how a cat tucks its head into its tail, and the quiet rumbling breath was deep and restful. Vali was more at ease, yet she was still cautious, the dragon felt intimidating. She knew Uroborus posed a far greater threat than Europeas did.

Odys pleaded with her to believe him. He tried to explain quickly, "Your grandmother Dola is my ex-wife. If Dola has harmed you, she has harmed me too, and your mother. You are not alone. I did not want to hurt you. I was hurting a lot myself over the death of my friend Europeas."

Vali felt her heart weighing in with compassion. She thought *the elf can at least be heard out. There is never any harm in letting others talk. He might reveal something I can use.* Vali was feeling a tug at her conscious mind, recalling her drawl on the word gramps. She felt suddenly guilty, *what if it's true?* She thought of Ilva's granny out in the woods. Livy was alive, why shouldn't Vali hope to find other family in the world? She considered her new information carefully, Odys nervously gave her time to process seeing she was deep in thought.

"I am sorry for killing Europeas." She knew it would be a respectful gesture that she had remembered his scaly friend's name. "I hope you can forgive me, I understand how difficult anger can be too, and I shall do my best to believe in your good intentions. Share with me your story, I will listen. However, if I find it to be fictitious, I may be inclined to not call you gramps again." This remark she said with a smirk, and it received a small chuckle from Odys.

He continued to smile, "You have wit girl. Have a seat with me then. This is a long story, genuine and sad."

Chapter 47

Odys began, "When I was infiltrating Karna, I was a soldier who moved up the ranks to captain, it took many years to do so. When I was captain of the Karna force, our troops were unmatched! I never lost a soldier. Dola was very impressed with my achievements, and regularly applauded my strength and loyalty. I was a stand-up soldier, devoted to my work. Dola often invited me to conferences with the High Lady, and she was as much a dog to her as I was to Dola. It was because of High Lady Alix that Dola became so prejudice of other races. She mimicked much of Alix's ideals.

"She was violent and angry. I do not know what made her that way, but as long as I have known her, she has been cold and relentless. Her love is not the kind of love you go seeking out. It's a madness. I'm glad to have escaped it. I had no idea you were alive, and I have no clue what your circumstances are, I just pray you do not take after her. I can't imagine how it must have been, growing up in Karna, I'm so sorry. I thought for sure when I saw the storms that you were gone, along with all of the troops, and your father.

"I wish I would have known you had survived the battle. I could have reached out to you sooner. I was exiled shortly after you were born. I used to have elves in Karna who wrote to me. Dola killed many messengers. Friend, foe and family.

"She is a dangerous elf. One who kills and hurts without thinking. She does not value the lives of others, only her own. She hired an assassin to murder a well-off family, just so that she could present their only surviving son with our daughter Vela as his heir. The rejection must have crushed that elf, for your mother loved a stolzite from the mountains. An elf named Rolk from my own clan here. This was how my secret got out."

Vali was now very interested in the story, she propped her head on her hand and continued to listen with sympathetic and heightened interest now. *True or not, it is interesting. And my father certainly had plenty of secrets. I barely knew him, he was always under my grandmothers watchful eye.* She admitted to herself.

"Dola was outraged when a couple of my soldiers, who were out scouting, dropped the young lovers at our feet. They explained how they had found them, making love in the forest. Dola was disgusted. When he raised his head he recognised me, and I him. He was not going to give me away, and I was grateful. We took their weapons, I had Vela's sword, Rolk was brought to the dungeon, and Vela was locked in an upper chamber. They tortured him. He confessed that Dola was also in love with a stolzite. Me. I was terrified at the reveal of my secret, it was a last resort to save his own life. In her fury at the discovery of her husband, Dola murdered every soldier in that chamber. She left Rolk to suffer in that dungeon."

Vali felt her face heat with emotion, tears forming.

Odys wiped her tears gently as they fell, the motion frightened Vali at first, and then she allowed it.

He went on, "I've let tears fall too, as my wife turned in that dungeon towards me. She was venomous as she approached me, her eyes were blazing with hatred and contempt. She had just killed several of her best men to keep her secret about our daughter being a half-breed. She came at me with all she had. I defended the crushing blows, using Vela's sword, I barely escaped her fury. The wall was now manned with the men I led, all of them willing at the snap of her finger, to shoot me down. I fled from Karna, leaving Vela and Rolk with that sick twisted bat, and I watched from a distance, the disasters that befell the city. Your father was barely healed when Dola found a use for him. He led the battle against Mila. He was a good fighter. Dola used you to manipulate him into silence."

Vali's eyes still glistened.

Odys waited a moment before continuing. "I did nothing to save my daughter. She birthed you and Dola killed Vela to keep the secret safe. I found out long after these things had come to pass, it took time to hire an informant. Your mother, Vela, many say she was reborn to the lake, that she became a Siren. A Siren with a silver harp. I used to walk by the lake trying to find her. I was almost drowned one day, I swear it was her, she let me go. Then I met Meliae, the Nymph of the forest. That was interesting. They told me I was the one who would help people in need, and that I was one who needed to live."

Odys drifted off into a daydream, recalling the Nymph.

They had a tall frame, all angles, dark skin, thick curly brown hair that stopped at their jawline, and stunning green eyes peeked out from under the ringlets. He found himself entranced by their stunning queer visage.

He drifted back, "So, I tried to help the refugees that ended up living in Nilfin Forest. Eventually we became a little community, and we found Evevale." He twisted his beard. "I wonder, what is your relationship with Dola like?"

Vali did not consider her answer much before releasing it from her mouth, "I can not say I have any love for her. I thought she cared about me, then I learned she just wanted to train me to play fetch. I suppose me being blind was a benefit to her at times. That angers me. I never thought she would do some of the things she has done. To be quite honest, I am at a loss of what to say about my relationship with her gramps." This time she said gramps with compassion and belief. Though she still felt unsure, she desperately wanted to hope that Dola was not her only family. The idea was comforting.

Odys finished telling Vali their family history. "Dola sought the artifacts, all of which possess powers beyond her control. She wanted to eliminate the other races of elves, believing silvers were the only elves of any substance."

The sleepy dragon nearby snorted smoke.

"Marka was once the home of the stolzites. We were nearly wiped out entirely when Lady Alix and her predecessor waged war. They used our old city for the growth of the silver race. There is much untold elven history, and the suffering we endured.

"My stolzite soldiers and I took as many of the sylvite elves back with us as we could before the war. We flew them group by group on the back of Europeas. He was their saviour. It was good timing too, for Dola sent troops into the city the very day that we finished the evacuation. She had no idea the sylvite artifact was still in the temple, but she knew the Wraith Wan was there, and she sent all of the elves she did not trust into the wastelands to die. We didn't want her to get her hands on any of the artifacts, yet we could not take it for ourselves, the magic was bound to only the ones who could use it. The sylvite mages, and the few we saved refused to return for it.

"Dola began accusing other leaders of stealing artifacts after the war, and she frantically searched and re-searched the city of Mila." He watched as Vali shifted uncomfortably, "How did you survive? There was a blast unlike anything I have ever seen, and storms filled the skies for weeks. Not to mention the Wraith Wan." Odys was eager to hear Vali speak.

Vali cleared her throat, "Well, the blast actually came from me. I think. I took the Sylvite artifact that the Wraith Wan had and some sort of power blasted out of me when I grabbed it. It was excruciating. My throat was raw. After the battle I could not see anymore. I was lost in the desert for what felt like months."

She thought about the knowledge Odys shared, and thought it only fair to share what she knew too. Perhaps he would answer more of the questions she had. "I just saw the Wraith Wan. Today. They came to me on the mountain before Uroborus scooped me up. They made me an offer, to bring them the three artifacts, and promised to restore my sight should I succeed."

Odys was perplexed by this. *Why does the Wraith Wan want the artifacts? What use are they to a shadow of a God?* He thought to himself.

She went on, "Is it wrong of me to want my sight back? Is it wrong that I want to bring them their desire so I too can have mine?"

Odys could tell Vali was struggling with her options, and he did not want to choose the path for her, he knew all too well that choosing another elf's path only sets them up to later blame you when things go wrong. It was not his place to weigh in.

He waited for Vali to finish asking her rhetorical questions, and came to rest a comforting hand on her shoulder. "I am sorry you lost your sight Vali. You must decide what you do for yourself. I can, however, tell you that you have a loving elf up in the mountains who misses you. I think whatever you decide to do, you should tell her. Love has no secrets."

Vali let this weigh heavy on her. She knew she should not abandon Ilva. Even if she is safe. Odys was right. About how much he was right, Vali did not know. If he was truly divulging honest tales while they spoke, then Vali would have much to make up for with her grandfather, and much more about Dola to despise.

Chapter 48

Ilva was busying her hands with every task she could to help out around Evevale. She assisted Bryn with the washing of clothes and dishes, she peeled potatoes and helped make lunch for everyone, and she served the kids who all greeted her with food filled smiles and many hugs throughout the day. Ilva felt useful, and happy. She felt like she could do no wrong here. Everyone seemed to help out. Even the kids did their own washing. The level of personal responsibility in this tiny under mountain town was amazing. She did not sense any real authority figure, besides Odys, but what was he to everyone? She did not know, his wife however worked tirelessly for all of her friends. That is what every civilian here was to her, a friend.

She realised her father had never had that with his authority. He had less elves, and they all cowered from him. He was feared, not loved. There was so much love in this mountain-top oasis, and so much beauty under the canopy of rock, houses and shops lining every few paces with strait rows and walkways. Every shop owner greeted her with conversation rather than a sales pitch. Laughter could be heard echoing in every corner of the magnanimous space. She loved it.

As she walked through the tiny town, hidden from the rest of Zoriya, Ilva noticed all the warm earthy tones around her, there were spice coloured sheers draped back and forth across alleys like giant streamers. Light did occur in the deep cavernous refuge. It came from glowing stones above, small blazing bugs flying overhead, and lanterns adorning each doorway, they all reflected through the streets in various fiery colours. Copper and gold shone off of the walls of rock.

The homes in Evevale seemed to be carved out of the inside of the mountain, until she noticed the points where clay and rock met. Everything blended in to give the appearance of a termite colony on a mass scale. Spires of rock still met with the top of the mountain inside, the homes and streets were built around these obstacles. Brick coloured paths in perfect curving lines spiralled the innermost part of the city, connecting to smaller thinner paths in between each home.

This made navigation tricky, yet also gave multiple routes to wherever you needed to go. Ilva had an urge to see what the city would look like from above. Too bad there was nowhere scalable above her, for her to climb up and see the marvel.

Ilva was content. She told Bryn about her family, and what had happened with her mother. She told her most of the journeying with Vali, leaving out the details that occasionally reddened her cheeks. She continued from them meeting in the forest all the way through to the mountain they were in now. Bryn listened intently as Ilva loosed all the thoughts that threatened to break her from within. She felt lighter after talking about everything. It was hard, then it was easy.

Ilva opened up more, about how her mother was with her before, and the regret she felt after her loss. How she was confused about her father, and who or what he was to her. Everything came pouring out. She really felt she could talk to Bryn.

She was so used to elves with stern faces and firm expectations. This is why she was always grateful when Vali smiled for her, and now she was grateful again, when Bryn recognized her pain.

After a while Bryn spoke, "That's enough. No more tears. Feel the good, accept the bad, and focus on the facts. What is in and outside of your realm of control here? That is the only advice I can give. You are strong, and I know you will take from these words what you need to. I have faith in your ability to heal your pain, Ilva."

Ilva stared dumbfounded at Bryn. For a brief moment she was a bit thrown off by having genuine good advice so simply put. Then she thought about the many ways that Bryn had been respectful while listening. She may have been blunt, but she was comforting to talk to. She listened well, just like Vali. Ilva appreciated the consolation. She embraced Bryn.

Ilva thanked her, and Bryn told her that anytime she needed someone to talk to, she would always have ears for Ilva. They continued working until a couple figures started moving towards the entrance, it was Vali and Odys. They had returned.

Ilva was overjoyed to see Vali. She ran towards the front of the crowded cavern. She had to dodge a little elf toddling his way along next to his mom, she did not want to trip on the wee guy. *Gosh he is a cute little one!* Ilva gushed to herself. This was the first time she had ever felt fondness towards children, these elflings exuded such happiness and it was infectious.

She reached Vali panting and hugged her, "Vali! I am so glad." Vali blushed a bit, she knew she was surrounded by other elves, she could feel their breath and hear their feet on the stony floors, it was awkward having their affections displayed with an audience present. She was glad Ilva was safe though. They embraced a moment longer, then Ilva released her and greeted Odys.

Vali listened to the conversation between Odys and Ilva, noting the easy wit and comfort level. She heard Ilva mention that Bryn was a wonderful hostess. She mentioned that he must be proud of this beautiful place. Vali was curious, but did not ask. She followed the sounds of their voices through the city as they talked, and after much greeting, everyone began to disperse again. Returning, each of them, to the chore or task they were doing before the excitement of a new face disrupted them.

Vali was glad they were not overwhelming her. She was worried when so many elves approached. They were an excitable bunch, but they were good fun to listen too. She heard many comical, lighthearted, and good-natured conversations going on around her as she wandered through the cave community. It made her feel, relaxed. There were no awkward silences when she passed, no one yelling "Thief" through the market square, no one calling out their prices or products. Was this even a town?

These elves were outrageously good natured. Vali was surprised that her grandfather held such authority with them. *If he was indeed the leader of this underground establishment, then he should be praised,* Vali thought. This elf, who has known hardship, loss, suffering, and burden, for him to be the one giving to others, and to this degree. His followers all seemed so peaceful. Vali's eyes glistened. She smiled with silent contentment. *So far, your story lines up, gramps.* She was honoured to be related to someone who was so remarkable. Someone who fought for dragons and elves of every race. *But am I worthy of such an honour?*

When Vali fully realised the repercussions of all her mistakes her feelings attacked her, *I don't think I'm so great. I killed an ally dragon, stole an artifact for a tyrant, started a war for love. I cannot even protect myself in this war. Why am I even here? Ilva would be safer without me near right now. I have brought her nothing but misfortune. I know she told me that she did not mean what she said, but what if she did? Am I really the reason for her suffering? Is everything my fault?* Vali's conversation with her conscience was unknown to Ilva, who would have been sad to hear.

Vali kept slandering herself. Forgetting anything she had ever done with good intention. Painting herself the villain in everyone's life. She imagined the sounds of war echoing in the caverns. She imagined Falil being burned to the ground and the citizens being enslaved. She imagined Ilva in chains, crying and hungry. All the most negative of thoughts, the worst of possibilities, played out in her mind like some hor-rifying reality to come.

Eventually her thoughts told her, *Ilva is happy here. Why did I come? I was worried for nothing. I should just go. I can get the artifact back and end this war. I should do that. Since I am the one who started this whole thing.* She took all the responsibility that was not hers to shoulder, and wore it heavily, allowing it to crush her into feelings of solitude and secrecy. She felt a sharp sting in her memories *"Love has no secrets."* She shuddered, and then sharpened her ears to listen to what her gramps and Ilva were discussing now.

Chapter 49

Ilva was, in fact, talking about food. She was going on and on about the delicious stuff they had eaten in Karna; a hot meat and veggie pie with chicken, peas, potatoes and carrots. She was gushing amorously about this blueberry pie with meringue on top, and how fluffy it was, "Like biting into ginger beer foam! Only if it were a touch firmer and made of sugar!" she exclaimed in delighted tones.

Vali was enamoured with Ilva's adoration of food. It was cute. Vali loved the sound of Ilva's voice when she was happy. It was like music for her soul. Vali felt a sensation of eyes on her, then it was gone. Odys, Vali, Ilva, and Bryn walked up to a hut at the edge of the cavernous town, and Odys opened the door.

He was still beckoning them in when they walked through the threshold. Ilva was darting her vision excitedly over all the different pieces of art in the room, and the massive shelves of books. The leather spines went all the way up to the top rafters in the hut. A ladder was planted against one side of the shelves, a bit sloppily. It irked Odys, who went and rearranged it. Picking up a few heavy looking weapons that were in the middle of the floor, clearly belonging to Bryn, and put them outside the door on a rack. The kitchen was disastrous, and Odys looked appalled.

"Bryn!" he thundered, "This is absolute chaos! Gods and goddesses!" He whined as he picked up a bowl from the floor with tiny little flies sticking to it, and floating above it. He looked as if he may throw up in disgust.

Vali was smiling at the theatrical voices that escaped gramps as he whizzed around the room clearly overwhelmed and compelled to clean.

Bryn seemed unbothered by all the excitement gramps was having over the state of their home. She went and pulled chairs up to a small table in the dining area, which was really just a square table against the wall right next to the kitchen. It was a small hut, and it seemed like the bookshelves took up most of it. A large blackish brown pelt lay upon the floor in front of the centermost part of the shelves. A tiny table sat with three short legs on the pelt, and a small stack of tomes atop it. There was a window across from the door they had come in through, and a tiny cupboard was under it, with intricate wooden designs.

The door had matching designs, and the kitchen was no contrast either. It was even more notably ornate being that there were so many of the tiny cupboards. Odys reasoned with Ilva that many small cupboards made more sense, with the two of them they only had two of each thing, so dishes needed little space. Also, the variety of kitchen items they had was vast, and none of the items would fit comfortably next to each other in large cupboards. Ilva only began to see the logic in this when Odys went clean crazy for the next couple hours, he straightened and dusted everywhere around the bookshelves and entry point. There was mud to be cleaned, and clothes to be picked up.

Bryn appeared to be a rather untidy elf, Ilva wondered why either of them needed so much stuff, she thought the question rude the moment she considered it. *Who am I to judge?* a voice in her mind sassed her.

Bryn had a barrel resting in the corner of the room, on the other side of the table from the kitchen. She walked over to it with a dirty cup and filled it with the contents that escaped a tiny spout. She snapped a flap back down over the spout, and pulled her drink to her lips. She took a big swig, and then walked back to the table. "Want some wine? We can share this cup while Odys cleans."

Ilva was good on the cup, she saw the horrors around the room. Vali did not and seemed to care little about the smell coming from the kitchen behind them. She took a gulp from the cup, and seemed happy for the gesture to share the wine with Bryn. Ilva tried not to be too grossed out over the cup, it was just a dirty cup. Odys, however, was thoroughly grossed out, and took it as a cue to begin cleaning dishes. He pumped what looked to be steaming hot water into a basin on the counter. Ilva was curious and came to assist him while Bryn and Vali drank their wine.

Vali was now fully aware that Odys and Bryn lived together. She wondered what her grandfather was to Bryn. *Maybe they are a couple? It does sound that way.* It was an enchanting thought, a break from her negative spiraling, Vali was pleased that Odys had others in his life, her guilt still nagging quietly at her about the death of Europeas. She went back to the dreary spiral.

Why, why did I kill him? Why did I not try to get Ilva to run away instead? Why did I slay him? She was racked with pain over it now that the picture in her mind was bigger. The wine seemed to be having the wrong effect on her. Her problems were being magnified. She was panicking, and she was overwhelmed.

Bryn seemed to sense this, and put a hand on Vali's. This pulled Vali back into the room, dragging her out of the mountain pass memories. She was smelling the wine again, and feeling the warmth from Bryn's hand on hers was bracing her somehow. It rooted her.

Bryn spoke to Vali, "Do not drink if you're hurting inside. It will make you hurt outside too, and then you will have something else to overthink about in the morning."

Gramps has a good friend, she thought before quiet words tumbled over her trembling lips. "I feel guilty about killing Europeas, and like I'm always making wrong choices," Vali confided quietly.

Bryn took that in. When it was clear Vali was still self sabotaging, she told her, "Everyone makes the wrong choices, and often more than once. That's life. Make a plan, and the gods and goddesses laugh." Bryn chuckled. Vali did not.

Bryn sighed. "Every choice you make affects something. Your choices can shape the world, the lay of the land, the air we breathe, the water we drink. Everything in this world has the power to be affected. Everything in this world also has the power to affect. We are all capable of making ripples, and sometimes we make waves. Wrong or not, choices will be made, and you will have to keep making them."

Vali considered all that Bryn had just given her to think on. She thought it was the most impactful thing she had ever heard in her life.

Chapter 50

When Ilva came up behind Odys he was so focused on his task he nearly turned and bumped right into her on his way to grab a dish rag and towel. She jumped back a step, and his eyes went wide at the almost collision.

"I was just wondering, well, would you like a hand?" Ilva chimed.

Odys beamed at the offer for help. "Absolutely! If you do not mind that is? I would really appreciate it. Do you want to wash or dry?"

Ilva thought on it, "Wash I guess?"

Odys was even more surprised, "Sure! The water gets pretty hot, so if it gets too steamy, we can wait a bit or add some of the water in the jug on the floor over there." He pointed at the end of the cupboards to a large glass jar that went up to Ilva's thighs.

Ilva walked up to the sink and put her hands into the basin. It was so soothing, having her hands in the warm water, her bones didn't seem to ache as badly, and her muscles felt looser. Soaking her sore hands and tired arms was immeasurably pleasant.

Odys saw and offered, "We do have a tub shed out back if you and Vali want to rest yourselves in the bath after?"

Ilva was positively glowing at the idea, "Oh that would be amazing! I do love a good bath."

"Wonderful!" Odys grinned.

Ilva was now in an inquisitive mood, "Where does the water come from? Why is it so boiling hot?"

Odys was impressed with Ilva's curiosity. He loved a wondering mind. "It comes from under the mountain. There are hot rivers and springs all underneath us here. We have found ways to take advantage, and provide the town with running hot water, when we release the water it goes into a different stream which leads to the sea. It is pretty creative, one of the sylvite elves here came up with the idea!"

Ilva registered what he said with thrill. "There are sylvite elves here?"

Odys laughed, "Of course! We try our best to all be equal here. Even my wife, Bryn, is a sylvite."

How many coincidences could there be in the world? Apparently, a lot. Ilva looked over to see Vali and Bryn having their heart to heart. Bryn's hand supported Vali's as she spoke. Ilva was glad to see Vali talking with her.

Bryn watched Vali, gauging how to react, and had given her the cut and dry approach to her worries. Which was nice and easy, for that was also how she got through to Odys most times. Especially on days when his compulsory need to clean overwhelmed him. Rationalising, and pointing out the things that were sometimes forgotten in moments of stubbornness or pain, this was Bryn's specialty.

Vali was suffering before Bryn simplified the concept of choice. The realisation that the world was bigger than her, yet still needed her, that she wasn't alone in her mistake making, was the most comforting thing in the world. All she could do was her best.

Vali understood well now that all of her actions would impact something, and she had to pick her battles carefully. She knew that someone would always get hurt, no matter which side of a fight you picked. That was becoming clearer. Choosing, often means to deny one course, which may have its own set of consequences. Sometimes she would lack the knowledge. Sometimes she would lack the skill. Life will not make way for those things. It will not give you another chance. Most of the time, when life demands you act, you get one opportunity to pick the action you go with. Then the conditions or situations change. All creatures are bound to make errors in judgement. Vali was no different.

Vali took a long moment to accept herself. To believe that she might be allowed forgiveness. Then the bars of guilt slammed her back into her fear.

Bryn knew what happened, she felt Vali tense again. She knew it wasn't going to be a lasting sensation, yet it was still important to have Vali feel it. It takes practice to believe in yourself. Vali would get there, she was smart, and had already felt the forgiveness settling into her heart. Bryn thought she was an incredible individual. She saw so much of Odys in her.

Odys and Ilva were finishing up the last few dishes, Ilva watched him placing each item in its own little spot in the cupboard. It was organized down to the last angle, everything the same distance apart, it was as if all the everyday items had suddenly come together to create a home that looked like art. Ilva was so impressed with Odys and all his fine attention to detail. The place was immaculate. It was only more impressive after seeing all the stuff that had been strewn everywhere beforehand. With it all tucked away now, the place looked cozy and inviting.

Odys mentioned the bath now again in front of Vali and Bryn. Vali seemed equally grateful to the offer, and followed Odys and Ilva out back to a tiny bathhouse.

When they walked in there was an immense amount of steam in the room. It was damp and warm and sweat began beading upon each of their brows. Odys explained how to start and stop the water pump. It involved a series of laborious looking actions, but was much easier in practice to do. Ilva ran the water and Vali gathered any of their belongings that weren't their clothes to give to gramps. He took them and said they could soak out here for as long as they liked. Before leaving he pointed at a couple of tasselled ropes on the wall. "If you want to change the scenery just pull the ropes." And with a small wrinkly wink he headed back inside.

Ilva was instantly curious and went to pull one. The first one made the ceiling change. She was amused at the moving of the panels. They appeared to be made of metal and shifted when the rope was pulled until they flipped into a new position. Each surface had a new pattern or picture. The metal pieces were revolving triclinic and prismatic plates, making the possibilities many. Ilva kept changing the ceiling until it was a vision of a starry night. The sky was blackish blue and stars dotted every inch. There were clusters of them, and then voids too. Perfectly detailed and a delight to Ilva's eyes.

She wished Vali could enjoy it with her. She felt suddenly guilty at her own enjoyment of such things.

She felt guilt nag at her again when she looked over and Vali was already undressed. She was stepping gingerly up to the tubs edge. The tub was large and appeared to be made of a sort of rocky material. It was smooth and polished, and round in shape. Vali stepped from the edge down into the basin, her body slowly dipping into the steamy bath. She looked breathtaking. Ilva was suddenly nervous. She began undressing too, and fumbled a bit. She didn't see Vali smile, sensing Ilva's struggle, realising she was beguiling her. The knowledge pumped her ego. Ilva finally struggled out of her shirt when Vali spun around in the bath to face her, and grabbed at her pants. "Need a hand, my love?"

Ilva blushed heavily. "Uh," she managed.

Vali gently pulled off the last of her garments and Ilva stepped up to the bath.

She plunged in next to Vali.

Vali cut through the water towards her and wrapped her up in her arms.

Ilva breathed deep, and let the hug soothe her.

Vali's face brushed Ilva's hair.

Ilva felt less concerned of being found out than she had before.

Vali treasured this moment after the week they'd had, she wanted Ilva to know, "I was really worried about you. I want to hold you close right now. You keep scaring me. I just want to enjoy these moments while I can. Before the next time we are apart."

Ilva felt the same way. She embraced Vali, their shoulders

met, and their bodies felt like magnets. Ilva's cheek pressed against Vali's as she squeezed her tighter. When they let go, Vali turned Ilva, took a brush from beside the tub, and began washing her back for her.

"You know," Ilva began, "we do seem to get separated a lot. I feel so useless whenever I'm not with you. Like I have no purpose, or like I can't make a move. I never used to feel like that when I was alone. Why am I so lost without you next to me?"

Vali's hand stilled a moment, then continued as she spoke, "I don't know. I feel it too sometimes. As if I simply need you near me."

Ilva spoke quickly, "I think we need to work on that. I don't want to be weaker when you're not near me. Gramps and Bryn are strong and independent, even when alone, they love each other deeply."

Vali fully stopped now and asked, "Are they actually a thing?"

Ilva said, "Yeah, Bryn told me a lot about them."

Vali suspected as much. "I'm happy gramps found somebody to fill the void Dola left in him. I guess I'm grateful to Bryn two times then. She is most kind."

Ilva nodded in agreement.

Chapter 51

When they had sufficiently soaked, they dripped out of the tub onto the solid floor of the steamy room, and dried off with a couple of towels that rested on a nearby shelf. Wrapping their hair, they stepped back into their pants and awkwardly shimmied into their shirts with the towels still on their heads. Emerging from the bath was an odd sensation. To step outside without actually being there. No breeze blew them, no chill destroyed their relaxed state. They walked comfortably back to the small hut where Odys and Bryn sat inside.

Before they went back in Ilva stated, "I'm going to train with Bryn. She said she can help make me strong. There is a stone elf here who might train me. She wants me to come with her to meet him tomorrow. I think we should do more things apart, so that next time we can both fight our own way out of whatever we face. I would still fight by your side, but I want to be able to fight on my own too, should I need to."

Vali nodded in agreement to this. "I think that's a great plan," she hesitated, "I want to collect all the artifacts."

As the words registered with Ilva, she asked, "What for?"

Vali didn't want to share the reason why with Ilva yet, it

was too personal, and as close as they had become, she wasn't ready to share every insecurity. "I don't think I'm ready to tell you, but I need to collect them and bring them to the Wraith Wan."

"What?" Ilva let the shock in her voice show.

"Trust me Ilva. I know what I'm doing. I have a plan, and I might need to do some of what I'm planning alone. Just say you trust me," Vali pleaded.

"I trust you," Ilva said, not missing a beat.

Ilva was so content to hear Vali's acceptance of her goals and aspirations, and to offer her acceptance in return for Vali's. She felt supported and loved in ways she did not know she could. Vali felt the same. Though Ilva still wondered about the things she did not know.

Vali thought to herself, *I am glad Ilva has her own plan. I think she will understand when I go. I want to tell her everything, she told me what she wants, why can I not tell her what I truly want? Why can I not just tell her what is on my mind? Why is it so hard to be as open and honest as she appears to be?*

They opened the door to Odys and Bryn's home.

Greeting them was a feast of delicate meats, asparagus, mushrooms and sweet potato, there was a thick red soup that smelled spicy, a pitcher of wine, and several types of breads, fruit and cheese stacked on wooden platters.

Ilva eyed the delicious looking spread.

Vali breathed in the savoury scents.

They both approached the counters and began filling plates at Bryn's urging. She was clearly waiting for them so that she could dig in herself. With full plates they all sat at the table, which was now pulled away from the wall to seat the four of them, and tucked into the food at the same time.

Ilva let out a groan of satisfaction from the moment she took the first bite. She hummed away merrily, and unconsciously, as she ate.

Vali smiled at the sound. *Ilva and food.*

~

Vali woke the next day to find Ilva and Bryn already gone. She rolled up from the floor. They had slept on the rug in front of the bookshelves last night.

Odys was in the kitchen area cooking eggs over the tiny fire stove. Odys explained that Bryn liked to train very early in the day.

Vali rubbed her face with her hands, as if attempting to rid the exhaustion from her expression. She sat at the still pulled out table, which had been cleared of wine cups and several spills that really only troubled gramps. Everything smelled freshly washed this morning.

Last night, before they went to bed, Vali and Bryn had played a few drinking games with the wine. It was as though they were also having a competition to see who could keep their composure best. The winner, and elf with the most tolerance for wine, turned out to be Bryn. Vali was shocked at Bryn's resilience. *The elf must do nothing but drink.* Vali thought. She smelled the eggs, and knew they were almost finished from the scent, and the sound of popping and sizzling. The scent made her both nauseous and hungry. A plate glided across the table, stopping right in front of her.

Vali admired gramps for his skill in the kitchen. She wondered how different her life would have been, had she known there was more family out here for her. Would she have been better off? She now thought she knew what Ilva felt upon discovering Livy out in the woods. The world is so much more connected than they had ever known. The discovery of this made Vali expand her idea of what she thought she knew. Every time she felt certain, she now questioned whether she was. It wasn't a bad feeling; it wasn't comfortable either. She accepted it for what it was.

Chapter 52

Ilva took a jab strait to her chin, and nearly somersaulted backwards. The pain rang across her even rows of teeth. The connection point stung, and she rubbed at her face tenderly. Getting back to her feet, she glared at Bryn. Determination set into her soul. She would lay a hit. She could do it. That's all Bryn had asked her to do. Hit her one single time. It can't be this hard.

Ilva was getting frustrated. That was her fourth attempt, and Bryn was getting rougher. Her defences seemed solid enough to keep a dozen elves at bay. Ilva wanted that strength. She wanted to be that tough. She felt a touch of envy creeping its way into her heart, as she raced towards her sparring partner again.

This time she tried to distract Bryn, she kicked a rock at her, then dodged to the other side that the rock was flying. Bryn caught the rock swiftly in hand, then brought it down on Ilva's leg, just as she was about to kick Bryn across the ribs. The smack of the rock hitting her thigh sent an ache through her entire leg, and her limb swung away from Bryn with almost the same force Ilva used to swing it towards her.

She surprised herself that she didn't stumble back. She held her ground, face to face with Bryn, who let the rock roll out of her hand and bounce across the stone floor. Ilva swung her fist, and Bryn grabbed it like she had the rock and began to squeeze. Ilva thought her fingers were breaking all at once. She squirmed under Bryn's grip, and jabbed her other fist towards her temple. She missed by an inch.

She thought she had improved, until she noticed that the near miss was Bryn's intention. She wasn't loosening her grip on her dominant hand either. She held firm to Ilva's closed right fist. Desperate Ilva tried to trip Bryn with her leg, and punch at her head. *Missed.*

Bryn grabbed Ilva's dominant forearm with her free hand and used her might to whip Ilva's entire body over her shoulder.

Ilva slammed into the stone floor, upon her previously bludgeoned shoulder she came down hard. The wind released from her in a small silent yell. Her whole body took time to register the shock. She trembled when it started to creep into her bones. Pain flared from elbow to ear. It throbbed and heat rushed the injured area. It was worse than when the boulder had struck her in the mountain. She got up slowly, after a few moments, remembering how to breathe.

Bryn could tell she was at her limit, even if Ilva could not. "Enough," she ordered.

Ilva was so worked up about not laying her blow to Bryn that she could focus on nothing but the nagging in her mind. It told her that it was nowhere near enough. It told her she could still succeed. She rushed Bryn. Her movements were slow, and weak. Her body sore and tired. She couldn't get any momentum, or power, but she landed a blow.

Bryn had let her.

When her fist landed dead center of Bryn's stomach, Ilva thought for sure she had finally managed to inflict some pain in return. It connected with hardness. The old skinny bat had abs of steel. Ilva's shock was instant, and Bryn broke into a big smile. Ilva's punch had not even made her move. Not a sound escaped from Bryn. She just beamed at Ilva, her pink eyes twinkling. Ilva fell to her knees, and then slumped sideways into a sitting position. She looked up at Bryn. "Help me become strong." She had never wanted anything more.

~

Ilva rubbed a cold cloth across her swollen cheek. Her gums felt like they had melted into her cheek from the relief. The place where the rock had connected to her thigh was purpling, becoming puffy and a bit hard. Her injuries were claiming much of her focus, so she did not see the male elf approaching them.

"Well hullo there!" he shouted out. "How are ya today Bryn. Who is this lass? She seems strong."

Bryn turned to the approaching elder, "Witl! Just the elf I wanted to see. This is a new pupil for you. Her name is Ilva."

Witl looked at Ilva. His eyes were evaluating, as he scanned every one of her injuries. He smiled at her.

His eyes were wrinkled, and baggy. His face reminded her of a tortoise with a massive grey beard. His facial hair grew in coarse waves, all the way down his tunic to his belt, and his mustache seemed to have grown into the rest of it. His eyebrows matched. His hair was knotted into a tiny grey bun. He was shorter than Bryn, coming up only to her shoulders. His eyes were a faded blue. They looked weathered with all the wrinkles. "Hmm, what do you know about your powers?" Witl asked sharply.

Ilva was confused, "My powers have never manifested. I have none."

Witl stole a disapproving glance at Bryn, then looked back at Ilva. "What do you mean you have none? Everyone has power! You are no exception to that. Get your sorry butt off that rock and show me what you do have."

Ilva was slightly triggered by his gruff nature, it brought out a rebellious fire in her soul, one she had forgotten about.

Chapter 53

Vali helped Odys with the washing when they finished breakfast. The house still smelled like food for hours after. They were nursing nearly cold teas now, chatting about the past. Vali learned more about her family, and felt a connection with Odys that she had never had with any other relation. She found it funny that both she and Ilva had more in common with the outcasts in their lives, than the elves who raised them.

Vali had many questions, and Odys was not annoyed about that at all. He frequently referenced books he had read, and knowledge he had attained. Vali was most interested. He began talking about the elements, and Vali's interest skyrocketed.

Odys knew about magic, and Vali needed to know more.

"I want to know about the mineral elements. Specifically, the arcane artifacts. Why does each magic need a specific race to wield it? Where does it come from?" Vali was filled with such longing for answers to these things.

Odys took a deep breath, and sighed it out. "Vali. Those are very important questions. I do not pretend to know all the answers and those particular queries, I am afraid, I cannot answer. What I can tell you is that magic is always mysterious and it needs more than a specific wielder to work. Artifacts that are not our own need sacrifices equal to the effect of their use. Only a few elves in our histories have tried this, and apparently you are one of them. In your case, your eyesight was the restitution for whatever spell you cast. It is actually quite miraculous that, that is all it took. You were lucky, that magic did not take your soul.

"As to where the magic comes from, none of us knows. There is no record and there is no history spoken of it. It has been around for centuries longer than any of us. The only one who might know, would be the Wraith Wan. The oldest living being in these lands. These secrets are dangerous, and if you are serious about uncovering them, be prepared for the worst."

Vali appreciated that Odys wanted to give her advice. She rarely listened to the council anyone gave her, the things Odys said seemed reasonable to her though. She accepted the kernels of truth and wisdom. Tossing her dark hair over a shoulder, she finished her tea, then walked to the sink, and deposited her mug beside it.

Odys watched her, and prepared to share a secret with her, "I wish to tell you how stolzite magic works. You must swear to never share this information though. You must also promise to keep our hideaway a secret. It's not the time to share that knowledge yet. Help me keep these elves safe."

Vali turned and leaned her backside against the sink as she spoke. "I have no idea what the stolzite powers are, I would love to learn. Your secrets have been very well kept from the world. You have my sincere oath. I will not breathe a word of this knowledge to any soul. I will respect your decisions in this, as the leader of this incredible refuge." She sighed, and added, "I am really glad I did not fight you that day. I would have won and it would have been a great loss, not only to me but to this whole community."

Odys burst out laughing. His stomach moving as he did. It was a hard laugh.

Vali smiled.

"You would have won eh? I will spar with you one time soon. I think you underestimate me. I just have a few questions before I tell you our magic. Question one. Will you do everything within your power to do right and good, and not allow shadows to tempt you, in your coming battles?"

Vali nodded.

"Good. Question two. Do you think the Wraith Wan can be trusted, and do you truly plan to bring them the artifacts?"

Vali answered, "I don't know. I feel untrusting with almost everyone. Who can you trust? And yes, I do plan to bring him all the artifacts. I plan to restore that which magic has taken from me, and I plan to right any wrongs that it takes to get what I want as well."

Odys stood and walked toward Vali. Reached out a hand, he gripped Vali's. He told her, "It's okay to trust those you love. Family, friend, lover. You can tell others your secrets. When you are ready. I'm trusting you with mine because of love and faith, Vali. I am one proud old elf to have you carrying on my bloodline."

Vali choked down fresh sobs. She cried a few tears, then managed to stop.

Odys hugged her, tightly, to stop her shuddering.

She cried more than few tears.

When she felt relieved after a few minutes, she straightened again and rubbed her face dry.

"Final question," Odys said. "Do you love Ilva? I mean really love her?"

Vali nodded fiercely. "With all of my heart, gramps."

A few moments later, you would never know she had cried. Odys was shocked by the quick change. After the various hysterics he had been around, and even Bryn's occasional tantrums, he had never seen someone wrap up their emotions quite like that. He wondered if she was really okay, or if she just had a master poker face. He offered to tell her more secrets and stories.

She nodded, and went to sit on the fur rug in front of the bookshelves.

Chapter 54

Ilva was sweating and swinging her fists wildly at Witl. Her movements had renewed a bit, but were slowing far faster than they had before. She hadn't eaten yet today and she was exhausted from a lack of sleep. It felt like she had been here all day, when in reality only a couple hours had passed. She was so frustrated that the fury was the only thing driving her punches. It left her open to attack, weakened her perception, and made her easy to take down. She was jabbed in the ribs, the chest, the legs. Her purple bruise had now blackened. She fell, and after a few sharp breaths through her teeth, she got up. Running back despite the pain. She aimed a punch at Witl's nose, he side stepped her. Ilva seethed.

He was just as efficient at avoiding her as Bryn had been, maybe even better. *He's so old! How can he be so impossibly swift?* She was furious. She jabbed again and again and again. Not a single hit landed.

He was steady, bending and swirling around her. Like trying to pick a tiny piece of eggshell, out of a broken egg.

Slippery old bugger! She tried something new. She lunged

in low, and shoved both of her fist's strait up towards the old elf's ribs.

This took Witl by surprise, he moved back a fraction, and pushed his own two hands out at the same time, clasping each fist. He pulled her up, and said, "You need training lass. I can tell you have fire. Are you willing to train both your body and your mind Ilva?"

She nodded despite her angrily gritted teeth. Again, to both elves this time, she said, "Help me become strong."

~

The hours passed. Ilva pounded a rock with her fist. Strait down. Her adrenaline was still pulsing through her, it was fading however, and she could feel her muscles weakening again. She had to pump herself back up. If only she could find the energy to do that. She steadied herself against the massive boulder she was sitting on. Bracing an arm on either side, she jumped down, breath escaping her lungs quickly, muscles throbbed, her body was shaking.

She thought the impact from the jump would cause her to collapse, landing in a squat, staying like that for a fraction longer than she normally would. Slowly she curled up, getting a slight head rush as she did. Her mouth was dry, and her lips cracked a bit. She seemed to hear an odd ringing sound. She focused on the old elf, who now walked slowly up to her, as if approaching a wild animal. *You are going down Witl!* Ilva cheered to herself.

She was set, determined. She would get strong, and as

fast as possible. No one would stop her. *Aside from maybe exhaustion*, she thought as she stumbled into a fists up fighting stance. Witl was close now, maybe four feet, she bounded out of the way of his kick, and sent him one of hers back.

"You are still too angry. Find another thing to fuel the passion for the fight. Pick something else!" Witl seethed.

Ilva was startled at the reflection, and missed a kick that landed on her arm. She rubbed the place below her elbow, then grabbed the next kick that came. She pushed Witl back and he bounced back into a relaxed pose.

Witl let loose another critique of her movements, "How can you ever expect to have control over a situation when you have no control over yourself? Come on lass, get a grip!"

Ilva snapped inside. *Get a grip? Does he really expect me to calm down while he is dishing up insults? Is this guy going to teach me anything? Why does everyone always want to tell me what I am doing wrong?* Ilva swallowed hard, feeling the lump in her dry throat, her body gave out on her then.

She fell sitting on her calves.

Witl approached her, and grabbed a bucket of water with a ladle, from a nearby rock.

Ilva graciously accepted the water break, and gripped the ladle with both hands as she drank. She was now spinning webs of thoughts, and did not even notice her own change in mood happening. Curious Ilva, was replacing angry Ilva, and she made the switch unconsciously.

Witl saw it though. He realised he had his work cut out for him then.

This guy does fight well, and he seems in control. How does he do it? Ilva's mind buzzed with thoughts and ideas, everything except the focus it needed.

Chapter 55

Vali prepared herself for gramps to talk more, crossing her legs comfortably on the rug.

He shared, "I believe stolzite elves have been around about as long as the silver and sylvite elves. Silver elves, as you know, use silver to craft weapons to master their powers with. There are also rare silver sirens, like your mother is whispered to be, you may also be one. It is not impossible anyways.

"Sylvite elves use their mineral to craft aesthetic accessories, their powers are usually derived from some sort of dance and a rare few can harness power from the sun. Movement is the key to them unlocking the sylvite, the mineral loves light, and when exposed in a sequential rhythm they can build up incredible power! No matter the strength a sylvite can muster, silver is far stronger. There has only been one instance of a sylvite elf defeating a silver elf, and she had built up power for days before releasing it, she won a fight against Dola. Sadly, she was captured after that, and she was sold to the stone lord. He paid an outrageous amount of gold.

"Stolzites are writers and illustrators. When we write, or draw, we are bringing into reality our own imaginings. For example, when I wrote in my little notebook back at the mountain pass, I imbued myself with stamina, I am normally quite weak to be honest with you. When I write, I write myself into being something more. I craft my reality.

"We could have extreme power in this ability, however, it does have limits. We can only write or draw a set amount each day. The amount depends on the quality of ink. Some ink is thicker and therefore fades faster, while thinner ink can be spread out for a longer duration. When our bottle runs dry, so does our magic, and the effect our writing or illustrations had. The creation process of the ink is lengthy and wearisome.

"I am particularly proud of our magical element, it is a secretive art, although you did already watch me use it once. Most elves who witness our magic either do not survive to tell, or are part of our community here. You will be the first to leave here with my trust."

Vali looked nervous.

Odys sympathised, "Yes, I know you plan to leave, I could tell you've wanted to since arriving. Keep this information safe, Vali. Because it is your history to preserve as well. You have stolzite blood in you. You are my kin. I sense you are in a rush to fulfill a destiny you are thrusting upon yourself. I will not stand in your way. It is your fate, and you will only succeed if you do it your way."

Vali nodded, and then she spoke as well. "I do plan to leave. Today actually. I have been thinking about it a lot. I must see to it that Dola does not use the artifacts to start another war. It is my fault she has the sylvite artifact."

Odys took in her grief. Then he offered, "Well then, I hope

the history I have shared with you teaches you something you can use. I do think that you need not take on so much, you can get help from others to reach your goals you know. I have this feeling you want to leave before Ilva returns."

Vali did not move. She did not speak.

Odys sighed. "Ahhh. Well, I cannot tell you how to have a relationship with your partner. Advice in any regard is essentially only helpful to a degree. Maybe you trust each other more than I am giving you both credit for, and who am I to give or not give credit anyways? I'm sure you will do whatever is right for you in every regard granddaughter."

Vali weighed the words of Odys carefully. She took in all the new knowledge she had. She searched subconsciously for the magic within herself, wondering how to use it well. Hoping she would.

Odys read her mind, "Your magic comes from you. Everyone uses theirs differently. You have the ability to create anything you imagine with the power of stolzite ink. In combination with your other powers. Vali, you are able to help shape the future, you and Ilva. You both possess special magic. Maybe you'll be the ones to bring everyone together. No more division or segregation."

Vali thought on this. "No gramps. I think the world will always find a way to divide itself. I will do my best with my gifts. Thank you for sharing so much knowledge with me. I appreciate the history lesson. The sylvite you spoke of...that is, was, Ilva's mother. There are secrets and mysteries and surprises everywhere I turn."

Odys could sense the wisdom coming off of Vali. He got up and walked over to the bookshelves to find the last thing he was going to offer her. He pulled a book gently off the shelf, ensuring to keep the cover facing up at all times, it was more than what it appeared to be. It was in fact a secret box disguised as a book. He felt he was doing the right thing sharing this with her. Helping her with her plan.

Vali stood up from the rug, stretched her arms above her head, let them swing back to her sides, and walked over to where Odys now stood with the secret book box.

He opened it to reveal what was hidden inside. It was a bottle of ink, a pen, and a fist sized stolzite formation. He brought them all over to Vali. "This is stolzite ink. We have plenty here for our own right now, this one is special however. It was one of the first inks to be bottled. It's far stronger and thinner than any other ink we have ever made. Here is a pen to use it, as well as our artifact.

"The stolzite artifact, from which all the other formations we turn to ink is powered, has been sitting here untouched for decades. Bottles full of ink sit in every stolzite home. I hesitate to hand over these treasures, however, I have always had the feeling that elves were never meant to possess all of this power. If you wish to bring these to the Wraith Wan, perhaps this will be the act that saves our world. Perhaps we simply need to remove these temptations from the paths of those who wish to use them for evil. At any rate, it is worth a shot. He has never asked for anything before. If you can gain his support, and if you wish to seek his help, then do so."

Although Vali could not see them, and she wondered how she would even use such a craft being blind, she accepted the gifts. Could she see them, she would note how the stolzite matched the colour of Ilva's golden brown eyes. The pen was crafted of a glass looking material, and the cylinder inside was stained with amber and bronze. Vali stuffed the chunky artifact into the bottom of her bag, then wrapped the amber coloured bottle of ink with a cloth and nestled it in the sack as well, finally she double wrapped the delicate feeling pen in another cloth and nestled it next to the ink. Also, in her bag she had still the small blanket and tin of candy from Llyr's tavern, as well as her water skin which had recently been refilled.

She shouldered the bag gently, pulling her hair from under the straps. The small silver knife was tucked into her boot again. She thanked Odys for the food, lodging, and the advice. She hugged him gently, and he had to press his lips together rather hard to make sure he did not quiver.

He did not want Vali to know she had moved him to tears with the gesture. Knowing he was the only one to see her off was just an added weight in his chest.

Vali knew this, and she even knew Odys was misty. She appreciated his silence, and his support.

She walked through town with Odys, they did not speak, even after the tunnels.

Odys continued walking with her. Not sure if the reason was because he was hesitant to see her go, or to provide her comfort. Perhaps both. He thought he would only walk her to the door, then he thought to the mouth of the cave, then he thought at the end of the tunnels. Steam swam around them in the warm damp air.

Vali and Odys exited the tunnels after about half an hour.

He tapped Vali's shoulder, when she turned Odys was holding out her mother's silver sword.

Vali sensed where he was, and did not at first realise he offered her something, his arms remained outstretched.

"Take this," he said.

Vali felt guilty at all she had already taken. She couldn't take more, yet Odys insisted. Vali reached out, and when her hand wrapped around the silver sword's scabbard, her face froze with shock. She felt the lingering essence, and a small voice sang into her mind, as she held her mother's soul bound weapon. Her silver sword.

Chapter 56

Ilva woke up, unaware that she had even fallen asleep. She shifted from an awkward bent over position, into a folded leg sit. Everything was tight and cramped, it hurt to move. She looked around for a sign of how long she had been out. Without the sun it was hard to tell what time of day it was, Witl was not in sight. She decided to stand, and was shocked at how difficult it was to do so. She staggered on her wobbly legs, which felt like they were filled with water.

She made it to the entrance of the training space when Bryn came in, and almost bumped into her. "Oh! Ilva. Here, have a seat. I grabbed you some food, and tea. It will help. You're already getting stronger."

Ilva didn't feel strong. She felt like a failure.

She had barely tapped these two elves with meek swats, and she passed out from exhaustion while fighting. She was pathetic. The worst brawler that ever tossed a punch. Who was she kidding? Did she really think she was going to become some sort of master bruiser right off the hop? "I'm a joke." Ilva's mind tore her apart inside, and that small piece escaped her lips.

Bryn slammed the food and tea onto the rock next to Ilva. "You think a good fighter is born knowing how to fight? If you want to be a badass warrior you've got to get up and keep going every day to be that! It takes guts and grit. You can rest, but you never get to stop if this is the path you pick."

Ilva took the words like a smack to her subconscious gears.

Her mind held still a moment, then when it whirred up again it started to think. *She has a good point. This is my first time sparing. I just need to build the skill! I can't believe I let something as small as a few defeats stand in my way.* She reached for the plate, grabbing a bunch of grapes and chugging the tea. Her expression was once again determined.

Bryn smiled cheekily to herself, *Ilva, you will be amazingly strong, you'll see.*

As soon as Ilva had finished eating, she walked over to the centre of the room and called out to Bryn, "Again!"

Bryn grinned wide as she walked over to face Ilva.

Witl came back into the small cave and watched from a distance as Ilva brawled with Bryn. He was amazed at how quickly she had picked up on technique. Just from watching and practicing today. He sensed more control in her movements this time. She seemed to have good balance, although Bryn was not attempting to derail her either. *It seems,* Witl thought, *Ilva is habitual at finding fault in her own character. Then again, who isn't? Cutting words get thrown around a lot when your opponent wants to end your life. I wonder how we can prepare her for that. To prevent her from overreacting in the heat of a battle.*

Ilva noticed Witl walking towards them.

Bryn almost locked a fist into her eye socket as a result of the distraction.

Ilva dodged her just in the nick of time.

"Good reflex," Witl complimented the evasive action. He pulled out a small box from a pouch on his belt. When he opened the box, it had two small stones inside of it. "Ilva. I will show you how to craft stone rings. After all, how can you find strength if you never harness your magic?"

Ilva was overwhelmed with the concept. Her stones. "I was not aware that our power came from the rings." Ilva admitted, and Bryn and Witl looked as if someone had just dropped a world ending truth.

"You what?" Witl exclaimed.

"How do you not know that? Were you born in the woods?" Bryn yelled.

Ilva felt suddenly uncomfortable. Before it was just knowledge she did not have. Now it was a point of ridicule.

"Well, if you don't know, then that's just one more thing we'll have to teach you. Gods and goddesses this job gets bigger all the time," Witl spat out sharply.

Ilva's boiling point of embarrassment popped. "I guess I should just have all the answers like you then eh? Come on Mr. Know-It-All! Teach me if you're so smart! I'm tired of being told how bad I am at everything. Why do you not show me so I don't suck as much as you all seem to think I do?"

Witl shrugged the shouting off. It seemed like it didn't matter to him at all that Ilva was upset.

This angered her more. "Why are you so full of yourself? I may not be good at fighting, but you suck at things too, you grumpy old relic! You are the worst teacher ever, and a terrible conversationalist!"

He sipped from the ladle he had pulled from the water bucket.

Ilva huffed out rage-filled breaths.

"If those are your opinions of me. I cannot change them. I personally do not care about that. I care about my own abilities to create. I care not what others think of me. This is how I have acquired my mastery. This is the mastery I want you to be able to conduct," Witl cooed.

Ilva still seethed. *Conceded old bastard! He thinks I have no control? I am totally in control!* Ilva walked angrily up to Witl, and knocked the ladle from his hand, which he caught mid-air and rapped across Ilva's open hand. It split the skin open. Ilva winced hard and let out a yelp as blood formed on the cracked skin.

He added confidently, "I will not train you if you think my lessons unimportant. I will not teach you if you believe I am inferior to do so. I am your best chance at growing into what you want to be. However, in order for you to become what you want to be, you must accept where you are at."

Ilva held her bleeding palm, and tried to rationalise Witl's teachings.

Chapter 57

Vali walked into the forest, her goodbye to her grandfather still lingered in the silence. His last words to her burned in her brain, "Come back to Ilva, and all of us."

She sensed the feeling of a breeze on her, it felt nice after the confinement of the caves. Many earthy sensations returned, and as she walked, she picked up on each of them. Birdsong and the sound of wind in the leaves, the smell of dirt and flowers and berries, the feeling of soft dirt under her feet instead of hard stone. She thought the air even tasted different. Cleaner. She was enjoying the delights to her senses so much that she almost didn't notice the presence out here with her. It hit her suddenly. The sense that there was someone close by.

She went on alert. She moved careful and cautious down the path, attempting to appear as relaxed as she had just been. She heard the steps, several paces behind her. When she thought her follower was close enough, she pulled the sword from its silver sheath and swung it around to point at the pursuer.

"Whoa! Hey stranger. Long-time no see. Fancy meeting you in the forest."

Vali tried to place the deep female voice, it was hard seeing how she'd only met this elf once.

"It's Llyr! Do you not remember me?"

Vali did recall her now. "What are you doing here? And why did you sneak up on me?"

Llyr took a moment to breathe, as Vali lowered and sheathed her sword. "Uh, I'm running from the war."

Vali was confused. "War?"

Llyr shot back, "Gods and goddesses! What rock have you been hiding under?"

Vali smirked at the irony in that question. "A big one," She jested back.

Llyr told Vali how the war had started. "Ediv came back from the sea with an army! He is leading them and all elfkind to war against High Lady Alix! He wants the entire realm for himself apparently. Something about it being the right of the stone elves to own this land and all the minerals that form here? It made Lady Dola go insane! I stayed in Ivarseas for a day or so, it's pretty much empty now. Ediv took every abled body with him to Falil.

As Vali absorbed this information, Llyr kept talking.

"I just made it to the forest today, been on the road a few. I saw you from some ways back, sorry if I came up and surprised you, I recognized your bag and dark hair. Nice sword by the way. Where have you been then?"

Llyr was as chipper as she had been the day Vali met her. She was grateful for the company, however, wary that she was now privy to secrets that she could not share. The 'rock she was under' being one of them.

Vali sank down and sat on a log along the path. Llyr sat

beside her. "That is a lot to take in. I had no idea it would come so quickly. I was waiting for Lady Dola to make the first move to break peace." Vali excluded the detail that she was granddaughter to the Lady Dola, feeling untrusting with all of her secrets. She kept talking discreetly to Llyr, "Ediv's army. Are they all elven?"

Llyr pulled out a small tin from her bag and began packing a pipe, a smell similar to a distant skunk rose up in Vali's nose. She would pass on the pipe if it was offered, she knew it made her hungry, and her food had to last.

She waited for Llyr's reply.

"Yes. They're elven. They're like me. I have a slightly blue tinge to my skin, it gives away the fact that I am different here. I am a sapphire elf. My kind have come here to fight in your war alongside Ediv. I do not want to get caught up in this mess. So, I'm on my way to the mountains. I'll wait there until this war passes. It always does, in time. The results are different for everyone. Having no ties to this country, no kin, and my tavern was just some run down old mill I made do with, this war does not affect me much."

This seemed to trigger a reaction in Vali. One she didn't understand. She snapped. "What do you mean? Does not affect you? War affects everything, everyone. It changes the world. Everything changes the world. We are all making changes with every step, every choice. What you are doing now makes a difference." Vali clamped her mouth shut before she said more. She felt more words roiling in her gut. She tried to digest them, and think about what she just said.

Llyr responded while Vali was still overthinking, "You're right. I'm sorry. Maybe I have been affected by it. But what can someone like me do? I'm just an outcast. No one on any side will trust me. Not Ediv, or Dola, or Alix, not even my own kind. I'm kind of a useless pawn to everyone."

Vali considered how it must feel to be in that position, and wondered to herself, *Why would Llyr be an outcast?* Vali had always been part of something, even if it was not her choice. To be part of nothing, and have no purpose. It must be so hard to find a fulfilling existence if all Llyr had was an abandoned piece of property and a few loyal drunks to keep herself prosperous. Vali silently marvelled at the resilience of this elf before asking her, "What did you do to be exiled from your home?"

Llyr took the question like a blow, Vali did not know who she was. She thought to herself quickly, *What should I tell her?*

She started explaining herself, slowly, and with her own discretion, "Well, I was once in high standing among the sapphires, and then there was a power struggle. I had too much to lose, and lose a lot of it I did. I had nothing left to stay for except power, which I don't really care for, and there were those who wanted it. I suppose you could say I let them have it. Status does not matter so much when you can't have the things you love.

"So, I took what I had left, and came here. I tried to start anew. There is nothing for me back there but threats and death. If they saw me fighting against them now, I would endure the same fate as I would have if I'd returned home, and fighting with the ones who threatened me also seems dumb. So, I'm picking another option. One that ensures this life will go on."

Vali wondered, *How can so many elves in this world not trust in their own abilities? How many have to run away from their problems? These are not solutions.* Conveniently ignoring the fact that she often did not acknowledge her own ability, and the fact that she had run from Dola. "Llyr, everything affects you here. This war uprooted the life you restarted. Do you not wish to fight for your right to have peace and freedom? You are not an outcast to everyone. I trust you. Will you help me end this war?"

Llyr smiled, "That is an interesting idea. I do trust you, Vali. Does this freedom flag group consist of just you and I?" A deep hearty laugh escaped from Llyr's widely open mouth.

Vali was suddenly nervous about how she should explain her plan. She did just say she trusted Llyr, and that statement now made her felt guilty. Trust and secrets could be terribly troublesome things to navigate.

Chapter 58

Ilva tried to accept that she was not as skilled at serving up punches. She tried to affirm that it would take time. It was hard to acquire things like patience and time though. She wanted to be strong now. Vali would need her help, and she felt absolutely useless. She kicked the rocky ground and pouted. Her moods had swung around a lot today. She thought they almost felt as exhausting as the fighting.

Witl snapped his attention on her, "Ilva," he started sternly, then softened his tone. "I think you have great balance, and you have almost mastered your stamina. You have already learned so much, the only thing you really need to work on is your strength of mind. I was very much like you when I started."

This caught Ilva off guard. Was Witl actually giving her a compliment? She thought it was not in his character to say such things, then thought better. She was doing the very thing he had just told her to try and train within herself.

Her first task with strengthening her mind was to avoid judgements that were not factual. Judging Witl's character was something she had no evidence to support. Therefore, she could not judge him. It was a hard lesson. The concept seemed so easy, and all her life she had believed in the concept of being non-judgemental. However, when it came to actually rerouting those thoughts, she found herself trapped in a spiral of false beliefs. Was everything she thought an evaluation? *Almost.* She felt discouraged.

Ilva was troubled when she realised how many conclusions in her head were fabricated. Her job was only to combat the appraisals she felt against Witl. In doing so, she realised she was also appraising Bryn, and Odys, and Vali, and her family. Everyone. Especially herself. It was a bit of a shock. She was not used to looking at herself this way. She was always looking at the behaviours of others. Observing, comparing. To now realise how subjective she was, made her feel strongly opposed of her own train of thought. It threatened to take the wind out of her sails entirely. It was exhausting fighting all these unverifiable verdicts.

Witl knew the effort Ilva was putting in, he also knew she was turning her judgements inward, and felt he should give her some encouragement, "Enough with the self loathing. Critique yourself, then move on. It's hard to look at ourselves, or others, objectively. No use getting upset over realising that your brain is full of opinions and observations. Just focus on improving any biases. Okay?"

Ilva was grateful. How lucky she was for this opportunity. Learning to fight, to strengthen her mind, to use her magic. Sure, some of the parts of this were uncomfortable, she still wanted to know all she could. Learning about her own mind brought her such clarity.

"Now, about your physical abilities. To put it simply, you are a weakling," Witl chided.

That stung. Ilva didn't let it bother her though. He could call her weak, but she wasn't going to stay that way. She readied herself for her next lesson.

Chapter 59

Vali fumbled with words. Keeping her story believable, while omitting details, wasn't easy for her. "Yeah, it is just me. There are other elves, just not here," Vali was not doing a good job coming up with a story.

"Oh, that sounds convincing," Llyr chuckled. "You can just tell me if it's *confidential*. I won't pry if you have things to protect. I can understand that. What do you need help with? If you were brave enough to ask, and not prepared for questioning, you must be about to do something pretty difficult, or stupid. Let me guess, you are currently acting on your own, and you need help, only you didn't want to involve those you love out of a fear of losing them. So, now you're trying to be some saviour, and you realise you're not prepared to do this. Am I close?"

Vali stuttered out several half words. The shock plain on her face. "How? How did you guess all of that?" She finally formed words into a structured sentence.

Llyr smiled at the memory of their first meeting. "Well, last I saw you, you were rushing off to be a hero. Now you have a sword, seem far less panicked, and ready to reap some revenge. You're protecting secrets, which I assume to be the location and conditions of your loved ones, you're alone again, walking into a warzone, with a weapon. I just painted a picture and took my best guess. If I was right though, my only question is; What do you need my help with? It looks like you're headed to Karna. Why?"

Vali nodded, "Yes. I am. You are most astute. I want to protect those I care about. I want to save myself as well. The parties engaging in this war are of little concern to me. The war starting is actually the perfect distraction for my plan."

Vali told Llyr only the parts that she needed to know and told herself *I am not lying; I am just omitting details.* The attempt at being permissive with herself only agonized her more, it made her consider how her intentions maybe weren't as honest as she wanted to believe, she still felt them necessary. So, lie and omit details she did. Vali carefully explained the events in Falil between Ilva's mother and Dola's guard. She then explained their camping in the woods and Ilva being abducted again.

Vali skirted over all the events in the cave and mountains by simply saying, "I found her though, and she is safe now. Turns out she can handle herself. Ilva's doing her thing, and I'm off to do what I need to do. It was a mutual decision I guess." *That is a lie.* Vali's thoughts attacked with venom. *You are a liar.* The thoughts slithered and hissed around in her mind. They would eat at her for the rest of the day.

They had gotten up from where they sat at the side of the path.

Llyr clicked her tongue and asked, "Well, where are we headed then, and what's our goal here?"

Vali snapped her mind to attention, focusing on her façade again, and stated, "I am off to retrieve something Lady Dola stole, and my bow. I left it behind. I must return to Karna, now that I have seen to it Ilva is safe from Lady Dola and Lord Ediv, and I will do it by whatever means necessary. I'll even kill Dola if I must." The last statement shocked Vali as much as it did Llyr. Could she do that? Kill her own grandmother?

She struggled to rationalise the statement when Llyr replied, "Do not expect me to stand in the way of whatever choices you make. Just do not ask me to kill anyone for you. I have shed enough blood in my time. You said you wanted my help, right? What exactly do you want me to do?"

Vali simply said, "All I need from you Llyr is to be my eyes. Can you help me find what I seek?"

Llyr nodded, "That I can do. Tell me where I am to guide you, and what I am to seek."

Vali explained to Llyr the arcane artifacts, and how she had to get the sylvite artifact, she also described her bow in detail. She felt empty when she talked about her weapon. She asked Llyr questions to keep her mind off of it. "How far away is your old country?"

Llyr was delighted Vali was showing an interest in her heritage and homelands. "Well it would be roughly three to five days by boat. Depending of course on how good the seas are. Really not that far at all. I was surprised when I arrived here, at how close I was to a new adventure all along. I've been here a while, and I didn't know this forest was so large. It amazes me what sights are just a walk or a boat ride away."

Vali took in the idea of the world holding more adventure than she gave it credit for. She thought of how she had been adventuring for months, and how this was all around her since birth. How little of it she felt grateful for, or had even had the chance to physically see. This made her feel a tad ashamed and then sad. She soaked in the energies of the forest around her. "You're right Llyr. The world is a place full of wonder. One can never be truly bored in a place full of so much adventure and magic."

They were slowly approaching the section of the forest where Livy's cottage resided, when dusk fell. It was getting dark, very fast. Llyr offered to set up camp for them, and Vali appreciated the gesture. She announced that she would go grab them a bite to eat and be right back.

Llyr grunted in understanding and the two of them set to their tasks.

Chapter 60

Ilva was sitting at a stone table in Witl's cave. He seemed to be isolated from the rest of the underground community. Ilva wondered why, and tried not to draw conclusions about the situation. Instead she worked on her stones at Witl's request. Ilva was swelling with excitement! She was tapping a chisel with a hammer, the sharp end chipping off slivers and shards of rock from the small stones Witl had given her. Stopping every now and then she examined the rock taking shape and managed, with Witl's guidance, to turn it into a small flat cylinder using a variety of tools. The next part was hard; grinding out the inner ring. All it took was a small change in the application of pressure to crack the ring entirely. She would have to focus and, hardest of all, be patient.

Witl coached her over her shoulder, "Apply more pressure," and, "You're on an angle," and other such helpful mentoring advice was proving beneficial.

Slowly she worked on drilling the diamond tipped driver through the stone. She picked up the ring and held it close to her eye. Inspecting it with the utmost scrutiny. She was surprised at her new craft. She gawked and grinned with newfound self appreciation. Her face a show of pure awe. Searching for imperfections, she found a few, and managed to clean them up with the driver. Then she smoothed the rough bits out using a small buffing wheel.

She stared with an appraising look at the ring. When she found nothing too major to criticize herself on, she was lost. She realised that wasn't a bad thing. She did something well and she was proud of herself. She still had one more ring to go though. *Still a chance to mess it all up,* her mean inner voice teased. She shut it up, and picked up the chisels.

Ilva was amazed. She stared at two perfect stone rings. After buffing them with an even softer buffing stone, soaking them in boiling water, and rubbing a polishing balm on them, the stone rings were the most rewarding thing Ilva had ever made. Ilva was transfixed. Her eyes roamed over the wavy layers in the rock's old formations. All the tightly bound lines running through each band.

Sliding the rings upon her thumbs was very satisfying. They were heavier than she expected, but she was used to them after only a few minutes. Resting perfectly, between her knuckles, were her own personal magical items. She kept giving herself a double thumbs up to inspect the details of her newest craft. She was now ready to learn how to use them. She asked Witl, "So what do we do now?"

He raised an eyebrow at her and walked over.

Out of nowhere he jabbed.

Ilva caught it. Her eyes grew wide. She was not surprised Witl was attacking ambush style, she was surprised at her strength and fast reflexes. She felt like she might crush his fist within her own. She squeezed a little, and Witl was suddenly breathing heavy, he winced.

He threw an elbow into the connection between their fists, and jumped back. He pulled out of his hip pouch two rings, and adorned his own thumbs with them. He also whipped off his tunic, exposing a surprising amount of abdomen muscles for an old elf.

Geez, Witl. You're a beast. Ilva's inner voice laughed at the sight of the old buff elder before her, ready and raring to go. "I can see I will need to get serious now. There you are lass. I knew you had something more impressive buried in you. Let's see what you got now!"

Witl launched himself at her, and threw fist after fist towards her, Ilva deflected each blow, letting them land all over her forearms. Her elbows flew up and down in a flurry of protective stances. When Witl had a break in his stamina, Ilva landed her blow. Strait to Witl's leg.

He went down, seething, it seemed like it was taking all of his energy not to cry out. He braced himself on his other leg and got back up. Leaning on the uninjured leg slightly, he held himself still. Ready for an attack. Ilva debated on where she should hit him next.

Ilva was not even breaking a sweat. She was starting to feel more like the master herself.

Witl was not surprised, he knew that training her before she formed her rings was proper. He had, after all, trained every stone elf in Falil. Ediv had sent them all to their death in the war. Witl was the only stone elf warrior, aside from

Ediv, who had survived Mila. Ilva was the only induction he had done since.

She was taking every hit without even a grimace now, and each one she delivered was devastating. She rarely needed to hit him more than one single time to take him down. They had to take several more breaks before the match was done. They both slouched, Witl clearly the loser of the brawl. His face and body bruised and bloody.

Ilva barely had a scratch from this trial. Her arms had a few purpling bruises, and her shoulder and leg still ached a bit from before. She was mostly just tired. She felt like she would sleep for days if she laid down.

Witl commended her on a job well done. "One day of training, and you're kicking my ass lass. You sure are something. I've never seen a fighter like you, then again maybe I'm just getting old. Get your rest while life allows you it. Eat well when food is plentiful. I will see you again bright and early tomorrow if you want to learn something new."

Ilva very much wanted to learn something new. She would never lose the desire for that.

She waved goodbye when she saw Bryn at the mouth of the cave waving her over. "Ready to eat?"

Ilva nodded with enthusiasm, "Am I ever! What a day."

"Day isn't over yet." Was the only response Bryn could give.

~

Ilva walked into the little inner-mountain hut, and looked around for Vali. When she did not see her, she thought to ask. She turned and saw the faces her hosts wore. Ilva knew then, and she turned to face the bookshelves, breathing in a deep sigh. She let it out. "Vali ran off, and told you to tell me not to worry, didn't she? I hope she succeeds. Let's train harder and faster, I'll get strong enough to join her in no time! I just need to focus on what I can do for myself."

At the last word, she wheeled around to face Odys and Bryn, who were both beaming with equally pleased and shocked expressions.

Ilva felt like she had learned more in the last ten hours than she had in the last ten centuries.

Chapter 61

Vali and Llyr were soon sitting around a comfortable fire, food in hand.

Llyr was pleased to have someone else do the food prep for her. Running a tavern, she was used to cooking non-stop and having to eat her meals quickly. She ate and enjoyed the forest and the fire in comfort. *This is different. I feel free. But, I'm not.*

Vali was also enjoying the forest and the fire. Along with the quiet company, which made missing Ilva easier. She simply soaked in what she could, the sounds and smells calming her. It made her feel comfortable here, and she felt she could trust Llyr. *At least*, she thought, *there's no reason for me not to trust her.*

Llyr had been reliable at building camp. She even helped build the fire, and had created a spit for the meat.

Vali thought to herself *resourceful, smart, a very good ally to have in the coming battle*. She hoped she could convince her to fight if the time came. She also wondered what kind of past Llyr had to cause her to reject the idea of fighting any battles.

They finished eating and drinking, and set up their bed rolls.

Llyr crashed into hers with force and appeared to be out like a light after a hastily huffed, "Night, Vali, see you in the morning."

Vali was mortified at the volume and intensity with which Llyr trumpeted out snores. *Note to self: Llyr is not a stealthy sleeper.* She was glad for the protection and aid of this great sleeping brute though. Vali laid down to sleep feeling totally content, until the thought popped up, *I wonder how Ilva reacted when she found out I had left her there. Without a goodbye.* Vali shed a silent tear. Laying down had made her exhausted body cumbersome, adding in the emotional toll and these tears made her body ache for sleep, soon delta waves dominated her mind, as the deepest of sleeps claimed her.

Vali woke up the next morning, and Llyr had already packed up camp and was ready to go whenever. Vali scrambled, despite Llyr telling her not to, they were on the road in less than five minutes. Vali silently scolded herself for not being more alert, *How did she pack up the whole camp while I slept?*

They talked about the animals in the forest, and other creatures like dragons and nymphs, and about the wastelands. Time passed very quickly. They had walked most of the morning, and were now very close to where Livy's cottage had been.

Vali kept smelling the air to see if she could catch a whiff of bread baking, she kept listening for the soft clucks of chickens, and tried to gather the direction it would be in. She guessed it was somewhere to the right and ahead, she went off the trail a bit, and Llyr asked what she was doing.

"I have a friend in this area," Vali said vaguely.

She hated that she could no longer use shadows of landmarks in the same way she used to. She had to feel things all the time now. When her feet were on paths, she could tell easily which parts of them she was on, attempting to not trip over roots in the forest, or fall down cliffsides, was harder. She had to glide her feet slowly, walking at a timid pace, mostly using her toes and nose to navigate. She was relieved when Llyr did not make her feel awkward about it, and volunteered right away to help her look.

The two of them searched for about twenty minutes, when Llyr said she had spotted Livy's cottage. They walked up to, what Llyr described to Vali as, an abandoned shack.

Livy was gone.

The chicken coop stood empty, the goat had vanished, the hut inside had been cleared out too. Everything. As if she had never been there at all. It was eerie.

Vali felt uncomfortable here all of a sudden, and they walked on, quickly. *What happened?* Vali wondered.

The pair walked steadily all week, until they were finally near the outskirts of Karna. The forest would open up soon, they were fairly close to the city, and dusk was fast approaching. They decided to camp one more night while they still had the cover of the forest, and so that tomorrow they would be well rested for whatever ventures they may find themselves in. They didn't bother with a fire tonight, the air was warmer and there wasn't any need for it if they already had food. Not to mention the fire would give them away.

Llyr offered her wine skin to Vali, who took it graciously. "Thank you so much," she said.

Llyr accepted the gratitude with a, "No problem."

They sat and drank and chewed their food. After the skin had been emptied and their bellies filled the two laid down to rest.

Llyr fell asleep the usual way, she plopped down and snored.

Vali was quickly behind her, feeling comfort and contentment.

Only Llyr was not asleep. She rolled up from her bed roll. After she was sure Vali was out, she grabbed at a bowl of dark coloured herbs that were stored, prematurely ground up, in her bag. She wafted the blackish purple paste, now smeared on a rag, under Vali's nose.

Her sleep became all the deeper. Then Vali was lifted up onto Llyr's shoulder and carried off into the night.

Chapter 62

Power surged deep within Ilva now. Her body resonating in a way it never had before. She understood what she felt, what she needed, what she was. Connections were being made, and despite being there all along, they were only now lighting up, and things became clearer. Dark alley's came to life in each corner of her mind, and she braved each one.

This kind of learning thrilled her. As her body was becoming sharper, she was eager to also train her mind. Ambitious to avoid thoughts of Vali leaving, Ilva desired to become immersed in every form of study she could.

She turned back to the bookshelves, "Odys, you did say I could read while I was here did you not? May I?"

Odys smiled even brighter, "But of course! What are you thinking of reading?" He was delighted to have an interested reader in front of his collection.

"I think I shall read this one if that is okay?" She held her book choice out to him after pulling it off the shelf she had stood in front of.

Odys looked at the ominous book, then at Ilva. "Are you sure this is something you want knowledge on?"

Ilva nodded.

"Very well. Take care with what you learn, do not push yourself. Read and digest this information slowly." With that Odys handed her the dark leather book, with the tiny pin clasp. The book, which bore no title, held secrets to a magic Ilva would soon discover.

Ilva clutched it to her chest, and curtsied gently down onto the bedroll that still lay in front of the center shelves. She read until she passed out with the book beside her.

~

Ilva awoke very early the next morning, and was ambitious as ever to resume her training! She was terribly sore, and she wanted to pretend she was not. She tried not to groan when she sat down, or when she got back up.

Bryn seemed only a little concerned.

Ilva was hiding her pain well.

Odys was piling food up on the table in front of them all. Little cakes, and fruit, and lots of eggs, sausages, and the most delicious drink Ilva had ever tried. It tasted of citrus and honey, and it was warm.

Once they were all full, but not bloated, Bryn and Ilva began walking towards the place they had trained the day before.

Bryn broke the silence first, "I'm surprised you are not more upset about Vali leaving like that."

Ilva turned her head, and smiled, "I worry about her. I don't want to think only of her though. I'm here training to focus on my own betterment. She's not even here to see that I am upset with her so what would be the point in expressing it?

"I can trust her. Even if she does things like this, I know her intentions are good, so, I leave her choices to her. I've got my own bad choices to make. Now let us go beat up my broken body some more!"

The two women laughed at this last comment until Ilva was wheezing and holding her stomach to stop. When Ilva caught her breath, she used it to say, "To be honest though, a goodbye would have been nice. I'll be sure to let her know how I feel about that when I see her next." They continued on to the training ground.

Witl was waiting for them there. He had his rings on again, and this time there were several obstacles placed about the cavern.

They spent the morning practicing her reaction time. She jolted her body around the course, and after every few obstacles there would be either Bryn or Witl aggressively attempting to throw her off. Ilva was dodging the blows and the rocks they tossed, as well as the objects and trials on the course. After yesterday's training, she was reacting well. Although her body felt displeased about all the extra strain on her tightly bound muscles.

When they took a break, Ilva rubbed the aches, hard. They seemed to release after several deep rubs up and down her thighs, hips, stomach and arms. She massaged every muscle group she could find, and sought the areas needing work by moving a body part and sensing the pain that emitted. She targeted each point and rubbed each until they felt loose.

Now she felt all wobbly when she stood though, and she worried she might have put her muscles to sleep a bit. She tried to stretch it out. She kept her hips still as she reached out to one side of the floor, then the other, before bending forward to place both hands on the ground.

Straightening, she walked to a nearby tray for a cup of water. She chugged it and filled it up three more times. She was ready to go again. *No stopping until I'm strong,* she thought. Ilva trained all afternoon on the obstacle course until she felt her body was going to rip apart with all the muscle tension. She fell, shaking, to the rocky ground, and surrendered by the end of the session. She felt disapproval at her own surrender, but she also knew it was just her limit. She walked back to the hut that night, sore and tired, and a little bit tougher.

Ilva woke up on the third day of training full of pain and panic. She was terrified she wouldn't be able to handle the brutality any more, worried she was in too much pain for her to do any good. It made no sense to her now why continuing training would strengthen her. It felt like it was just crippling her. She was doubting herself, and the doubt was turning her fears into realities.

She was overwhelming herself with all of this when Bryn walked up. "Ready for today?"

Ilva almost broke into tears, "I am in so much pain."

Bryn felt bad for Ilva. She asked her what hurt.

Ilva tried to explain how all of her muscles were tingling with dull pains, how using the muscles made them feel as though they might tear open, and how her bones ached.

Bryn knew of things they could do to relieve the cramping.

So, before setting off for training, and after unhelpfully stating that the muscles were indeed tearing and that is how muscle builds, they had a morning of self-indulgence.

Bryn ran a hot steamy bath in the tub room, and made tea for them. She grabbed up some incense burners and a basket of herbal remedies she kept in the kitchen. When they were in the tub room Bryn gave Ilva a few leaves from the basket to chew up, and she began pouring stuff into the bath. Salts and crystals and drops of liquid oils. She gave Ilva her tea, and insisted upon her entrance to the tub.

Ilva felt her whole body melt into the heat.

She almost dropped her tea. She sat it on the tub ledge and just let her entire body soak. She felt every muscle ease, her face relaxed, and she thought she even felt her jaw change position. Her eyes were suddenly so heavy. She wanted her tea, so she reached for it and took a big gulp, her eyes were not as heavy then. She savoured the taste of peppermint and sweetness, and it kept her awake in the bath. She drank up the last of her tea and climbed out of the tub reluctantly once the water had cooled.

Bryn was sitting on the bench reading a book, and she looked up to ask if Ilva was refreshed.

Ilva gushed at how much she was.

Bryn nodded, and said "Good! On to training then."

Ilva let out a groan of displeasure.

Chapter 63

Vali woke with a start. She knew instantly she was no longer outside. She was trapped in a room, she recognized it right away. She was in the dungeon in Karna. She knew it by smell, and by the door she now placed her hand on. She had been here before. This was how her grandmother grounded her growing up. This was her childhood prison. She felt so small. Her cell was right below the room where she last spoke to Dola.

She was frightened now. Where was Llyr? What had happened to them? She felt nauseous, and hungry. She curled up on the small bed roll on the cell floor. At least there was that. She was awoken the second time to the sound of the cell door unlocking. She was more alert this time, she felt plenty rested now, but she was still so hungry. Was that food she smelled?

A guard clanked in, dropping the platter of food onto the floor. Rice, beans, and bread flew off the plate onto the dirty ground.

Vali walked towards it unfazed. She knew it was a threat, she did not care. She was hungry, and it was food.

The guard spat on the rice.

Vali's blood began to boil hotter. She was bursting at the seams. What is this elf's problem?

"Traitor! I hope you rot in here." The female guard turned to leave.

Vali focused on the voice, it was different, hoarser and so weathered, but could that have been Jyke? Vali remembered now all the elves whose wrath she would suffer, all those who were slain by them in the village of Falil, how her and Ilva were the only ones to survive. She was worried now.

She thought she had a chance, and that her grandmother was more distracted. Was she deceived in the forest? She must have been. It was the only reason she could think of for being alone in this cell. *Llyr.* It all was coming together, it was the only explanation. Vali considered it unlikely to be coincidence that Llyr had met her in the forest. Vali could not sense other prisoners here in the hall full of cells. She had been here often enough as a child to know when the cells were inhabited. By sound mostly, but also the fact that she was the only one who was brought food.

It was a small dungeon, with only a few small cells. Marka's dungeons were ten times larger. Normally in Karna prisoners were executed quickly, or in Vali's case when she was young released for use by Dola. She thought this time it wouldn't be the same liberation she got as a child. Would Karna be attacking with Ediv? Was the part about Ediv even true? Was Llyr lying to her?

Vali was full of seething anger. It showed in her shallow breaths and a hissing she occasionally did through her tightly clamped teeth. She hated lies, even when she told them. Especially when she told them. They made life so confusing. She didn't rationalise that they might not be lies, and that Llyr might be in real danger too. She was convinced she had been betrayed.

Pacing and pacing in her square prison, she was becoming increasingly bored and irritable. She would rather face any confrontation than this boredom. She tucked in the urge to yell out the tiny barred window. She sat on her frustrations all day. At night her second meal came. As did Dola.

Vali knew it was her the moment she strutted in. Her toe taps were unmistakably arrogant, and the aggressive aura Vali was much acclimated to floated into the cell, it still chilled her to the bones. She was sitting on her bed roll. Feelings of control masked her fears. She tried to portray them onto her face. She wanted to come off as cold, and unperturbed.

The tray was tossed upon the floor as the previous one was.

Vali did not care, she ate the bread off the floor and the whole tray just became her bowl. *No matter how bad things are, they could always be worse.*

Jyke stood on the other side of Dola, eyeing Vali.

Vali could feel their eyes upon her. She was picking at a small chicken leg, when Dola spoke, "I see you have been busy. Found a safe place for Ediv's daughter, did you? That will not change the fact that your relationship is unnatural. You belong to different magic classes and are unable to produce children together. This is shameful, Vali."

Vali's jaw locked, she could not bring herself to chew. She

thought she might choke in her anger. She found the will to swallow, it almost brought a tear to her eye when the chicken lodged in her constricted throat a moment. Ignoring Dola's insults and bigotry, Vali steeled herself against the oncoming slander. She took another bite. A big one, and chewed slowly.

Dola was furious, "Tell me why you are doing this? Why are you protecting that elf? She cannot live. She is a problem that needs to be eliminated before it's too late!"

Vali was ever the more curious, though her expression stayed detached. She had a few questions answered in Dola's rambling. There was indeed a war, and Ilva is a problem to Dola. *They see something dangerous in her? What could that be? She is just sweet soft Ilva. Giddy and childish about everything.* Vali could not imagine her being something to fear. Yet what she felt from Dola, was that she was most afraid of Ilva. *Interesting.*

"Well, I don't know much about this war that is going on. Enlighten me grandmother. I am also wondering what happened to the elf who was sent to abduct me? That blue elf. What was her name? Llyr?" Vali tried to sound carefree and relaxed about her state of imprisonment. The statement still held an ounce of venom.

Dola seemed to feel more like the prisoner now. This enraged her. She walked over to her granddaughter. Grabbing her by her tunic she yanked her up off the floor with one fist. She suspended her uncomfortably, yet Vali tried not to pay it any mind, her face remained blank. Giving herself a small fraction of control over the situation.

"Bit dramatic don't you think? Why are you getting mad? I

only asked you a question grandmother." The light innocence Vali drizzled on to provoke Dola was working.

Dola let her fall.

Vali let herself crumple making her act all the more believable. It was an act within an act. She listened to the footfalls in the cell. *One. Two.* In one more moment she would have an opening. She readied herself.

However, Dola had noticed the preparative movement and looked around. She realised that the guard who had brought the tray moved, and was inspecting the bathroom stall, the dungeon door was open. Dola was too late when she looked back at her pitiful prisoner.

Three! Vali was lunging under her arms for the door.

Jyke had prepared for this though.

Vali was shocked when a fist connected with her stomach. She curled and sunk down. A second fist connected with her face. She flew back, slamming the base of her skull off the floor. She felt desperation clawing at her. She was throwing her arms wildly around her seeking her opponent. She felt like a younger sibling in a fight against Jyke. She was embarrassed. She knew it was her as soon as they started fighting. She hated how her old friends were now her enemies.

Jyke stood up, and kicked Vali in the ribs with all her strength.

Vali coughed and coughed.

The guard, Jyke, and Dola took it as their cue to leave.

Vali cried. Days turned into weeks. Time was moving, and she was not. *What will happen to Ilva? Will I see her again? How will I ever get out of this?* Questions rattled around in

Vali's mind. Tormenting her. Driving her slowly mad. The isolation she used to be adjusted to, now only burned at her. It ate away at her and made her crave for Ilva's company more and more each day. Each lonely night was agony. *Will I ever hold my Ilva again?*

Until one night the doors banged open, and she could hear a struggle. She wondered what was going on, when the guards shouted, "Get in there you little blue devil!"

A small male voice shouted shrilly, "Screw you, big dolt! Ma is going to wreak havoc when she gets loose from those chains! Just you wait!"

Chains? Ma? Blue skin... Vali was playing super sleuth again. *What does this all mean? Who is that little elf?*

Chapter 64

After doing stretches and slower exercises all of yesterday, Ilva woke today feeling like her body was impossibly tough. She pounded the rock that Witl had instructed her to attack. She thought it a strange request, yet as she was doing so, her fists did not give, her arms did not slack. Her body went full on into each strike.

Several hours were spent punching the X etched into the boulder, which was twice her size, before she understood her task. Ilva felt the rock under her fists begin to give way, she thought she was imagining it. Then the rock suddenly spilt into several fragments. In half but also a third of one half fractioned off of the massive sphere. Ilva looked on with astonishment at what she had just accomplished.

She split a rock twice her size in three. Was this real? She was ready for the next task, she turned to Witl and made the rock warrior stance she was taught; fists together, thumbs over her knuckles, knees bent and feet apart. "Now, I feel strong."

Witl smiled wide and shouted, "Gods and goddesses lass! You really are! I was getting sore with you beating up on me, I figured you should see why you no longer train with Bryn or myself. You are something stronger than either of us. Even at half strength with your rings you could break off one of our arms. You have not realised that you have far surpassed our strength, have you? I am not sure what else we have to teach you,"

Ilva looked toward a blushing and frowning Bryn.

She avoided Ilva's eyes.

Ilva turned back to Witl, "I suppose you also failed to notice that you broke my nose yesterday, or that I lost a tooth. You have surpassed your teacher's lass. All I can do is help you do things to control it. Now that we know you are plenty strong, have fairly good reaction timing, and are a skilled observational fighter, we will work on your weapons training.

"Please try to focus on movements less than defeating me, you may actually kill me if you get carried away. Practice control. I am sure you will use plenty of force when the time comes. We will start with footing and form. It will be more of a dance than a fight, think of it that way for now. Oh! Also, Bryn has a gift for you. I am curious to see if it enhances your power further."

Bryn walked up with a small leaf wrapped pouch. Tiny enough that it fit within her closed hands. She brought it over to Ilva and placed the tiny pouch in her palms. "These seemed more your style than the fans your mother had. I made them for you. It seemed right since you are Syli's daughter."

Ilva unwrapped the leaf to expose a pair of small delicate earrings. She hadn't adorned her ears in years, and hoped it wouldn't be a struggle to get them in. She pulled the tiny piece of wood off the back of the pin, then pushed it through, it was only a little hard to get in. She replaced the wood backing, then repeated this with the other ear. She asked them both, "How do they look?"

Her observers gazed kindly, "Brilliant!" Witl exclaimed.

"They look great on you." Bryn spoke with pleasure. "You are as beautiful as the archmage herself."

"Archmage?" Ilva wondered who Bryn meant.

"Yes, your mother. The strongest sylvite who ever lived. I have always looked up to her. Since I was a small girl in Mila, we were good friends, I miss her. She was my reason for becoming strong."

Ilva blinked, dissociated, *this world is all so much. So many centuries before me have passed. What really happened? What is to come? What is real? What is not?* Ilva noticed the strong feelings of overwhelm, squeezing and releasing her fists, her toes curling and uncurling, she tried to focus on the much larger muscles in her body. Flexing each one in turn, thinking of what she should say in this moment.

Bryn was waiting for her response.

Ilva, finally, looked up with searching eyes, "Please, tell me about my mother. Before she was a slave."

Bryn wore a haunting smile as she told Ilva the tale of two girls in a desert city. How, with other children of Mila, they had played and worked and smiled.

It made Ilva happy to hear about her mother's childhood. To know her life hadn't been all bad. She wished her mother could have been here now. With her childhood friend, watching her daughter find strength, feeling the freedom she hadn't had in over a century. But her mother was gone. She would never have a chance to make her proud now.

Bryn was aware that Ilva had been mourning the loss heavily, and despite not knowing exactly what Ilva felt, she spoke from the heart, "Ilva. Syli would be honoured by you. Spreading such love and laughter, working hard, showing everyone kindness and understanding, even those of us who are hardest to love. You are absolutely everything a mother could ever want in a daughter. Be proud of who you are."

Ilva was filling herself with confidence now, brimming with affection, she felt like she glowed. Her face felt bright and hot. She reached up and touched the earrings. Gratitude and newly found pride came off her in waves. She smiled at Bryn, "Let me do my best then, and continue to honour her."

~

She was trying hard to imitate the movements Witl and Bryn showed her. They were majestic and made it look so easy when they held the hilts of swords and moved in sync with the blades. Almost as if the sword was just an obstacle in the hand of each dancer, and they wanted to get rid of the annoying weapons without dropping their own. Ilva thought fighting poetic then. She was entranced by the beauty in it. They swapped swords for axes and then hammers, showing the different styles for each.

Ilva was ready to try herself now. She held a small hammer and a stone shield. She lifted the heavy items with ease, her new strength a cloak of protection as well. The shield was barely needed. The hammer swung this way and that, and

Ilva only felt self-conscious for a moment. Then she found a groove, and moved with it.

It felt good to her, swaying herself out of line of a blade, then swinging herself back up and delivering her own blow. Using the weight of the weapons to propel and exaggerate her movements. Her hammer flew sideways and almost struck Witl. She held back at the last moment, knowing that could have been a deadly blow. His eyes were wide. She panted and swung her arm back.

"Good battle instincts, and amazing control lass! Come on, keep it coming!" He threw another sword swing at her.

Ilva pulled her body back just in time, and found herself dancing around the cavern with Witl and Bryn with much enjoyment. She loved this type of dancing. Her earrings caught the light of the fire in the cave, they glowed, and her rings felt cold. Ilva was shocked when she realised both the sylvite and stone were colouring her skin.

Her ears were glowing copper, the reddish orange leaking in lines onto her face like cracked watercolours darkened in their crevasses when wetted. Her hands were graying, fogging up her arms, her skin felt like stone. She felt her power overwhelming and strong. She was connecting the two powers and she couldn't keep rejecting it. They merged, the watery lines of golden orange spilling down her, met with the grey cracking stone skin reaching up. The power turned her whole body rigid. She let out a small silent scream, and her body seemed to snap into being again. The colours on her vanished in a flash when she screamed. She stood there staring at her hands. At her rings. "What just happened?" she asked both Bryn and Witl.

Bryn and Witl both had no idea what had occurred. Stumped as they all were, Ilva felt stronger than ever and proved it by walking up to another rock twice her size, slamming her fist into it once, and it split. Strait down the center this time. As smoothly as if it were cut with a knife.

Ilva stared at it while announcing with confidence, "I think I'm strong enough now. I'll leave soon to help Vali."

Bryn and Witl both simply nodded at this, Bryn had her mouth wide open as she nodded. They both starred at the changed elf before them. Was this really the same elf that they were afraid of breaking weeks ago? They had spent a month training and perfecting Ilva's strength. The strength she buried all this time out of doubt. It was incredible how much power was stored up inside. How much her confidence and belief had released her from the prison in her mind. She was now hardened, learned and housing a new kind of magic within herself.

Witl and Bryn both secretly wished her luck on her journey. They hoped with all their hearts that she would take care with her new found abilities. They had no idea how to direct such a powerful force, and it was not their burden to bear. It was honourable of them to give Ilva this choice, but terrifying all the same to see their pupil prepare to face her destiny.

She would have thanked them for their understanding, had she known it lay there between them. She turned and walked back to the small hut where Odys had been working away all day on writing and other such things. She walked in and he was furiously jotting down word after word onto pieces of parchment.

He was dabbing and scrawling, dabbing and scrawling.

Ilva decided not to disturb him, and went to the shelves. She browsed the books until she came across one she hadn't read yet that she thought was useful sounding. It read '*Herbs: a Guidebook*'. Ilva flipped through the pages reading about herb after herb. There was information on everything from medicines to poisons. She was especially interested in the ones that could soothe burns and cuts. They were common plants she had seen in the forest often.

Some things she wished she had known about during those years of fending for herself. Like herbs that can help with colds, and stomach aches, and rashes. All sorts of fascinating facts. Ilva was pouring over the notes for hours, and did not realise when Odys came and put away all of his books and work materials.

She only stopped reading when she smelled dinner cooking. *Mmm, food.*

Chapter 65

When Vali was sure the guards had gone, she called over to the cell the elfling boy was in, "Hey, I'm Vali, who are you?"

The voice was barely audible; he was so short behind the door. "My name is Bior."

Vali was going to need to ask more questions. The little one was not too forthcoming. "Did I hear you say your ma is here too?"

"Yes."

Vali thought about a more conversation provoking question. "Where is she?"

Bior began to cry, "They have her in chains, lots of them! She is in the main room upstairs. They were beating her. They wanted her to give them information on an army that is coming. My ma will not tell them though!"

Vali thought about this. Then asked, "What is your ma's name, Bior?"

"It's Llyr."

Vali was struck by the statement, despite having drawn that possible conclusion herself before asking. She listened to make sure no one was around to hear before saying, "Do you really think she can break out and save us? Or do you want to help me save her? We can make a plan from here."

Bior seemed to be thrilled at the idea of being the hero. "Let's save her!"

Once they had assessed that there was nothing in the cells to aid their escape they started talking about the door. It was made of wood and had a small window with metal bars. Vali was glad of Bior's help when he came up with the idea to use the bed roll and yank the bars out with it. Vali tried it. She wrapped the strong hide through the bars, then pulled on the thick material. The bars creaked but didn't move, she even lurched on them several times. Pulling the bars harder and harder. They were really in there.

She put the roll back on the floor and paced in front of the door. A few moments later she heard the click of a cell door. Then there was a rattling at hers. "Kid?"

"Shh." Came his tiny voice on the other side.

She was full of anticipation. This was it. She had to be ready. *How did he unlock the door?*

Her cell door clicked and Bior opened it gently and quietly. "Come on."

Vali did not need the coax, she was already walking out. "I need to get some things first, then we'll save Llyr," Vali said.

Bior wanted to protest, but then thought it better to follow.

"How did you unlock the doors?" Vali asked silently on their way up to the main door for the dungeon cells.

"Easy! These locks are old. I just moved my shirt pin around above the keyhole and popped the lever off the lock."

He proudly pointed at a pin on his vest Vali could not see. He seemed to not realise Vali had no eyes to see with.

She opened the door a slit and listened. Coast seemed clear.

They both bolted down the hall to their left.

Vali was holding Bior's hand and they walked briskly to the guard station where her leathers and knives were stashed. No one was in the room so she gathered her things and hurried out. She was strapping them on familiarly as she walked, wanting very much to avoid any confrontations, as she traced her steps from memory. They were almost to the main floor entrance when two guards nearly walked right in front of them.

Bior shoved Vali into a space behind the door, and the two guards walked past the hall without going down it. Bior then pushed the door open and they continued to sneak stealthier down the way the guards had come from, they made their way up several flights of stairs to the top floor of the keep.

It was night, and dawn was coming fast. Vali sensed this by the smells of breakfast foods beginning to cook, and the sounds of guards waking from slumber in many of the rooms they passed. They had to hurry if they were going to get this done as smoothly as she wanted. She raced to the end of the hall and opened up a small door with decorative engravings. This was where she and Ilva had slept. The bag Ilva carried from Livy's cottage, stuffed with their provisions was still stashed under the bed where she put it before leaving.

Next, they trailed down the hall to another similar door. This was her mother's old room, and in the last hundred years it had been her room. She felt around for the aura of her bow. She sensed its magic coming from the wall near the wardrobe. She grabbed her bow off the weapons mount it still sat on, and the arrows were on the desk chair nearby, everything still right where she had left it. Her bag, with the ink in it, wasn't here though. She was not sure where it was, and she was feeling guilty and regretful for accepting such a precious thing, and then having it stolen.

Bior came to warn her that guards were just outside the door.

They waited by the door for the guards to move on again, then they slipped out and took another route than the guards took. Vali knew the direction they were headed next. The main hall.

With everyone still asleep they could break Llyr out more easily, she thought searching rooms for her bag after everyone left the rooms to be wise, she may even have a couple extra hands to help after freeing Llyr, or at the very least a good distraction with their escape.

They crept along the halls and made their way to save the sapphire elf.

Chapter 66

Ilva was up early that day, before the sun would have been in the world outside the caverns. She thought it would feel weird to leave this world behind when she went. She liked living in the mountain. It was nice never having to worry about the weather, yet she did miss the sun and the fresh outside air.

She considered how she would get to Marka, and decided to take the way past Falil rather than past Karna. She shouldered her bag full of supplies and grabbed a wooden staff she had chosen last night from the weapons rack. It had a blunted stone tip and was made of very strong wood. She thought it might come in handy. She also grabbed a small knife and tucked it into her belt. She was ready. She wanted to say goodbye to Bryn and Odys, so she waited.

They awoke right before the dawn came. Ilva thanked them, offered short and teary goodbyes, then left. *Any goodbye is better than none*, she thought only a bit bitterly. She jogged through the village, through the cavern passage, down the mountainside, and through the woods. In a half a day she was at the mouth of the Nilfin Forest, and by the second half she had made it to her old cave. She camped there for the first night.

The next morning, she woke, ate, and left the site with haste. In a couple more days she exited the forest. It opened up onto a trail full of tents. A war camp. There were triangular canvas dwellings lining the road all the way to Falil. *What is going on?* Ilva thought. She was suddenly worried she chose the very wrong way to come.

She skulked along the edge of the lake and avoided the road. Most of the warriors were waking up still, tiredly meandering about. Ilva felt safe as long as none of the soldiers spotted her skirting the shore. She kept creeping along. The closest of the many camps were a good twenty yards from the lake, she was still careful not to be spotted across the open expanse of land from here to Falil. A siren swam up beside her. Its crackled skin was like plaster slowly flaking off a brittle statue.

Its eyes were inviting.

Ilva had to stay focused and avoid looking or listening. She jammed her fingers into her ears to be safe. She was glad the siren was only stalking her and not luring with its harp of silver. Ilva could not help glancing now and then.

The siren so resembled Vali.

Soon Ilva was out of range of the warrior's encampment, and the siren had vanished. She wondered where all these soldiers had come from. Why Falil was suddenly so popular. She had seen all the ships at the docks and knew they were not from Zoriya. Just who were all these elves? She was curious, but she didn't want to become distracted. She had a task to carry out and she was seeing to it that the task would be done. She was going to help Vali get what she wanted. She was going to take down High Lady Alix and get the silver artifact for Vali.

She had no idea where Vali went, to Marka, Karna, somewhere else. She did know what Vali sought, however, and would not sit by if there was a chance she could help her with her goals. So, she raced along the remaining stretch of road for days. She was close. So close. If only she could get there faster. She had to find her patience now though, she knew it was wise to accept that this was as fast as she could travel. This was a very calculated operation she wanted to pull off. It was going to require all of her efforts and skills. She could use this time to plot.

After running another entire day and most of the night, she stopped under a grove of fruit trees for a quick break before attempting to sneak into Marka. She was only one more day's run away now. Time had moved swifter than she expected as she planned her moves. She was so anxious, she thought she might be sick. *No getting nervous.* She scorned herself. *This is it. Now or never. You break boulders with your bare fists! Do not cave to your fears.*

She sucked in a deep breath to calm herself and ate away her worries. She decided to take a quick nap before the next days run, and then she planned to sneak into the city under the cover of night. She found herself a hidden spot beside some trees and hills, it provided great cover for her. She nestled in by a rock near the biggest hill, concealing herself from all but the sea, and slept soundly in the last few hours of moonlight, soothed by the familiar distant sounds of waves breaking upon the shoreline.

Chapter 67

Vali entered the main hall after listening for any movement. Bior guarded the door. All she heard was the soft clink of chains. She was infuriated when she realized Llyr's position. She was wrapped up in so many chains that they had to weigh three times as much as her. Vali was pulling and pulling. Layer after layer. She soon found the places where the chains were locked and asked Bior if he could work his magic on those locks.

He enthusiastically yipped a, "Yes," and went to work.

As he did that, Vali sensed around the room for the sylvite artifact. It wasn't here. She expected that. She did hope it would be that easy for a moment though. One could always wish there was an easier way.

She sighed, and heard the first clink. It was promising, that sound. A few moments later she heard another. One more to go she thought. Then she heard a third clink, but not the clink of a chain lock. This was the clink of a door.

Jyke had just entered the hall and what she saw looked to her like more treason. Jyke advanced on them quickly, sword drawn she ran at Vali.

Vali grabbed her knife and ran at the assailer. A few

slashes into their confrontation and the third clank of the chain locks was heard.

Suddenly Llyr seemed to light on fire!

Blue flames licked off her skin, walls of heat emitting from her as she walked over to them and closed a hand effortlessly around Jyke's throat. She squeezed and Jyke's eyes began to water and distort.

"Stop!" Vali yelled when she understood the situation before her.

But Llyr did not listen. She popped Jyke's neck inside her fiery fist, crunching the bones inside.

It was terrifying to hear, and Vali was glad she didn't have the ability to watch the ordeal.

Bior seemed unfazed by this display of gore, but Vali was frightened. Llyr crumpled to the floor with the body still in her grip. She released it with seized fingers, and looked at her hand.

"It's okay ma. You're free." As if the child had said those words to her before.

Vali was shaken to be in the presence of these two now. *What kind of magic was that? What did I get myself involved in?*

She jolted when Llyr spoke. "Thank you, Vali. I'm sorry for the suffering I have caused you. I hope you will find it in you one day to forgive my lies, and actions. I appreciate you saving my son. I am eternally grateful. We are not safe here though. We were to be used as leverage in the coming war. My son and I must leave. I wish you luck, Vali." With that Llyr and Bior got up to exit the great hall, and escape Karna.

Vali was on her own now. She gulped, and began heading

towards the hallway to Dola's chamber. She would sneak in as soon as Dola left the room. The Artifacts and the ink had to be there. *Dola would have kept everything important in her own chamber,* Vali rationalised. She waited behind a pillar in the hall for what felt like hours. It had actually only been twenty minutes.

Once Dola's door clicked open, and shut again, and Vali heard her tapping toes exit the hall, she moved swiftly and silently for the door, opened it slow, and scurried inside. She felt around the room for anything, casting her hands about in every direction. She felt pulled to a table at the edge of the room. There was a box on top and when she opened it, there it was. The sylvite artifact. She grabbed it with hasty hands.

Now just to find the ink. She was rummaging through every drawer when she discovered the strap of her bag at the end of the bed, by almost tripping on it. Then she heard the shouting in the great hall.

They had discovered Jyke's corpse, and the escaped prisoner. She had to hurry. Vali pulled the bag out from beside the bed. All the contents were inside still. The ink and all the stuff from Evevale. She shouldered that bag right over top of the other one. All she needed now was an escape plan. Dola was sure to have jumped into action already. She could be in this room any moment. Vali wanted to be as far away as possible now.

She opened the veranda door, and knew she wasn't too high up. It was only the second floor. She could jump and land in the flower garden below. She knew right where it was. She sightlessly swung her legs up onto the edge of the overlook and jumped down. It was a soft landing, and she was glad she judged it well. She began quickly rushing around the perimeter of the property, and then was soon near the base of the mountains behind Karna.

She was a full day from Marka, and about half an hour outside of Karna now, when she heard Dola's scream cut across the land. It frightened her to her core.

Dola must have just discovered the artifacts were gone.

She kept moving, and decided to take the long way around and give herself time to rest and recover, as well as more cover from potential pursuit. Night was coming on, she could feel the dew through her thin soles, and hear the crickets chirping. She needed a plan before she headed into the city. She set up a small fireless camp, and slept.

Chapter 68

Once Ilva was rested and rejuvenated, she stretched her arms high, stretched her legs and hips out, then began her sprint across the last expanse of land before Marka.

As she approached the outer wall, stars were just starting to come out, and so was her ambition. She walked casually into the city, that clearly had no knowledge of the war to come, after being questioned by a guard who spent more time attempting to flirt with her. *Well that was rather uncomfortable.* Ilva cringed.

She entered the quiet streets, there were still stragglers wandering, and the odd bar was still full of shouting and sloshing and drinks on shoes. Ilva stayed away from on-lookers, and refused to make eye contact with anyone. This seemed to be normal to those around her, she imagined the large city was full of shiftier characters than her, she simply looked like a lone female elf fearing her own safety in the nighttime hours. She sneakily drifted down an alley near the palace and it was a sight to behold.

Gawking at the massive pillars and walls, she felt only a moment of hesitation, then she climbed the side of the wall.

She had to be brave. She had to get into this palace. Higher and higher she climbed, driven by adrenaline, and she was almost to the towers balcony when her shoe slipped. It fell off her foot and tumbled into the street below. Landing right behind a guard on patrol. Luckily, her shoe landed softly enough that the sounds from the bars drowned it out, and the guard walked on none the wiser.

Looking down only reminded her of how high she was. She forced her footing to survive the last few grasps of the wall. Hauling herself over the edge of the balcony, she tried to make her landing as soft as possible. In spite of the exhausting climb. She took off her other shoe and stuffed it into her bag, continuing barefoot.

This was a very poor plan. She had not a clue which part of the castle this tower was, or, where the High Lady slept. She was determined to find the silver artifact though. She slunk into the room the tower contained. There was no one here, it appeared to be an old observatory. The items in the room were fantastically elaborate, and Ilva was filled to the brim with curiosity.

Forcefully she recollected and reminded herself that there was no time for her wonderings. She scouted out the staircase and began waltzing down the pivotal decent. When she reached the bottom the hall before her was empty, and very grand. Nearly four times the size of the great hall at Karna. Ilva felt lost in the castles grandeur and it took constant effort to remain on task.

It took several hours to scout without being seen, Ilva found her way through the first half of the third floor of the castle. She avoided many guards, and witnessed a few suspicious activities, including a kitchen elf and a guard frisking each other rather unprofessionally. She was glad for the size of the place, it seemed many suspicious things were going on, and so it wouldn't be hard for her activity to go unnoticed. As long as she wasn't seen snooping, she could do this easily. Though she worried about someone finding her shoe outside.

She thought there was someone behind her frequently and it felt like every hair on her body stood on end. She was paranoid and constantly sensing for, and imagining eyes on her. She created a mental map of every turn she took, she wished she had an actual map.

She was walking down a corridor with many white roses decorating pedestal vases. This hallway was far more elaborate than any other on the top floor. The room at the end of this hall had double doors and silver was on absolutely everything. She slowly turned the handle, and it took her all of three seconds to realise she was entering the High Lady's chamber.

Alix lay before her in a massive canopy bed, with silver adorning every inch. A stream of moonlight swept into the room and over the bed, and it made everything shine and shimmer. Even Lady Alix, her face so serene, seemed to be made of silver herself.

Ilva approached with caution. She was gazing all about for any sign of the silver artifact. *This is the most likely place for it, close to its keeper.* Ilva spotted a large decorative wardrobe at the end of the room, and she thought to try there, she stepped gingerly, one foot after another, around the bed to the far side of the High Lady's chamber. She opened the wardrobe with a soft click, and peered inside.

There was nothing but an outrageous amount of clothing. She turned to see a small white satin cloth draped by the bed-side table. It was hidden from the entrance point. She turned and walked up close to the side of the bed. She pulled the cloth back and there it was. A large silver hunk sitting on a suspended platform. Ilva plucked it off the little stand, and dropped the cloth back over.

Then she tucked the fist sized silver hunk into her bag, and began to retrace her steps back out. She made it to the corner of one of the beds four twirling posts, when the floor-board beneath her groaned.

Lady Alix sat up in the bed, slowly like a creepily roused sleepwalker, her cold silver eyes shot directly to Ilva.

Dear gods and goddesses. Ilva thought. *What now?*

Chapter 69

Vali was about an hour's walk away from Karna, she had gotten a few hours of sleep, and that was enough. She was too anxious to sleep long right now. Being so close to her goal, and surrounded by dangers. She was really about to do this. The last artifact. She thought of how she could get close to Lady Alix. She had of course heard the rumors of the high lady's great prowess, her masterful battle abilities and her terrifying weapon.

Shaking debilitating thoughts from her mind Vali re-focused on her plan. She took up all the courage she could muster and walked towards the dark city, forming her plan in her mind as she went. She was preparing for the fearful encounter to come, not knowing that Ilva was already doing the dirty work required. Vali had no idea, that at that exact moment Alix and Ilva were face to face.

~

Lady Alix gracefully swept her legs out from under the satin sheets, pulled herself upright with delicate finesse, and laid a dainty hand on the unmade bed. She seemed to be sleek and skilled in her catlike movements, as she glided around the corner of the bedpost, eyes not leaving Ilva's.

Ilva did not want to give her a chance to arm herself. She came at her, walking swiftly across the room to close the gap, not running to alarm others nearby. She shot her staff, then a fist out at Alix when she was within range, and Lady Alix casually leaned to the side, twice.

Her cold silver eyes mirrors of everything. Her face did not move. Not a wince, or a parting of the lips. It was as if she could do it in her sleep, eerily enough, it felt as if she never woke.

Ilva felt suddenly quite outmatched. She swung a few more fists, and the staff, at Lady Alix's face. She missed, and missed, and was becoming very annoyed. She took a deep breath to refocus, remembering her training, and not letting her frustration take her out of this moment. She had to stay present. This was not training anymore. This was the moment that mattered. This was what she had staked everything on. The battle to end it all. She would be the one to take down the elf all others looked to overthrow. In this moment, somehow, she knew it had to be her.

She felt the warrior within her rise to meet the challenge. She slowed her movements, and met Lady Alix's calm with equal repose.

Ilva stepped with Alix. They might have looked like they were floating on their gently sweeping feet, had it not been for the occasional assail that proved they were grounded. Ilva took in every movement, and felt a good match for Alix now. As her confidence in herself grew, the more intense the fight became. The two of them were soon sweaty.

Finally, Alix showed an expression. It was small, but noticeable.

Ilva was breaking into her opponent's stoic strength. *I can do this! I can win!* Her confidence grew and grew. She became careless and let Alix retreat a few steps. She didn't consider that Alix may have been plotting rather than retreating. She was so confident thinking she was winning.

As Alix began lazily pulling out a chain from beside the bedpost, dragging most of it out from under the bed, something scrapping the floor on the other end.

Ilva was afraid to see what it was. She was frozen by the realization that she had given her opponent the very few seconds she needed. She was unsure and intimidated when the final bit of chain dragged out from under the bed to reveal a curved blade attached to the end.

Alix seemed to be used to this fearful response. It was the fear of facing an unfamiliar fighting style that she used to manipulate her enemies. It was working for her now too, as Ilva stood before her, eyes wide on the kusarigama. Alix approached Ilva, swinging the chain-sickle in a slow controlled circle, the blade whipping around and around.

Ilva was hypnotised. It was her turn to retreat a few paces.

As Alix got closer, Ilva noticed her expression was still fixed. She was not smiling conceitedly as Ilva had. She was cold and calculating. Her expression was almost as formidable as the terrifying weapon she was now expertly drawing circles with. Alix whipped the sickle a little harder around and then it was flying.

Ilva barely dodged the sharp edge as it shot over her

shoulder. It came back though, and sliced a sharp cut across her arm before it returned to Alix's hand. Ilva's staff fell, and rolled across the room.

Alix held her weapon where blade and chain connected.

Ilva felt the sting of where she had been cut, she tried to block it out and think of ways to next avoid the attack.

Before she had a chance to consider her first defense strategy Alix was advancing again, with the curved blade in one hand and the chain wrapped around the other. Her face still solid and eerily focused.

Ilva felt her confidence draining. She was frightened, and knew her fears could ruin her chances of winning. So, she fought to stay confident as she bolted through the room. She lunged for the bed and scampered across, ducking behind the mattress slightly, hoping the four posts would prevent the blade from swinging so freely.

When Ilva looked back she caught what she suspected was a twinkle of amusement shining in Alix's eyes.

Chapter 70

As Vali walked her legs began to ache. She hadn't been able to fall asleep fully. Her body now reminded her of why sleep was important. Her muscles felt tired and they protested every step of the way.

She drank the last of the water that was in her skin, and stuffed it back in her bag. She felt moody and her temples were throbbing. She carried on a few more minutes, then rested beside an apple tree. Picking apple after apple off the ground until she came across one that felt smooth and mostly unblemished, she bit into it. Her jaw hurt as she chewed slowly. She craved sleep. She craved peace.

Vali knew however that she would not have it until her tasks had all been complete. She agonized over the fact that her body was failing her in her greatest need of it. She cursed herself. *Why! Why am I so tired? I have gone without sleep before and not felt this way!* Forgetting that she had experienced other trials recently. She ignored the possible reasons and rationalizations, and chose to focus on the irrational and unreasonable. Setting herself goals that would be unobtainable, and damning any consequences that may result.

She was set in her mind; no matter how impossible it was, she had to do it, and she had to be successful. Her sight, and her future, and all of her dreams rode on this. She would never give those things up. No matter the cost. She believed these things had to work out, all of them. And so, they would. Somehow.

Vali got up and tossed away her apple core. She walked again, closing the gap. In less than half an hour she would be in the city. She pulled her thoughts of agony in, and focused on her feelings of need. Of want. She thought of nothing except her wish to see, and how the only things that now stood in the way of that were this final artifact, and the long hot walk across the desert sands.

As she walked, she felt the dampness of the dew soaking her shoes again. She felt the chill of the night air. Then soon, she felt the glow of the approaching city on her skin. She knew she was almost there. *Almost there. Almost there.* She coaxed herself onward. She was now filling herself with anticipation, and exhilaration. *It will be over soon.* She was so ready for this conclusion to her long-lived quest, she felt her body shaking.

As Vali entered the city, she heard a sound. It was loud, it echoed over the city. *That sounds like...oh no.* Vali knew this sound. She knew what followed. She was entering the city, just as the battle was about to begin. The sound was the war horn. A warning that the city gave off just as an army approached it. Vali suddenly found herself in the throes of crazed elves, running hard around the streets.

Doors were flying open, screams filling the city. Vali was

full of anxiety too. She rushed through the crowds, who seemed to have no idea whether to flee the city, seek refuge, or fight. They scrambled around her, as she kept moving fast and determined towards her destination. She was bumped into by a panicked elf, and knocked to the ground.

Feet were pummeling into Vali, and tripping on her. She knew she had to get up fast or she would be trampled. That was not the ending she wanted. The elf who had tripped over Vali now lay next to her on the ground, being trampled in the madness. Vali heard her cries of desperation and reached out to grasp her arms. They pulled themselves up together. Vali shouted, "Run!"

The elf girl took off. Vali grasped her stomach, which had met someone's foot in the chaos. She steeled her body and pushed harder through the masses. Not letting another elf knock her from her feet. She pushed back against the hustle. Drilling her heels into the ground with every step, she advanced on the castle. There were hordes of civilians slamming their fists on the doors of the castle, the sounds echoed in Vali's ears. She wondered, *How will I ever get in now?*

~

Ilva looked at Alix. She seemed unconcerned about the bed in her weapons path. She swung the chain back and forth looping it around one arm and then the next, in a rather dramatic display of mastery. The blade swept up, making slicing sounds through the air, the chain rattled as it moved back and forth, around and around. It was doing figure eights between them. She was envious of the skill Alix was using to control her weapon. It took Ilva by surprise when Alix shot her right leg forward and her blade swung from her right arm in unison.

The blade flew between the bed posts, landing on the mattress, shredding it. Alix swung the blade around once it returned, and thrust it harder than before, wrapping around the two bedposts upon the footboard, and she yanked. The posts turned to splinters.

In seconds she had done the same to the posts at the head-board. The whole canopy collapsed. Leaving Ilva squatting behind the mess that used to be a bed. She stared at the destruction, realising how little Alix cared about the room.

Then, Alix spoke. Ilva was beginning to wonder if she even could. "Did you really think you could sneak into my chamber and steal that which is bound to me?" Her voice came out as a coo. One that might be used to manipulate a child.

Ilva swallowed before replying, "If you mean the artifact that is already in my bag, then yeah, I did think I could do that. Your castle is not very secure lady." Her response was filled with the same defiant tones that she had used against her elders since the dawn of her life. Finally, Ilva witnessed a full faced expression grace Alix's features.

It was grotesque. It was a sneer that made her appear far older, and far less attractive than she had when she was stoic. Ilva realised now what weakness Alix had. Pride.

"That's high lady, little rat. I will slay you with ease. You have no chance of victory." Alix spat these words out.

Ilva ducked as another swing of the chain sent the blade

her way. Once again, she misjudged. The chain dropped behind her, and then flung back and dragged across her spine. Her back felt as if it was peeling open. The air felt cold and the blood, now running down her, felt hot. Then the pain hit. It was searing, as if the air was hurting her more than the blade had. Her open wounds were now drawing all of her attention. She wanted to reach back and touch her spine, but fear and horrified shock prevented her.

Alix laughed. Her laugh was childlike and playful. It was frightening to hear. "You are pathetic. I will end your life painfully. I will torture you until your last breath." She leapt in two gentle bounds over the crushed canopy bed, and was less than a foot behind Ilva in seconds.

Ilva reacted far too slowly as her assailant vanished behind her. The stone elf's eyes were wide with panic. Before Ilva could turn around the chain came over her head and bound her arms to her sides. Alix pulled her closer until airy breath drifted across Ilva's shoulder. The high lady's arm slid over Ilva's bicep and pointed the tip of her blade down at Ilva's chest.

Alix stood behind her, breathing excitedly against Ilva's hair and neck. "I want to feel it, the moment you give up, let me feel you crumble in despair."

Her blade began sinking in.

Ilva cried out.

It was moving slowly into her flesh. Ilva could not believe how intense the pain was. The blade sunk into the center of her chest, and then it was yanked out. She could feel Alix, breathing in pace with her, heavier and faster. As Ilva was struggling, Alix was relishing. She found another tender point below Ilva's collar bone, and pushed the blade in again, shallowly and slowly.

Ilva began to cry. *The pain. The ungodly pain*!

Alix was giggling gleefully. She was enjoying this far too much.

As Ilva was about to submit to her defeat, she heard a sound booming throughout the castle.

A horn bellowed through the halls, and the whole chamber seemed to reverberate with the sound. Alix stopped laughing, and her blood-soaked blade went still.

Chapter 71

Vali roared in frustration as she tried to help pummel the doors down with the civilians. The army Ediv lead was making their way deeper into the city. She could smell the blood, and knew it would not be long until all those around her either surrendered or were massacred.

She decided to find another way. She exited the mass chaos at the front door, and shoved around the side of the castle walls. When she finally got away from the crowd she felt with her hands around the brickwork. "There must be another way," she whispered aloud.

Guiding herself with touch, she found a spot where the dirt that once rested on the bricks was smooth. She felt a higher spot and there it was again. The smooth feeling of dirt having been shifted. Someone had scaled the wall here. If they did it, then she could too. She stepped back, adjusting her bag, and stepped on Ilva's shoe that had dropped. She picked it up.

Realising what it was, she thought, *the climb must have been hard for whoever did it. I had best be careful.* She dropped the shoe, with no idea it was Ilva's, and began climbing. She lifted herself with her strong arms, her feet feeling over and over for footholds. She had no idea where she was climbing too, yet she climbed on and on, higher and higher.

The wind got stronger the higher she went. She felt all the spots the elf who went up first had used. It made her climb all the easier. By doing this she also knew she could find the place the other climber had ascended to.

She felt like she had been going up for a long time. She could hear the shouts and screams of terror below. Some grunting that sounded closer than the other sounds too. She assumed others would have seen her climbing by now and be right behind her. She only hoped they would not ascend too hastily and bump her on their way past. She tried to pick up her own speed while full of anxiety at the thought. *What if someone is waiting at the top to battlements? What if they shoot me down? What if I slip?*

The wall she climbed now echoed with booming vibrations, she heard a consistent crashing along with a chorus of, "back," and after a pause, "forward," which was followed by the tremors she sensed in the bricks. The army had a battering ram, and they were smashing the front doors down. Up and up she went, fingers feeling the reverberations every time she gripped the next brick.

Vali made it to the top of the tower, and swung herself safely up over the ledge. She walked through the observatory slowly, listening for any potential guards or occupants. She heard sounds deep within the castle, they echoed through the rounding stairs. She found them easily with the rebounding sounds.

As she descended the steps, the shouting grew. She knew she would not be able to avoid being seen once inside. How would she get to the High Lady? How would she find the artifact? She was frustrated with her lack of a plan, and inability to see the confusion around her. She listened so hard her ears were aching from the strain.

She heard a male elf shouting, "Get to the armoury! We need all of your help. You there! Arm yourself too! Maid, you are not an exception, do you hear me?"

Vali was shaking. She had not considered how dangerous the situation she put herself in really was. She had trapped herself in a war zone. She felt sick. As she rounded the bottom steps, she felt the frenzy before her.

She knew she was in a hall full of frantic elves, all rushing to and fro. A maid bumped into her, "Oh sorry milady, pardon."

Vali nodded and decided to ask, "Where is Lady Alix?"

The maid stuttered in a wary voice, "I think she is still in her room. She would be preparing for battle no doubt. We all are. I am to fetch more weapons from the armoury. Please excuse me."

Vali felt her bowing quick and jittery before her. Vali nodded again and asked, "Which way is her quarters?"

The maid seemed very unsure now, but she replied, "Last hall on the left"

Vali could not believe she got such an easy reply, "Thank you." She began sprinting through the hall, past all the mad men and women fastening armour, and fixating on their current situation. She heard a variety of voices as she navigated with sound. Some were fearful, others brave, many sounded confused and lost. It seemed that not many of them had the strength, or the ability to remain calm in the midst of a storming raid. She tried to keep herself calm, as she rushed to the last hall and turned.

As she rounded the corner she slammed right into a broad chested elf. "Whoa there!" he shouted. "You alright? Keep your head!"

Vali shook herself and stammered, "Yes, sir."

He eyed her suspiciously. "Hey! Do I know you?"

The calm Vali had tried to feel vanished.

Chapter 72

Ilva sucked in a breath at the sound of the horn. She knew it had distracted Alix too. She felt a sudden burst of adrenaline shoot through her at the sound. She wanted to live. Her whole body burned with the desire. Then she saw it. The sun. It was rising, and it shone straight through Lady Alix's window, and it was shining on her now. Her face soaked in the warmth and then her ears were on fire. *The earrings.* Ilva suddenly knew what she was capable of again, and her skin began to harden.

Her fists clenched tight, began fading to grey stone. It ran up her arms and over her body, from her ears cracks of gold wove themselves into the grey, they spidered out across her entire body.

The gold cracks filled every injury, healing her with blinding light that crackled loudly. Her eyes shone. She grabbed Alix's arm and pushed the sickle out of her now stony chest etched with gold.

"No!" Alix screamed. "What is this?" she wailed in confused frustration.

Ilva turned to face her.

Alix lunged at her with her kusarigama, she slammed the curved blade off Ilva's chest, and the reverberation caused her to lose her grip.

The blade bounced off her stone body and the tip was now not as fine as it had been.

Alix grabbed for it, and thrust it out again, this time the blade bent a bit more. Alix wrapped the chain around Ilva's arm, and yanked. She was trying to break her arm, and had no success. Not even an ounce of give. She pulled harder and harder. Then the chain broke. Alix stared at Ilva in shock. "What are you?"

Ilva's shining golden eyes pierced Alix's soul with fear. She grabbed her and threw her across the room. She slammed against the brick wall ten feet away, and crumpled from the blow. She lay there bloodied, and beaten. Nearly every bone was crushed on impact. The force of her throw was the same force that had spilt boulders. Ilva had, unknowingly, killed High Lady Alix.

Ilva answered, believing her opponent still lived, "I am strong."

After checking on the artifact, and wrapping it neatly in her bag next to her shoe, Ilva went back to the entrance of the now desolated bedroom. She walked out, her body still fueled by power.

Before her was Vali, face to face with a large brooding elf guard. He seemed to be questioning her.

Ilva decided to act first, and ask later. She walked fast down the hall to them, when she approached she shouted to Vali, "I have it. We have to get out of here!"

Her voice came out strangely, it was grinding out in a

possessed and otherworldly tone. The guard turned to Ilva, and was clearly shook by the sight of her, for he backed away with eyes wide, then ran down the hall toward the preparing troops.

Vali knew the sound of Ilva's voice, despite the change in pitch, and was so relieved to hear it, yet also stunned. "Ilva?"

"Yes, Vali, we need to run! Come on! We need to escape before my father gets into the castle," Ilva pleaded, her voice gradually returning to normal.

Vali was wearing the most adorable look of confusion and surprise, Ilva relished in it. Even Ilva was a bit surprised by herself.

They needed a way out. Ilva decided they should run straight down the hall ahead. It was abandoned looking, and away from the main doors. She grabbed Vali's hand and they sprinted off down the corridors. They came to, and descended three flights of stairs, Ilva's barefeet slapped the steps. They twirled down them, and with the speed they were running, they felt slightly dizzied. They rushed to one of the westernmost corners of the back of the castle.

They found themselves in a kitchen, there was a big wooden door to a cellar, Ilva wondered if it had an outdoor cellar entrance. She opened it and seen some of the kitchen staff huddled inside. They were preparing to escape as well. Some of them were filling bags with food. Ilva thought this a good idea at the sight of it.

"Please! Don't hurt us!" A young elf screamed in terror.

Ilva's skin was still stony looking, but it was fading away slowly. Her adrenaline was ebbing. "We mean you no harm, we are looking to flee the castle too. Pay us no mind, and we will do the same for you." Ilva began stuffing fruit and vegetables in her sack, she took some drying herbs down from overhead, she grabbed a bunch of nuts too and a loaf of bread, finally she grabbed a string of meat hanging above them and shoved it in too. She noticed a pair of old work boots near the bottom step, they were a bit big, but she yanked them on her feet.

She swung the bag back over her shoulders and went to the back of the cellar. She creaked the overhead door open a sliver and peeked out. The kitchen staff almost gave them away yelling, "What are you doing?" Ilva pulled the crack shut and swung a finger to her lips in a shushing gesture.

There were soldiers approaching. Only a few.

She whispered very low, "We need to run now. The soldiers are scouting around. They will find you. You must flee if you want to live. We are escaping right now. Be quiet or you will give us all away."

The elves hiding in the cellar trembled and looked like they would not survive even if they did run. Ilva felt a pang of pity, before pushing it away to focus. These elves would have to fend for themselves. She listened from behind the pantry door before peeking out once again. The soldiers had moved to the far end of the wall. Ilva opened the slanted door more, and it let out a loud creaking groan.

The soldiers whipped about and faced her.

"Shit," she mouthed under her breath. She decided they had to make a run for it. She lunged from the hole in the ground cellar, Vali in tow. They ran hard towards the wastelands. Straight across the grass filled fields, seeking the land ahead with the cracked earth, and sandy winds.

As they ran, they heard shouting behind them. Without slowing down Ilva stole a glance, and saw the soldiers laying on the ground. The kitchen elves stood over them, pots and pans in hand, heaving heavy breaths.

Those elves all took off running north.

Ilva had no idea what was to the north. She found herself curious. They had their own destination though. Ilva was not sure where it was yet. They just had to run for now. Harder than they had run since first facing Uroborus.

As they ran Ilva kept stealing glances behind them, as if having to make absolutely sure, over and over again, no one had come after them. She was relieved when an hour or so later, their legs shaking and their breath running out, she could not even make out the fighting anymore, or the horses, or most of the city. They were almost to the base of the mountains that skirted the wastelands. Ilva wanted them to at least make it there.

They pushed on at a slow jog. Panting heavily, their knees trembling with every step. They pushed themselves hard and in just over ten minutes, they made it to the sheltering protection of the foothills.

Chapter 73

They set up a camp even though it was still the morning hours. They needed rest no matter what time of day it was. They were both tired, and had done much these past days. Vali and Ilva sat in their hastily made campsite, and began shoveling the bread and a couple sausages into their faces. They each wanted to eat more, but their jaws ached from chewing. They drank gulps of water, straining to not toss up what they just scarfed down.

Vali was the first to speak, "Ilva, I," her voice catching, "I'm sorry I didn't say goodbye. I abandoned you. I let you down."

Ilva was not expecting this to be the first thing they talked about. She had built an idea up that the first thing Vali would mention might be Ilva's newfound strength, or her dependability as an ally. She still found herself wanting the apology that Vali offered.

Vali went on. "I didn't want you to worry about me, and I knew you would either way, I thought not saying anything would be easier. I thought I might worry less about you, if I didn't see your concern for me," Vali reached inside herself, finding the right words to admit her confession. "I didn't know how guilty I would feel. I tried to push it away. I tried to tell myself you would understand and not resent me. I was wrong to leave you without explanation. I'm so sorry." Vali took a shuddering breath before adding, "I don't want you to get tangled up in my fate. I don't want you to have to fight for my destiny. You have your own dreams do you not? Why are you doing this? You could have died!"

Ilva took in all that Vali had said. "Yes. I could have."

Vali seemed to be tearing up, and her expression was cracking into one of heartbreak.

Ilva knew the feeling. "I was not okay with you not saying goodbye. I pretended to be. It really hurt."

Upon hearing this Vali stiffened a bit. Shame burned her face.

Ilva spoke more gently now, "Please do not distrust me in the future. If you want to do things alone I can very much understand that. I was the ultimate loner before you spirited me away on the adventure of a lifetime."

Vali was trying hard not to sob.

Ilva continued, "I can help you though, and I did help you, that does not make your success any less victorious. We have our own goals and those destinies we both have can coexist. I do have my own dreams, and helping you achieve yours is helping me to achieve mine. Together we are so much more than we ever were apart."

Vali's face went from sad, to contemplative.

Ilva went on when she saw the switch in Vali's comprehension, "I wanted adventure. I wanted to see more of this world. I wanted to be loved. You already give me everything that I want. Do you not see that?"

"But you might die following me on this path." Vali confessed her fear.

"Death does not frighten me. Living a life confined is terrifying. I want to live a life filled with adventure, and I want to live that life with you, Vali." Ilva concluded.

Vali now cried harder than she ever had before.

Ilva thought for a moment that perhaps she had said the wrong thing, then she realised Vali was smiling and laughing in between the harder sobs. Ilva crawled up to her and hugged her close as Vali cried deeper into Ilva's arm. Tears wetted Ilva's clothing. She did not care.

Vali sniffed hard. Wiping her eyes aggressively. She kept sniffing until she was able to breathe through her nose again. She took a few shakier sobs, before saying, "Ilva, I love you, deeply and assuredly." She pulled harder into the hug as she said this. A few new tears streaked down her cheeks and soaked into Ilva's now damp tunic.

Ilva was crying too, not as hard. She let a few sobs escape, a handful of relief filled tears. She sniffed a few times herself.

They laid down in the warm afternoon sunlight. Ilva was nestled into Vali's shoulder, her leg over Vali's, her inner hips pressing against Vali's outer hip. "We have all the artifacts."

Vali sighed with contentment.

"So where are we heading now?" Ilva queried.

Vali responded with an answer that weighed heavily for a moment, "Deep into the Vexian Wastelands, to meet with the Wraith Wan."

Ilva stilled, then relaxed. "Let's have ourselves an adventure then,"

They lay there, enjoying the embrace they had both been

longing to feel for weeks. The one they had grown semi-dependent on. Holding each other was one of the greatest joys they knew. The soft comforting entwinement of their bodies lulled them both into a sleep as deep as could be.

Chapter 74

Somewhere deep in the Nilfin Forest, an old white-haired elf with dark eyes converses with an ix.

At the base of the Vozrek Mountains, Bior and his ma are face to face with a griffin.

In Marka, Lord Ediv kicks over the corpse of Lady Alix, his blood honour to rule unfulfilled.

In Karna a blue-eyed elfling weeps for his fallen mother, and a silver lady plots revenge.

A dragon slumbers in a mountain that remains hidden.

And the Wraith Wan awaits two travellers, in the Vexian kingdom.

The adventure continues...

EDGE
Book II in the Stone Souls Series
COMING SOON!

ACKNOWLEDGEMENTS

Writing ETCH was a bit of a random affair. In 2019, during NaNoWriMo, I jumped in and pantsed this project. No outline, no idea where I was going with it, and no clue how to write fantasy. I just loved reading it and I had some fun ideas. Ideas that would have never come to fruition without the support and encouragement of everyone I'm about to mention.

I wish to thank my husband, Bear, my very first reader and my ultimate cheerleader. I didn't think my work was worth sharing. It was destined to be hidden in a folder amongst other secret lost projects. I'm glad he read it, and then encouraged me to let my friends read it as well.

Speaking of those friends; I would like to thank Sylver Michaela, Chelsuu Kilroy, and Kelsey VanRaay for their helpful feedback, uplifting words, and positive vibes. Without them I would still have a lot of self doubt and uncertainty. I'm grateful for the candid and wholesome conversations we had around my unpolished first draft, and I can't wait to give them copies of this book now that it's become something more.

I want to thank Mallory McCartney and Teighan Gibson, a couple of local authors in my city, who have both been such good friends. Before I even thought about writing my novel, these two were beacons guiding me to this place. I super appreciate them giving me advice and inspiration on my journey to becoming an author.

I can't thank enough my incredibly talented cover artist! Cora Graphics went above and beyond my expectations with the execution of my cover. I'm delighted that I found such a wonderful creator to help make my vision a reality.

My fabulous editor Kayla Grey, a pleasure to work with, taught me a great deal. Her attention to detail, understanding, and well written critiques made this experience much more comfortable. With her guidance and coaching I feel far more confident in my work. There was so much about dialogue structure and grammar that I had to become educated on, and Kayla is the best teacher.

I would like to thank all of the family and friends who have supported this spontaneous adventure I'm on. Thank you to all of you that have been excited with me about my debut. Thanks to Coles in Sarnia as well, for giving me an opportunity to learn about and work with books. Special Thanks to my colleagues, Shannon and Michelle, for being beta readers of my second draft. I love my entire bookstore family and I look forward to visiting them all very soon.

Thank you everyone. I am immeasurably grateful.

ABOUT THE AUTHOR

J. A. L. Solski, parent to Milo, partner to Eric, has found sanctuary in books since childhood. Scholastic book fairs of the 90's, the local library that was more of a post office really, and school libraries fueled a passionate interest in fictional worlds.

They volunteered for therapy research as a PTSD test patient, donate to the local shelters they once resided in, and attempt to walk every therapeutic path possible. Including creative writing and a never-ending list of ever-changing interests and hobbies.

The author and their family reside in Ontario, Canada. Still frequently loaning from the library, seeking out adventure, eating and reading gluttonously, and quite often discovering, as they have in this moment, that their tea has gone cold, again.